AF335449

No Flags Did Wave

by Timothy F. Klie

© Copyright 2019 Timothy F. Klie

ISBN 978-1-63393-940-0

This is a work of fiction. The characters are both actual and fictitious. With the exception of verified historical events and persons, all incidents, descriptions, dialogue and opinions expressed are the products of the author's imagination and are not to be construed as real.

Published by

 köehlerbooks ™

210 60th Street
Virginia Beach, VA 23451
800–435–4811
www.koehlerbooks.com

NO FLAGS DID WAVE

TIMOTHY F. KLIE

VIRGINIA BEACH

CAPE CHARLES

"No brass band played,

no flags did wave,

when we came back to the 'Home of The Brave.'"

"Dunk's Almanac" by Maj. H.G. Duncan USMC

AUTHOR'S NOTE

The characters in this work of fiction are loosely based on real people and events. The story is an amalgamation of this writer's imagination and occurrences during the Vietnam War. It's a tribute to the Marine Corps and its brave warriors who struggle on and off the battlefield to protect our country.

PROLOGUE

24 SEPTEMBER 1969

**BELMONT BAY MARINA, UNIT B3 RIVERSIDE DRIVE,
WOODBRIDGE, VIRGINIA.**

THE BALLPOINT PEN WOBBLED in his unsteady hand. His penmanship was as messy as his mind. Salty tears fell silently on the spiral notebook paper, words blurring in the dome-shaped drops. The ink oozed into black fingers as the droplets were absorbed. The emotions were more difficult to control than the words were to write. And the words were impossible. He knew his future depended on the accuracy of his journal, yet he doubted his ability to remember all the details. They were as twisted as a honeysuckle vine around an old plantation fence post.

These feelings surprised him. He never cried. He was Mr. Control. Now every sentence seemed to take an eternity to put on paper. The words felt like red-hot fishhooks twisting and pulling in the gray matter of his brain. Each word extracted was mental agony. He sat motionless, paralyzed with fear.

He'd been working on the narrative for over nineteen hours straight. Recrimination and anger had eaten at his resolve. The task was futile. His frustration came to a boil, and he impulsively threw the notebook against the wall. His future was preordained by his past actions. His case was hopeless.

He turned off the desk light and sat in the darkness of predawn. Wearily he struggled with past demons. He could no longer keep the ghostly creepy crawlers from infecting his mind. Pictures suddenly materialized out of the darkened room. He remembered the cigarette lighter carried by one of his dead Marines. The shiny metal rectangle floated in front of his face. He remembered flicking the flint and watching the flame dance, then clicking the top closed, smothering the light—doing that repeatedly in a time better forgotten.

As commanding officer, he had the unpleasant responsibility of sanitizing the personal effects of each Marine killed in action before the personal effects were shipped back to the States. Normally, the first sergeant ensured this task was performed. The Corps didn't want the bereaved parents or family members receiving a sea bag or footlocker from their Marine with pornographic material or letters to an unknown girlfriend in Bangkok. This was especially true if the Marine was married.

The commander had picked up each article and inspected it. He had to determine whether to send or trash. That could mean reading each letter, looking at all photos, and examining every piece of clothing. Nothing left to chance. The process was painful, often heartbreaking, always depressing. He had to ensure the Marine's image was never tarnished; the reputation of the Corps was at stake.

He relived now, in detail, the day he sat on the ammo box sorting through the dead Marine's duffle bag. A Marine he could not remember. What flashed in his mind was the PFC's silver cigarette lighter. It was an ordinary flip-top Zippo, but what was engraved on the case was extraordinary. At the time, it meant little to him; now it was a profound statement, something to think about before he made his final decision about what to write in his journal:

Lord, give me the strength to accept what I cannot change,
The courage to change what I can change,
and the wisdom to know the difference.

Reluctantly he pulled himself from the deep cocoon of the couch and retrieved the journal. His life was the Corps. No matter the cost, he would finish the journal. *Semper fidelis, semper fidelis, semper fidelis,* his mind screamed.

CHAPTER 1

WELCOME HOME, BAD ASS

THE SLEEK COMMERCIAL JET flew into the August sun out of the midnight-blue western sky. The plane's exhaust crystals trailed in the Pacific sunrise. Countless men and woman had prayed for this metal bird. Others thought the moment would never come. Many passengers rubbed lucky charms. Some had carefully crossed out 396 days on a crude helmet calendar. Several smiled knowing the rosaries around their necks had protected them. A few stared out the plane's portals in shock; they survived while others had perished.

When hunkered down in some deep, dark, smelly foxhole, they all prayed for the Freedom Bird, no matter their beliefs or faith.

Banff Airlines Flight 169 was a charter from DaNang via Japan and Alaska to Norton Air Force Base, California. Most passengers were Marines who had finished their thirteen-month tours in Vietnam's I Corps. They were excited and relieved to be back in the world. Some looked like they had just stepped out of the boonies, with dirty camo jungle uniforms and scuffed black to tan boots. Others wore the short-sleeve summer service Charles uniform. A few individuals were in full summer service khaki Alpha uniforms with ribbons. Most had slept during the long flight to the States. Several talked quietly. One captain read throughout the flight, occasionally chuckling at a passage from the book. His laughter was disconcerting to the majority aboard. It seemed antithetical to a battle-hardened Marine.

The return of the warrior elite was a cherished ceremony honored by a grateful nation. They expected to be welcomed home like their fathers with open arms and parades. That dream would soon be shattered.

The shapely, round-eyed flight attendants in their short skirts politely asked their passengers to ensure all seatbelts were fastened. The shimmering airplane banked and straightened out for the approach to the smog-shrouded runway. The final flight path was a new beginning for those aboard, a breath of life in a world now full of peril. These travelers were unprepared for the transformation of their beloved homeland, now filled with anarchists. Radicals filled the streets shouting slogans on college campuses while burning classrooms and America's flag. The dissidents said the war was wrong, the government corrupt, and that vets were dupes of the system. Returning war veterans were portrayed as unclean degenerates, wanton killers, and social lepers. They were scorned, humiliated and discredited.

"These war-weary killers must be cleansed from our nation for a new government to gain legitimacy," anti-war activists proclaimed.

After a screech of wheels, the huge cylindrical sarcophagus with wings rolled to a stop. All on board erupted into applause. Some men covered their faces and sobbed. The gleaming plane taxied to an isolated staging area. An Air Force ground crew hustled to move a rolling metal staircase to the plane's passenger door. After an agonizing few moments, the hatch popped open. The applause increased. Catcalls, whistles, and hoots of joy filled the air. The Marines smiled, thankful to be deboarding with arms and legs intact.

As the Marines stepped off the ladder and touched the tarmac, an Air Force sergeant directed them to dull-gray transit buses designed for standup passengers only. The vehicles carried the Marines to a cluster of dreary concrete-and-steel hangars. The Marine reception area was within the confines of the airbase but surrounded with security chain-link fence topped with razor wire. A group of senior citizens holding a droopy paper banner stood in front of one structure. They looked like escapees from a hospice facility. The banner read *Welcome Home* in large colorful script. As each Marine got off the buses, one of the seniors gave him a stale glazed donut and paper cup filled with lukewarm coffee. Some Marines said "thank you" to the geriatrics, but the vast majority acted like zombies after the thirteen-plus-hour flight. They just took the refreshments and moved with the crowd toward the inside assembly area.

The converted steel hangar they entered was a Cold War relic. The Marines moved from the hazy California morning sun into a darkened cavern lit by huge, florescent, upside-down mushroom globes. Under the light, everyone looked jaundiced. A stiff-backed Marine gunny sergeant with a hatchet face and a half dozen hash marks on his sleeve gave the order to form ranks and dress right. All but a small group of senior enlisted and officers quickly formed ranks. The junior enlisted were lectured about contraband, military protocol, available transit housing, civilian dress, and travel. A very young first lieutenant addressed the officers and senior enlisted. He didn't look old enough to drink liquor at a public bar, let alone lead men into battle.

The first lieutenant was neat and pressed in his summer service uniform. His trousers had a razor crease. His short-sleeve shirt was perfectly starched. All accouterments were squared away and correct. The ribbons on his chest indicated he'd been in Vietnam, receiving a Bronze Star with *V* for valor and three Purple Hearts. He proved that warriors came in a multitude of shapes and appearances. The silver bar spoke to the senior NCOs and officers in a commanding deep baritone.

"Gentlemen, welcome back to the world. Processing begins in the next building. The NCO clerk will require your military ID, a copy of your travel orders, and declaration forms if you have any war trophies. After processing, there are vehicles available to take you to the transit facilities or connecting transportation. You may pick up your luggage in the processing area. Any questions?" No one said a word. The first louie shouted, "Outstanding."

The small group picked up their carry-ons and walked toward the second building. Captain Mike Z. Ruhawk, who had been reading and laughing on the plane, didn't move. He stood like a sentinel in the Superman pose, hands on his hips, chest out, and chin up. His uniform fit him as if tailored by the best on Seville Row in London. His black leather shoes gleamed. His hair cut to Marine regulations, high and tight, his outer façade hid the inner fierceness of a natural born warrior. His destiny was leading Marines in combat. He felt all the traditions of the Corps were his responsibility to uphold. His religion was honor, his sacrament was courage, and his life was commitment to the mission. He looked at these returning soldiers as "his" Marines, a guardian on duty watching his wards. The captain listened closely to the NCOIC lecturing his Marines.

The Marine gunny was finishing his spiel to the troops. "Between this building and the processing building is an amnesty box. It looks like a blue Dempsey Dumpster. Trash any contraband you are carrying, or you will be prosecuted under the Uniform Code of Military Justice. You will not have a second opportunity to discard any illegal goods before inspection. Any questions? . . . Corporals and above, claim your luggage from the baggage cart and proceed through the doors marked Bravo 23. Lance corporals and below: As your name is called, fall out and retrieve your luggage. Abbot, Adicski, Arnold, Bahraini, Bennett, Brown." Marines began to fall out, grab their gear, and file through the green steel double doors. Posted on the door was a large standard USMC plywood sign with four-inch stenciled yellow letters on a red background. The sign read:

ILLEGAL CONTRABAND:

Drugs – *hallucinogens, narcotics, marijuana, heroin, LSD, non-prescription malaria pills, formaldehyde, & drug paraphernalia etc.*

Pornography *–nude pictures/photos, sex illustrations, sex toys, nude statues, dildos, inflatable dolls, body parts (ears, fingers, noses, etc.), body fluids, etc*

Ammunition *–ordnance, artillery rounds, mortar rounds, blooper M-79 rounds, LAAWS, 50 cal, 30 cal, 7.62, 5.56, .45, 38. etc.*

Weapons *–pistols (without DD603 authorization), automatic rifles (M16, AK47, etc.), machine guns (M60, PKM, etc.) mortars, and parts thereof, knives, swords, hatchets, machetes, brass knuckles, spikes, clubs, chains, throwing stars, nunchakas, ninja paraphernalia, etc.*

Explosives *–C4, Detcord, TNT, grenades (smoke & frag.), pyrotechnics (star & illum.), Claymores, toe poppers, Bouncing Betties, M-14 and MD82 anti-personnel mines, anti-tank mines (M15, TM46, etc.), celebratory ordnance (fireworks, firecrackers, sparklers, etc.), etc.*

Chemicals *–CS, heat tabs, defoliants, paint, gas, bug repellent, camo face paint, lighter fluid, etc.*

Foods – *fish, meat, fruits, nuts, berries, grain, can goods, etc.*

Animals – *cats, dogs, monkeys, snakes, mice, etc.*

Insects – *bugs of any kind (dead or alive), etc.*

**Violators prosecuted under
The Uniform Code of Military Justice**

***(All war trophies must have Form DD603 completed
with command endorsement)***

The returning NCOs watched the ramrod-straight Captain Ruhawk observing the group. He was not handsome in the *GQ* sense, but manly in the outdoorsmen style, his face deeply tanned with squint lines around his eyes. He looked like he was in his late teens even though he would soon be twenty-seven. In civilian clothes, he might be mistaken for a college athlete. He'd been a collegiate all-American lacrosse player, a first-team attacker with the size and speed of a football linebacker and the smarts of a chess player. There was a quiet confidence about him. Some would say he was unflappable. Calm, cool, and controlled were terms on his Marine fitness reports. The most notable feature that overshadowed everything else was his eyes. They were ice blue. Captain Ruhawk scanned each Marine. Some troopers thought he was the officer in charge of the returning Marines. Others did not care who he was. They just hoped he wasn't there to screw with them. When the final Marine passed through the heavy metal green doors, the captain followed.

The two converted hangars were connected by a double-wide concrete walkway. Next to the doors leading into the second hangar was the large, battered blue dumpster, its top open. Several Marines had stopped and tossed items in the trash before proceeding into the hangar. Captain Ruhawk waited. After the last Marine entered the hangar, he investigated the trash container. The dumpster was half filled with a variety of contraband. He shook his head in amusement. Marines never failed to surprise him.

Building B-23 was a newer prefabricated replica of the first hangar. The steel support structures looked like the bones of a huge beached whale. The enlisted were ants in the gargantuan building. They formed several lines in front of the inspection tables. The long banquet-style tables had worn, tan Formica tops. Behind each inspection point was a stand-alone enclosed room with a huge mirrored wall facing the tables. The NCO processers asked for orders, IDs, and luggage. Marines began emptying their jungle utilities, uniform pockets, carry-ons, and bags. After reviewing documentation, the NCOs began inspecting the contents of each piece of luggage. Sometimes they pulled apart the lining of the suitcase. At one table, the inspecting NCO raised his hand. Quickly two very large Marine MPs with gunmetal-gray Colt 45 automatic pistols strapped to their hips and white-maple belly clubs in their hands appeared. The MPs positioned themselves on either side of the returning Marine the NCO was searching. The Marine became agitated and yelled, "What the fuck do *para-fin-nail-ya* mean?"

The OIC of inspections, a chief warrant officer who sat behind the two-way mirror in the center standalone room, shook his head in disgust. The jarhead causing the *paraphernalia* commotion had to be one of McNamara's One Hundred. The OIC could spot them two clicks away.

■■▮▮▮▮

Secretary of Defense Robert McNamara had this great idea of integrating 100,000 substandard recruits into the armed forces to meet the needed quota for the draft and to uplift the unemployable marginalized citizenry. That would help the constant need for cannon fodder in the Nam and address President Johnson's war on poverty at home. McNamara patterned the initiative after the Israeli Army's program of ethnic assimilation of immigrants into the armed forces. The Israeli project worked because their recruits were physically fit and mentally capable. In contrast, the US 100,000 project, also known as the Moron Corps, recruited the unfit. These individuals did not have the minimum education and/or could not meet the physical requirements for the services but were allowed to enlist. This social experiment in the middle of a war proved catastrophic. McNamara's Moron Corps comprised 10 percent of the Marine Corps Nam force but caused 90 percent of its personnel problems. The "paraphernalia" soldier was a poster child for that substandard group.

Gunner Zorba, a warrant officer, knew in his gut that this experiment would have long-lasting negative effects on his Corps. He doubted he could make it three more years to his thirty years for max retirement benefits. Drugs, racial discourse, McNamara's idiots, drafties in the Corps, and Nam itself were albatrosses around the Corps's neck. Every day the gunner could feel the internal pressure building.

Exasperated, Zorba struggled out of his chair to face yet another human pustule infecting his beloved Corps. His morning was going to be devoted to explaining what *paraphernalia* meant to a fifth-grade dropout who probably read at a third-grade level. The discharge paperwork would require several hours of night work. All for someone who should never have been allowed to wear the Marine green with the Eagle, Globe, and Anchor.

After the commotion, the paraphernalia Marine was escorted through the doors behind the inspection table by the MPs, his luggage and all personal effects put on a rolling cart. The inspecting NCO pushed the cart through the doors the MPs used. Later, the "McNamara turd" would be transported to the detention center with other "brig bunnies." These problem children were becoming the new bowel blockage in a military judicial system struggling with the "Nam" crap cramp.

A new inspector appeared from a different door and took the place of the departed NCO at the table. The inspection continued. Soon, every order was stamped and all luggage repacked. All arriving Marines departed except the ever-watchful Captain Ruhawk.

He approached the inspection table and put his battered, drab-green Valpak, cheap brown plastic zipper valise, red USMC gym bag, orders, and book on the table. He began to empty his uniform pockets. A poster-perfect staff sergeant approached the tables.

"Excuse me, Captain. You don't have to go through this inspection."

"Why is that, Sergeant?" asked the captain.

"You're an officer, sir."

Captain Ruhawk laughed with a deep-in-the-gut rumble. "You and the Corps know all officers are above reproach, correct?"

"Yes sir," said the E6 with a smile.

"Sergeant, please have one of the corporals stamp my war trophy DD603 form so all's shipshape per USMC regulations. I have a Tokarev 7.62 TT 51 Chicom pistol to declare with two magazines; no ammunition."

Quickly the sergeant got the attention of one of the NCO processers and checked the captain's orders and trophy forms.

"Sir, all's shipshape."

"Thank you," said the captain.

"Welcome home, sir."

The captain picked up his novel, *Catch-22* by Joseph Heller.

"Sir, how do you like the book?"

"After Nam I think it's more autobiographical than satirical. A fun read. I would recommend it to anyone that wanted a good FUBAR laugh." *FUBAR*—Fucked Up Beyond All Reason.

"I need a good laugh and some fun, sir," said the sergeant with a hint of sadness.

The captain looked around. "This looks like a party place. It's sure better duty than humping in the bush."

"Yes sir. Did my time in '67 with 2/1 on the Rockpile, and this is definitely better duty. Expecting orders for a second tour to Nam any day."

"Good luck. Oh, before I forget, you might like to look in the Dempsey Dumpster between the buildings. The EOD people may be needed," said the captain.

"Yes sir," said the surprised sergeant.

■■■■■

"Good eyes, Sergeant," said the Air Force explosive ordnance disposal tech. "There was some interesting shit in the dumpster, but the M-26 fragmentation grenade could have spoiled your whole day. How you saw it among the other crap is amazing."

The sergeant just nodded.

The EOD group moved their vehicle and the very large funnel-shaped bomb-disposal trailer with the grenade inside away from the dumpster. They would explode the fragmentation grenade downrange. One of the processing NCOs came up to the staff sergeant after the truck and trailer moved out and asked how he knew the grenade was there. The staff sergeant explained.

"You mean that weird standoffish captain who watched everyone like a brig bull?"

Sergeant Quinn turned to face the corporal who'd spoken. "Jerkins, before you run your mouth you best do a recon of his ribbons. That captain has one Silver and two Bronze Stars and four Purple Hearts. His campaign ribbon has six stars. He's no REMF." Aka a rear echelon motherfucker. "He's a bush Marine and badass to the bone. Now get back to work."

A dull-gray school bus stopped in front of another colossal aircraft hangar. Above a single man door cut into the huge metal hangar doors was a sign: *Officer's Transit Facility.* Captain Ruhawk grabbed his belongings. The Air Force driver informed him the bus ran on the half-hour service and stopped at 2100. After scheduled hours, a base cab could be requested at the front courtesy desk in the TOQ, the transit officers' quarters. The captain nodded and stepped off the bus. The bus crunched gears and sped off. Captain Ruhawk stood a moment and did a 360-degree appraisal. This area of the base seemed deserted except for several old Quonset-style hangars that could house mega-airplanes like the B52. The buildings were probably vintage Korean War or earlier.

The surrounding concrete deck was cracked and neglected. The captain got the feeling the Air Force didn't like the idea of housing transit officers. These quarters were not the outstanding Air Force officer quarters that were the pride of the air service. Looking at the sky, the captain figured it was about 1300. He looked at his watch to verify the time and realized he was still on Okinawa time. With a smile of amusement, he picked up his gear and went inside the hangar.

Captain Ruhawk felt like he had walked into the lobby of an upscale hotel chain. The lobby was ultra-modern with tubular chrome tables and black leather chairs, the walls painted off-white and adorned with black-and-white photos of every fixed-wing plane the Air Force ever flew. There was a young female attendant behind the welcome counter wearing Air Force blues.

"May I help you, sir?" said the enlisted E2. She looked young and healthy. With a little makeup, she could be pretty. Her hair was pulled back and set into a severe bun, giving her a no-nonsense demeanor.

"Yes, I need a room for several days," replied Captain Ruhawk.

"May I see your orders, sir?' she asked.

While the receptionist looked at the captain's orders, he set his watch to LA time. The overhead digital clock read *13:16*.

After review of the orders by the clerk, he signed some check-in forms and received a key, a packet of information about the base, and directions to his room. The TOQ was a series of prefabricated modular rooms that were perpendicular to hallways off a long central corridor. The multiroom facility was one floor, windowless, air conditioned, and sterile—a cost-effective dormitory. To the captain's surprise, his room was large, furnished with a king bed, metal nightstand, metal dresser, small metal writing table with metal chair and flex-crane metal desk light. Next to the desk was a comfortable-looking Air Force–blue Naugahyde sitting chair. The bed was made and there were clean white towels in the adjoining bathroom. A fruity smell assaulted his nostrils until he realized it was a disinfectant smell and not something rotting. Slowly he undressed and hung his uniform on fat hangers in the closet. After he stripped off his underwear, he stood in front of the full-length mirror attached to the closet door. Captain Ruhawk surveyed his body.

He was thin, too thin. His five-foot-eleven frame had once carried about 180 pounds. He had a swimmer's build—narrow waist and broad shoulders. Now, at 156 pounds, he looked more like a long-distance runner who had missed too many meals. He could put the weight back on his body but would have to work to ensure most was muscle.

He refocused on the marks the war had left on his body. One scar zigzagged from the inside of his right knee to his upper thigh. It looked like a cartoon lightning bolt. The new skin was mahogany red. A scimitar-shaped scar ran from his forehead through his left eyebrow and across his nose. The scar was like weathered fishing line and blended into his tanned face. A white pencil-line scar ran from his left collarbone down his chest and under his right nipple, ending with a hook in his right side. Then there were the red measles-looking scars that peppered his left side. He remembered the pain of each mark. The physical scars were easy to recognize. His brain was a different matter.

Captain Ruhawk had a love affair with war. The camaraderie, the demands of body and mind, and the intensity of battle were addictive. That was the upside. The downside was the price he paid to the bitch Bellona, the ancient Roman goddess of war. She demanded payment in flesh and bone plus compound interest on the psyche. His physical scars were a daily reminder of the cost. His mental scars were to be determined.

Marine training prepared him for the academics of war but not its psychological effects. Now, somewhere deep within his soul, Captain Ruhawk had embraced the physical and mental carnage of the battlefield. He rationalized his passion for combat as a coping skill to handle the brutality and heartlessness of the deadly arts.

Those skills didn't account for other feelings—the terror before the attack, and the exhilaration during. The captain felt intoxicated by rage in close quarters while shooting, stabbing, and slashing. Afterward, being alive never felt so fantastic. Light, sounds, smells, even plain water was wondrous. He enjoyed them as if he were a newborn babe. He liked the sensation, but his emotions disturbed him. Was a sadistic person lurking in his rail-thin body, wanting to brutalize others? What had General Lee said during the Battle of Fredericksburg? "It is well that war is so terrible, or we should get too fond of it." Would he be damned because he was "fond of it"?

Stop thinking. Your war is over. . . at least physically.

Moving away from the mirror, Captain Ruhawk went to the nightstand and put his wristwatch on the table. His mind tumbled like a clothes dryer. Suddenly another image appeared in the small dryer window—the watch his mother had given him. It reminded him of their trip together to New York City.

He had just completed The Basic School for Marine officers and had his orders to Fleet Marine Force Pacific and Nam. Lieutenant Ruhawk had three days of in-transit time. It would only take him a day to fly to the West Coast, so he met his mother in the Big Apple for a pre-birthday outing before he shipped out. They stopped at a high-end jeweler on Avenue of the Americas and purchased the stainless-steel, French-made Tourneau wristwatch for his twenty-third birthday. The watch had a simple black face, iridescent numbers, one to twelve, and in the background twelve to twenty-four, with a black nylon band. His mother insisted on paying for the high-end timepiece. He insisted on the engraving on the back, his name, service number, service, and date of commission: *M. Z. Ruhawk, 0105186, U.S.M.C., 01-04-65.*

After an awkward lunch of things not said, mother and son picked up the watch. This would be the last time they saw each other. After goodbyes at JFK Airport, Ruhawk would fly to Danang, Viet Nam, and she to Cleveland, Ohio. He thought he was flying to his death in

French Indochina and his mother into an agonizing period of prayer and waiting. Instead, she passed away from cancer in a hospice run by French nuns, and he returned home hoping to find peace.

Wearily, Captain Ruhawk walked to the bathroom for a refreshing shower. He loved hot showers. The psychological muck and stink of Nam would never wash off, but the ceremonial cleansing made him feel better. After the long, stinging, blistering-hot shower, he toweled off and slipped between the clean white sheets. Captain Ruhawk's last thought before drifting off to sleep was of the sensual pleasure of lightly starched, clean bed sheets contrasted with the dirt-encrusted, smelly, sodden poncho liner he left in the "Arizona Territory" of Quang Nam Province.

The rain. The fucking rain. The cold fucking rain.

Mike Ruhawk was more miserable than he could imagine. He sat alone under a poncho liner in a chill, water-filled hole in the middle of triple-canopy jungle. The monsoon had started eleven days earlier—eleven days of unrelenting rain. The sky was darker than India ink on black paper. All Ruhawk could hear was the rain hitting leaves. There was something out there. Of that he was certain. His eyes tried to focus.

Ruhawk reached for his M16, but nothing was there. The breath of the beast filled his nose. It was hot and rancid. His olfactory memory struggled to identify the smell. Synapses snapped between the smell of rotten dead dog and fish-head sauce—*nuk baum*. The thing rose up and engulfed him. Terror choked him. He was shivering with fear. Ruhawk flung aside his poncho and ran. The black void swallowed him.

He wasn't sure if he was asleep or awake. There was no noise, just silence. He blinked. Everything remained the black of a deep abyss. No light; this darkness was the total absence of light. Grabbing the tangled sheet covering him, Ruhawk flung it away as if it were a funeral shroud. His hand hit a solid object. He spotted the iridescent watch face. Instantly he realized where he was: the officers' transit quarters, Norton Air Force Base, San Bernardino, California. He fumbled for the light switch.

The bedside lamp cast a soft light in the sterile room. He looked at his watch. The hands indicated it was 1606 hours. Captain Ruhawk wiped the perspiration off his chest with the damp fallen sheet. Feeling slimy, he took a quick shower. He hoped the hot water would take the chill away and calm his panic. As he dried, he looked through the *Welcome to NAFB* packet. An information sheet indicated the officers club was open from 0530 to 2300 weekdays and 1200 to 2400 weekends. Lunch served after 1200. Evening meal served from 1600 to 2100 weekdays and 1700 to 2200 weekends. Sunday buffet 1100 to 1330.

Run first, eat second, and then plan. That sounded like an excellent course of action, thought Ruhawk.

The captain dumped his red bug-out bag on the bed. He pulled out his khaki Navy Underwater Demolition Team shorts, black running shoes, and a faded green cotton T-shirt with the *1st Marine Division* patch stenciled above the left breast pocket. He dressed and stretched. He planned to run two to three miles, return to the TOQ to shower, shave, put on his Alphas, and go to dinner at 1800 hours; a good, simple plan of attack.

Key in hand, the captain walked down the corridor to the front lobby desk. The TOQ was deathly quiet, the corridor's walls painted a muted blue. The overhead lighting dimmed to a faint glow. He could barely hear his running shoes on the thick, dark-blue carpet. There was no one at the check-in counter. Captain Ruhawk didn't stop. He pushed out the front doors. He was stunned for a few moments.

Instead of being greeted by a sunlit California sky, it was zero dark thirty. He turned around and walked back into the lobby. He looked up at the digital clock above the reception counter. It showed *0432*.

A different airman appeared behind the counter. He looked a little unkempt like he had been napping.

"May I help you, sir?" the airman asked.

"Jetlag, I think. I just slept fourteen-plus hours, thought it was afternoon," answered the bewildered captain.

"Are you flying 52s or tankers, sir?"

"Neither, just in transit."

"The confusion seems to get the long-haul pilots more than jet jocks. The TOQ has no windows or room clocks. The facility has soundproof rooms. The detail that works here calls the TOQ the *tombs*," stated the airman.

"Maybe you could help me. I would like to take a run, two to three miles. Are there any measured distance courses nearby?"

"Nothing officially marked, sir. But if you take a right out the doors and stay parallel to the hangars, the first paved road you meet is Perimeter Road. Take a right; follow it until you reach a traffic circle. That's about a mile and a half, maybe two miles. There should be very little traffic at this hour. I should warn you about the high level of assaults on base. Race relations are a problem—black power versus white control and all. A base directive has been issued by the CG advising personnel to travel in pairs after dark." The CG was the commanding general.

"Thanks for the info," said Ruhawk.

The captain followed the directions and ran to the traffic circle. There was no traffic; the temperature was in the low seventies. The ambient light from the airfield provided enough light to avoid any pitfalls. He ran alongside the paved road on dry, crunchy, water-starved grass. By the time he reached the traffic circle, sweat drenched his shirt. He estimated the distance closer to two miles than one and a half. He walked around the circle several times to slow down his heart rate and stretch out the burn in his lungs and legs. Headlights from a sedan stopped at one of the circle's intersecting roads blinded him for a moment. The dark two-door coupe slowly drove around the traffic circle, then stopped in front of Ruhawk. Two men dressed in civilian clothes emerged from the car. The passenger spoke.

"Ain't too smart for a cracker to be walking alone out here in da nite," said a tall, well-built man in sweatpants and a black hoodie. Captain Ruhawk couldn't see their features.

The other man, smaller but more muscular, said, "I think we'z should teach this honkie a few lessons. What's you say, boy?"

Ruhawk didn't say anything. He just rolled his shoulders.

"Bro, I think we'z got a skinny white pussy," said the tall driver as he approached.

Captain Ruhawk moved backward in slow, measured steps, thinking he could outrun the pair. He did not want anything to spoil his leave and personal mission. A confrontation with these thugs would just add to the difficulty of his new mission.

Ruhawk turned and sprinted. The pursuing passenger was faster than Ruhawk had expected. Suddenly, in midstride, the captain twisted, swinging his right elbow in a savage downward arch. The tip of his elbow caught the running attacker square on his right temple. With a thud, the man dropped face-first into the concrete curb. He was out cold, bleeding from the mouth. The driver looked at his friend, then turned and ran to the car. Before he could get the car door fully open, his face was smashed into the door jamb. His nose made a loud pop, and blood poured down his dark-tan zippered jacket. As he slid down the door, Ruhawk caught him under the arms and pushed the driver's arms through the open window Then, he opened the door and cranked up the window trapping the driver's upper arms. The man moaned in pain. Ruhawk carefully closed the door and dragged the other attacker to the car. In the same fashion, he locked the second assailant's arms in the passenger-side window frame. The two men looked like chicken wings draped on the carcass of a dead bird.

The captain started to walk away when the driver screamed, "Motherfucker, you can't leave us like diss."

"Payback is a medevac," Ruhawk said as his fist pounded the driver's jaw. The driver's head snapped back and his body went limp.

Standing next to the TOQ lobby counter, the sweating Captain Ruhawk opened and closed his right hand. He would need some ice to slow the swelling. The sleepy airman appeared behind the counter.

"How was the run, sir?"

"Great, more like four miles than three. I think you should get the shore patrol or whatever you call your military police to that traffic circle. There seems to be two people that need medical assistance. And do you have an ice machine?"

CHAPTER 2

MIA

CAPTAIN MIKE RUHAWK STOOD outside the TOQ watching the sun peek over the San Bernardino Mountains. The morning was going to be Hollywood glorious; bright sun, blue skies, and clean air, with the temperature in the upper seventies. It was 0601. The captain had been waiting for more than a half hour for the base taxi. He took the time to enjoy the sunrise and relax. It had been a long time since he felt safe. The constant anxiety of unseen booby traps, enemy snipers, and tree line ambushes had vanished. He no longer felt he had a target pasted on his helmet. He took a deep breath and let the air out slowly, savoring the moment.

The moisture of the steaming tropics was replaced with the dry fresh air of California. He no longer tasted the decay of jungle, the sour smell of fallow rice paddies, or the putrid odor of the unwashed. He had enjoyed the long shower, shave, deodorant, and cologne.

Mike considered himself almost Marine Corps presentable. His uniform needed a professional press and cleaning, but the steam iron he found in the room did an adequate job. His shoes shined brightly. It was as if he'd never left the comfort of the States. When the dented yellow taxi finally arrived, he smiled. He asked the driver to take him to the base officers' club.

The club looked like a massive Pacific Palisades ranch house, all white stucco, terracotta-tiled roof, narrow floor-to-ceiling windows, and a wide wraparound screened veranda. The surrounding area was landscaped like a tropical island in the middle of a concrete ocean. Palm trees swayed, huge ferns made a lush green border around the club's exterior, railing boxes were filled with yellow ginger lilies, and the brick pathway to the entrance was bordered with red Katie Moragne. Inside lights gave the dwelling a glow like a garden lantern in the early morning shadows. Mike passed hanging lipstick-red bougainvillea in bloom next to the front doors, the bright-red blossoms sprinkled with dew.

The interior was just as lush as the exterior. The captain walked into the wide travertine hallway. His dress shoe heels clicked down the polished floor. Per military protocol, the captain went to the club's business office. In most military officer clubs, patrons signed a paper chit for all meals and drinks. The bill was tallied at the end of each month, and the officers promptly paid or stood tall in front of the base commander. The club's office was small, and a middle-aged female civilian clerk helped him register. Captain Ruhawk filled out the necessary personal information card, paid his fifteen-dollar annual membership fee, and received his club membership number. The four-digit code could be used at all base support facilities except the commissary and exchange. All he had to do was put his number on the chit and sign.

The captain chose seating on the screened veranda. Hanging flowering plants and tropical ferns decorated the outdoor space. The wrought iron table was set for two. Gleaming sterling silverware lay on a bright-white linen tablecloth. Sparkling crystal Waterford glasses and fresh-cut red carnations adorned the rectangular table. *Only first class for the airdales,* thought Mike.

The club sat on a knoll providing an elevated panoramic view of the base and flight line. It was 0642 and the airport was busy. Every type of plane was moving, from prop mono-wing planes to huge passenger jets. Captain Ruhawk enjoyed the view and activity as he savored his second cup of coffee. A one-star Air Force general and an elegant woman took seats several tables away. Captain Ruhawk acknowledged their presence with a "Good morning, sir." The brigadier general acknowledged him with a smile and good morning. The neat, thin, well-coiffed woman with the general gave Ruhawk a withering stare. Soon a young woman joined them, dressed in form-fitting chinos and a loose-fitting turquoise blouse accessorized with a multicolored scarf. Her hair was cut wedge style, known as the Dorothy Hamill cut after the Olympian gold medal winner. She looked like a young professional business executive or a catalogue model. The captain thought her quite attractive. She sat next to the general and they soon were in a lively discussion.

Captain Ruhawk refocused on his breakfast. Three eggs, slab of bacon, hash browns, and all the white toast with butter and jam he could eat. *Real food!* Hopefully he had eaten his last C-ration. Pushing the cleaned plate away, he felt well fed and relaxed. It seemed like an eternity since he had been able to eat a meal with pleasure. He was reaching for another cup of coffee when the general spoke to him.

"Excuse me, Captain, would you please join us?"

The young woman said, "Daddy, let the captain enjoy his breakfast. This is a family matter."

"I believe an outside voice of reason is in order. He's a Marine officer and outside my sphere of influence, so his input should not be tainted."

"And only God knows how large your sphere of influence is, Daddy Dear," interjected the sarcastic young woman.

"Sir, I'm a simple infantry officer returning from my overseas tour. I doubt if I can add anything of value to your family discussion," the captain said.

"Nonsense! You are an experienced officer. Please join us," said the general in a very demanding voice. It was, in essence, an order.

"Oh my God, you're unbelievable," said the petulant daughter.

Captain Ruhawk numbered and signed his chit and approached the general, who rose.

"Captain Mike Ruhawk, United States Marine Corps, at your service, sir." They shook hands.

"Brigadier General John Esposito, my wife, June, and my daughter, Angela."

"My pleasure, ladies."

"Please sit, Captain," said General Esposito. "May I call you Mike?"

"Sir, yes sir," replied Mike as he sat down next to Angela. For an awkward moment, his leg touched Angela, who did not seem to mind.

Turning slightly in his seat, Mike met her eyes. She was inspecting him as if he were some snack about to be devoured. She flashed a flirtatious smile. Mike's eyes diverted to the four empty cocktail glasses in front of the general's wife. She showed no signs of inebriation.

"Reconnaissance completed, Captain?" asked the general.

"Yes sir," answered Mike, somewhat embarrassed.

"My curiosity needs to be satisfied," said the general.

"Sir?"

"As the base commander's XO, I read the night's incident reports before I go to breakfast. One report piqued my interest. Two known race agitators were discovered severely beaten and immobilized in their vehicle earlier this morning. A Marine captain doing early morning physical training reported their plight. Would you know anything about the incident?"

Mike covered his swollen hand. "Yes sir. I reported the two men needing assistance."

"I'm sure the provost marshal will want to speak to you. It would behoove you to stop and see him today."

"Yes sir."

There was a long pause as the general's eyes never left Captain Ruhawk's face.

"Here's the situation. Our daughter is a junior at UCLA and wants to quit to get married to some hippie musician."

"He's not a hippie," said Angela defensively.

"As I was saying, we are not thrilled. I have asked her to finish school before she decides to throw away her life. She is doing very well in a pre-med program."

"Let's get the story right," said Angela. "You are not happy. Mom could care less. She's fucked up about Peter."

"Young lady, two things I will not tolerate is that language and any disrespect for your mother. We are not talking about Peter now, but you," the general said in a deep, menacing voice.

"I would like your opinion about Angela and school," General Esposito said, turning back to Mike.

For the first time in a very long time, the captain felt out of his realm. All he wanted to do was walk back to the TOQ, put on some civvies and go to the PX.

"Sir, I am in no way qualified to give an opinion."

"Give one anyway, Captain," insisted the general.

"Yes sir." Captain Ruhawk pondered the question for a moment. "From my own experience, you can never have enough education. Education can be formal like an institution of higher learning or practical as in the field. Complete school. Finish what you start. Second, all life decisions should be made only after examining all options in the appropriate amount of time. All decisions should be on the spectrum of the best-case and worst-case scenarios. If you have difficulty handling the worst-case scenario, you must re-evaluate the problem. Third, always remember there are more spectators with opinions than the leaders who make the decisions. Make a decision and move ahead."

"My God, you sound like Peter," said Angela, stunned.

Mrs. Esposito dropped her glass on the table and started to cry. The bloody Mary cocktail splattered on everyone at the table.

"Christ almighty," said the general. "Angela, please take your mother to the ladies' room and ask the manager to get some soda water for the captain and me. I'll be able to change at the office, but I doubt Captain Ruhawk has another uniform."

"Come on, Mom, let's get you cleaned up. As one of Dad's great Army commanders said, 'I will return,'" Angela piped.

"That did not go as I expected," said General Esposito. "My own fault, as you can see. Our family is a little dysfunctional. We aren't dealing very well with our adult daughter's rebellion. And our son's MIA status is driving us over the psychological edge."

He paused, then explained. "Our son is an Air Force captain flying F4 Phantoms from Ubon, Thailand. Seven months ago, he did not return from a raid over Hanoi. Other pilots confirm a parachute opening but, as of today, no confirmation of his status by the North Vietnamese."

"A difficult situation, sir," said Mike.

"I see by your ribbons that you've been to Vietnam," said General Esposito.

"Yes sir. Finished my second tour and on my way to MCB Quantico, Virginia, sir."

"What's the ground situation in Nam?" asked the general.

"Sir, my knowledge of the overall situation is negligible. My tours were with the 1st Marine Division, I Corps. I was an infantry platoon and company commander."

"You must have an opinion."

"Yes sir."

"Captain, opinions are just those—opinions. I would be interested in hearing yours from the viewpoint of a company-grade officer on the ground."

"Yes sir." Mike paused. "The Viet Cong and NVA we fight are determined and experienced. In a conventional confrontation, we roll over them. They are no match for Marines. However, as an irregular force—guerrillas—they are difficult to find, fix, and destroy. If history is any indicator, this war will be long, costly in both men and material, and unwinnable, sir."

"Do you consider yourself a defeatist, Captain?"

"Absolutely not, sir. I'm a realist. We will win every battle. But strategically, unless political policy changes, I believe this will be the first war we lose, sir."

"Are you implying my son's efforts are in vain, Captain?" the general huffed.

Angela walked to the table and stood directly in front of the general. "Daddy, you need to take Mother home. She has passed out in the bathroom."

General Esposito dabbed his mouth with a napkin and slid back his chair.

"Captain, we will have to carry on this most interesting conversation. I will reserve a table for 1730 tonight at the club; be there. Now, if you will excuse me."

"Thank you for returning," Mike said to Angela. "I'd dug a deep hole and your father was just about to bury me."

Angela's face lit up.

"Anything for our men in uniform," she said

"Thank you."

"Do you have plans for the day?" she asked.

"I have to get to the paymaster and PX. Now I'd better check out of the TOQ. I'm not having dinner with your father, nor am I talking to the provost."

"Do you have a car?"

"No."

"Great, I need a mental health day from school. You need a driver and someplace to stay."

"I don't want to impose."

"A breath of fresh air will do both of us good—you away from the military, and me away from my family and school. Let's go grab your stuff and visit the admin building and PX."

━━▪▪▪▪

Angela was excited about the possibility of an interesting day with a handsome Marine officer. Mike was excited about the possibilities of spending his first full day back in the world chauffeured by a woman that could be on the cover of a fashion magazine. Angela's car was a 1961 black VW bug with manual shifting. Mike had loaded his luggage into the back seat after checking out of the transit officer quarters. Next stop was the paymaster. Angela knew her way around the massive base and drove Mike to the redbrick building that housed the Air Force Financial Administration Office of the Paymaster. Mike cashed one of his government checks, carefully putting the crisp twenties in his plastic, zippered folder.

They arrived at the Post Exchange. Mike's shopping list was short. He needed some colored pocket T-shirts, a pair of dark-blue or black slacks, a couple of button-down short-sleeve collar dress shirts, some tighty-whitey briefs, tube socks, toothpaste and a road atlas. Angela guided him through the mammoth PX.

"Where to now, Marine?" asked Angela.

"I need a couple pair of well-worn jeans and a good pair of cowboy boots."

"At your service, and I know just where to go. It's on the way to my apartment."

"Outstanding!"

They drove for a half hour through heavy LA traffic. Angela fiddled with the car radio as Mike gazed out the window. He felt jittery with all the bumper-to-bumper traffic, skyscrapers, and the pulsating humanity. He had spent the last year yelling at his troops to stay ten yards apart to avoid multiple causalities from mines. Here, people packed the sidewalk without cover or concealment. They just walked about looking like they didn't have a care in the world. Cold sweat trickled down his back.

"Are we going to stop soon?" he asked.

"The shops are just around the corner. Are you feeling OK?"

"I'm feeling a little claustrophobic. I'll be OK once I get out of the car."

She pulled the VW to the curb. Before it came to a complete stop, Mike was out.

"I think it would be a good idea if you took off your uniform jacket and leave it in the car," she said.

Mike gave her a perplexed look.

"We're near campus. College dissidents and anti-war factions are confronting anyone who supports the war. Your recent badass behavior would probably get both of us into trouble. And that's not how I want to spend the rest of the day—or night—with you."

Night?

Ruhawk carefully took off his blouse and shirt and put them on the back seat. His white T-shirt, khaki trousers, and shiny black shoes would still be a giveaway if someone noticed, but the streets were filled with weirdos, and somehow he blended in.

After visiting several vintage clothing stores, Mike wore faded, torn, bootcut Levi's and a jean jacket. His prize find was a 1940s Cleveland Indians faded gray wool baseball hat. The *Chief Wahoo* embroidery logo had seen better days, but the hat fit. Now he looked the part of a civilian but still felt like an outsider—just one wearing civilian camouflage.

"Well, you certainly don't look like a squared-away Marine anymore," said Angela.

"Thank you. All I need now are some boots."

"Just a couple more blocks. Let's walk."

They turned a corner and walked into another world. Captain Ruhawk felt like he had stepped into the center ring of a bizarre five-ring circus. There were young people everywhere. They had beards, mustaches, long hair, and no hair. They wore bell-bottom pants, flowing tie-dye dresses, short-sleeve T-shirts with slogans calling for *Group Sex Wanted, Peace Not War, Gay Power, Burn Your Bra, Free Mandela,* and *Fight VD not VC.* There were braless girls and people dressed in saffron robes with shaved heads handing out flowers. Individuals were on street corners standing on stepladders, preaching everything from the end of the world to "save the whales." The pedestrian traffic enveloped them. Mike became extremely anxious.

Mike felt people pressing in from all sides. A giant invisible hand was squeezing him. His breath came in short gasps. He was spinning in a stream of lost souls. His vision narrowed and focused on the cracked sidewalk. The white concrete began to undulate like some creature from the depths of a burning lava pit. Suddenly in the middle of the sidewalk stood a very large black man with a beanie pulled down on his Afro. On his black shirt was a screen-printed clenched white fist. The T-shirt stretched tightly over his bulging muscles. His huge arms hung at his sides, his oversized hands balled into club-like fists. He looked like a human boulder. Angela was pushed by some pamphleteer and fell against the huge man.

"Watch were ya go'n, bitch," snarled the man.

"Excuse me. I think you owe the lady an apology," said Mike.

"Say what?" The man's face screwed up in rage.

"The appropriate response is 'pardon me,'" said Mike.

"Listen, you jive ass white turkey. You want some of dis?" said the man as he started to raise his fist.

Before the man could smash his balled hand to Mike's face, the captain quickly snapped his arm out and hit the giant man square in the sternum. The effect of the *Vo thuat Binh Dinh,* Vietnamese martial arts open-hand technique, was devastating. The gargantuan body recoiled as if hit with a wrecking ball. The man's head snapped forward. Mike crouched and sprang up, delivering a punishing uppercut. The giant staggered backward a step and fell, hitting his head on the concrete with a thud. Mike then kicked the man's side as if he were punting a forty-yard field goal. Angela quickly pulled Mike into the crowd of bystanders and hustled him down the street.

"What the hell's wrong with you? You can't attack everyone who has a problem," said Angela.

"He threatened me and disrespected you," said the Mike as he unclenched his re-swollen hand.

"That may be, but you'll be the one that goes to jail. For God's sake, he's known on campus as a leader in the Black Panthers. They take shit from no one," said Angela.

Mike smiled. "Neither do I. Now, let's get some boots." They quickly darted down the street as a large crowd gathered around the moaning Panther.

Mike bought a pair of snip-toe, two-toned, black, stirrup-heeled cowboy boots, and a pair of fancy multicolored knee-high cowgirl boots for Angela. She insisted she didn't want them, but he said they were payment in lieu of a chauffeur's fee.

"OK, cowboy, you ready for some lunch?" asked Angela.

"Sure am. How far are we from La Palma?"

"About an hour more or less depending on the traffic; what's over there?" replied Angela.

"I have a family to visit."

"It's only about one o'clock civilian time. We can stop and pick up something to eat and be there before three."

"This stop may take some time. I think you might feel awkward and I don't want to put you in a difficult situation," said Mike.

"Why not let me decide?" answered Angela.

"Look, I lost Marines in Vietnam. I'm taking my forty-two days of accrued leave and visiting as many families of my fallen Marines as I can. The first family is Corporal 'Double D' Dan Diamond. He was my radioman, good friend, and excellent Marine. His father and mother live in La Palma."

"Oh," responded Angela. "I think we should stop for lunch and talk this over."

"OK," said the captain.

They stopped at a small mom-and-pop Mexican restaurant in Los Nietos. They sat across from each other on well-worn red vinyl benches with a distressed wood table between them. He let her order for them. She spoke fluent Spanish, to the delight of the waiter.

"We're going to have chicken fajita, refried beans, and a couple of Pepsis, OK?" questioned Angela.

"Excellent," said Mike as he looked down at the paper napkin, stamped steel fork, and thin metal spoon. The silence became awkward as he fumbled with the utensils. Finally, Angela spoke.

"So, if I understand you correctly, you're on a quest to visit families of your fallen comrades."

"Yes."

"I assume the Marine Corps have grievance personnel that handle these types of visits."

"Yes."

"But you feel you have a special bond with these men and by visiting these families you can mitigate some of their grief."

"Yes."

"Had you given any thought that another visit by a Marine may make the grieving process more difficult?"

"Yes."

"Are these visits more for you than the families of your fallen Marines?"

Mike chose his words carefully. "I'm trying to bring closure to the families and myself."

"Your visits may bring you some closure but may reopen or worsen emotional wounds for the Marines' families. Have you thought of that?"

"This is something I have to do, for me and my Marines."

"I'm trying to understand. I get your reward, but I think you are a little arrogant to think you can bring any emotional relief to the families. You might even aggravate the grieving process. Instead of providing some peace, you may agitate some bitterness aimed at you and the Corps. You lived. Their son died. It's much more than a Marine thing."

"Sage advice, so noted," the captain said. "But this is my mission. I will perform to the best of my ability. These men were my responsibility. Their families need to know their stories. So, their combat commander is taking the time to visit their families to say their Marine son, brother, or husband was special. He made a difference, making the ultimate sacrifice for the Corps and country. I owe them that tribute."

"Who am I to deny a Marine captain's destiny?" said Angela sarcastically. They ate in silence, neither making eye contact during lunch. Mike paid the bill and Angela left a tip.

"Give me the La Palma address, please," said Angela.

"Are you sure you want to accompany me to Double D's?"

"Given some thought I'm sure I could find other things I would like to do, but this may give me some insight into what may happen in the future. MIAs have a way of turning into KIAs. I'd like to be prepared if it's possible," said Angela.

"All right, here is the address," said Mike. He pulled a small green government memo pad from his back trouser pocket. He flipped through the lined pages, ripped one out, and handed it to Angela.

After what seemed like an endless drive in a built-up industrial area, they entered a dilapidated business district.

"Are you sure of the address?" asked Angela.

"Absolutely!"

"It should be coming up on the left." She did a U-turn and parked in front of a long, 1920s-era two-story brick building. It needed some basic repair and paint. A large plateglass window covered most of the front of the first story and was painted with the Harley-Davidson motorcycle logo. In script below the sign was *Doc Diamond's Cycles* engulfed in ice-white flames. Wavering in the breeze above the glass doors were three flags—the Stars and Stripes, a California state flag, and a USMC flag.

Mike looked at the window and remembered the hours of conversation he had with Dan about motorcycles. Mike grew up in the Ohio countryside riding dirt bikes through fields and streams. Danny grew up in his father's shop fixing and riding street bikes. Their conversations were lively about the pros and cons of both pursuits. They had planned to tour the USA on Harleys after Nam. The VC changed those plans.

Now that he was here, Mike was unsure of how good his idea really was. *Maybe Angela is right*, he thought. He would stir the emotional pot. Nevertheless, Dan and he had made a commitment to each other. If one of them didn't make it home, the other would visit the deceased family. It was to be a testament of unity, faith, and the Corps. That all sounded good then, but this was now, and Marine captain Mike Ruhawk was not prepared. Angela stood next to the passenger door.

"Having second thoughts, Captain America? Where is that Marine gung-ho sprit I've always heard about?"

Do or die, thought Mike. He got out of the car. They pushed open the dirty glass doors of the dealership.

The inside of the store was early machine shop industrial. The floors were smoothed concrete painted maroon, scuffed bare in areas most traveled. The inside walls were distressed red brick. All the glass windows and doors had rebar welded to the inside of the metal casement frames for security. A long countertop of diamond plate steel ran parallel to the street. On it were several manuals and parts catalogues in quick reference stands. Centered on the counter was a large retro NCR cash register with a paper ribbon dangling over the edge. Between the front doors and counter were twenty or more motorcycles—all Harleys. Mike could identify several, like the 1916 HD 1000cc, the 1928 Single Banger, and the 1950 HD with the black-and-white-checked gas tank. Other HDs were stock 1960s mixed with a few customized choppers.

In one corner of the shop was motorcycle apparel, all in black: leather jackets, vests, chaps, gloves, boots, belts, hats, black leather everything. All the apparel embroidered with the HD logo. There were circular clothing racks filled with T-shirts with slogans like *America . . . love it or leave*; *Sniper–one shot one kill*; *The Few the Proud the Marines*; *Born to be Wild*; *Harleys Rule*; and *If you can read this, the bitch fell off*.

From somewhere behind the counter in the parts racks a manly voice yelled, "Be out in a flash. Look but don't touch. Chuck is watching."

Chuck? thought Mike.

Suddenly, appearing at the end of the counter was a king-size white German shepherd. The dog immediately sat. Mike had some experience with trained K9s in the Corps and stood still. Angela approached the dog. She was met with bared teeth and menacing growls.

"I think you should back away from the dog," said Mike.

"Ya think," Angela said as she slowly retraced her steps. The dog immediately licked his chops and wagged his tail.

A heavyset man appeared from behind the counter wiping his hands on a blue shop towel. He wore a grease-stained red Marine T-shirt, dirty jeans, and a small, brimmed, black leather Harley cap. His wire-rimmed half glasses were perched on a thin nose planted in an oval face surrounded by full salt-and-pepper beard. His gray ponytail was held back with red rubber bands. Peering up from his hand he said, "What are you looking for a—" He stopped mid-sentence and stared. Without another word, he went to the front doors and locked them. Then, he turned over the cardboard *Open* sign on the door. The sign now read *Closed, gone riding*. Next, he walked to Ruhawk, stuck out his hand, and said, "Welcome home, skipper."

They shook hands. "Thank you, Mr. Diamond."

"Please call me Eddy. And this is?" he asked, turning to Angela.

"My friend, Angela Esposito."

"Any friend of Danny's CO is a friend of mine," said Eddy.

"What was the giveaway? My buzz cut with white sidewalls, uniform, or—"

"That and the pictures we have of you and Danny, mostly the Marine bearing—*Once a Marine*, and all that. I've been expecting you for about a month now. Danny told us about your death pact. I was hoping that it would be . . . well, you know," said Eddy.

"Yes sir, I do know," said Mike with a trace of sadness in his voice. He felt a cold nose and wet tongue against his hand. It was the shepherd.

"Sit, Chuck! The white wolf is Danny's dog. He usually is very leery of strangers. Won't go near them, just growls. He sure has taken a liking to you."

Mike leaned over and scratched the dog's ears. Chuck leaned into Mike. His tail swept the floor rapidly. Angela approached.

"It's OK, boy, she's a friend," said Mike as he petted the dog's head.

Chuck calmed down and started to lick Mike's hand again.

"I'll be buggered. That's a first," said Eddy, looking at the dog.

"Eddy," said Angela, "my curiosity has gotten the better of me. I would expect your shepherd to be called King, Max, Brute, or something like that . . . not Chuck."

"Danny named him. He said it was a Marine thing," said Eddy.

"I'll explain later," Mike said.

"Come on upstairs. I want ya ta meet the wife," said Eddy.

Behind the counter and through the parts racks was a well-lit motorcycle garage. There were two bikes on motorcycle lifts. Parts were on several pyramid-style dolly carts next to the bikes. Tools littered the floor. In the back near an overhead garage door were several more cycles covered by a silver canvas tarp. Next to the white steel garage door was a metal man door. Adjacent to the man door were punched steel tread stairs leading to the second floor.

Eddy yelled up the stairs. "Ma, a couple of Danny's friends have stopped to visit."

"For goodness sake, invite them up," a sweet, mellow voice replied.

The aroma of sugar, cinnamon, spice, and vanilla welcomed them. Through the wooden eight-paneled door at the top of the stairs, they entered a California-style kitchen. The avocado-green kitchen appliances, sunflower-yellow Formica counters, and white breadboard cupboards were the essence of 1950s California modern.

"Welcome, welcome, welcome. I'm Sally Diamond, and you are?" said a woman who looked like a young Mrs. Santa Clause.

"I'm Mike Ruhawk and this is Angela Esposito."

"Oh my! You're Danny's commanding officer, aren't you?"

"Yes, mama."

She hugged him like a long-lost child, then held him at arm's length. "He's written so much about you, and here you are. Please, please sit down. I have some warm snickerdoodle cookies ready. They're Danny's favorites. I don't think I've burned these." Carefully she opened the oven and pulled out the fresh batch of cookies.

"Would y'all like some coffee?" said Eddy.

"Yes sir," replied Mike.

Angela shook her head no. She was watching Sally pull a tray out of the oven.

"Doggone it. I burned a few," said Sally. She took the pan to the large trashcan near the sink and scraped several dark-brown cookies into the overflowing container, filled to the brim with charred cookies. A few burned treats fell to the checkered vinyl floor. Chuck quickly devoured them.

Sally put the platter on the round chestnut kitchen table as if it were an offering to an ancient god. With a waving of hands, she announced in a loud theatrical voice, "Let's all sit down and have some cookies and milk. Papa, get a plate for Danny. He'll be here anytime..."

━▪▪▪▪▪

They drove in silence. It took over an hour to get to Angela's apartment. She lived in a neighborhood of California-style ranch houses not far from campus and had a one-bedroom apartment in a converted garage behind a cedar-clad ranch home. They pulled the car onto the crumbling asphalt driveway.

"I'm going back tomorrow," Mike proclaimed.

"Do you want to talk about the Diamonds in the car or inside the house? I would prefer to go inside and sit on the couch," said Angela.

"Inside would be great. Lead the way."

They got out of the car and entered the apartment. The living room was small, just enough room for a couch and single chair. The kitchen was even smaller, with a bathroom and single bedroom beyond. A loud window air conditioner struggled to cool the living room. Angela dropped her over-the-shoulder brown leather purse on the tiny kitchen counter and turned off the noisy window unit. The AC clunked and sputtered, then made a painful squeal before shutting off. A musty mildew smell seeped into the apartment.

"Want a beer?" she asked.

"That would be great," said Mike as he sat down in an abused, oversized chair that was a secondhand-store rescue. Taking the beer, Mike said, "That's one scenario I didn't imagine."

"You mean total denial?"

"Yeah, she's been cooking those cookies every day thinking Danny was coming home. My God, is that some sort of mental illness?"

"I'm no psychiatrist, but maybe it's a temporary coping skill."

"Interesting way to cope. I told Eddy I would stop by tomorrow to talk with him. He said anytime. Sally has a doctor's appointment in the morning and plans to stay with her sister the rest of the day."

"I have school, but I could drop you off when I go to class."

"Outstanding. I'll find a way back."

"That'll work. Now let's talk about tonight," said Angela.

Over several beers, they talked about families. Mike talked about growing up in rural Ohio, the only son of a stay-at-home mother and a college English professor father who taught Shakespeare. Angela talked of being a military brat who lived in five countries before she graduated from high school. She went to UCLA because her daddy was stationed in Texas and the possibilities of his being assigned in California were minimal. Then he was reassigned to Norton AFB when she was a sophomore. By that time, her brother, Peter, was flying jets. He was an all-star in high school, both academically and athletically, a real three-letter man with a 4.0 GPA. Of course, he went to the Air Force Academy, graduating near the top of his class.

"He is the favorite child," Angela said.

Angela admitted to a fling with one of the musicians living in the adjacent house, but it was over. She was just bull-baiting her dad with the possibility of dropping out and marriage. Mike listened but remained silent. *Be a leader, not a whiner*, he thought.

As the sun set, Mike got hungry and suggested they find a hamburger joint. He wanted a big juicy cheeseburger, fries, and a chocolate milkshake. That was his idea of an ideal American meal. Angela knew of just the place. It was a classic Southern California drive-in with servers in tight satin blouses, short pleated skirts, and roller skates. They chowed down in the car watching LA traffic cruise Wilshire Boulevard. The sights and sounds seemed alien to Mike after over two years in the bush of Nam. Mike became sullen and conversation stalled. To restart the conversation Angela asked about the Diamond's dog.

"What's the story with naming a dog Chuck? You said it's a Marine thing?"

"It's really a Navy thing that the Marines adopted. In the Marine Corps, we only have green Marines; some are lighter green, some are darker green. When groups of darker Marines talk, they sometimes refer to their lighter Marine friends as *Chucks*—not in a derogatory way, but just to distinguish them from their other friends. Now, when a group of light Marines talk, they sometime refer to their darker contemporaries as *Splibs*. Again, only to distinguish between the two groups."

"Splib? What does 'Splib' mean?"

"There are several definitions. One of my squad leaders, a dark green Marine, gave me a definition I like: 'Superior, Positive, Legitimate, Intelligent Blacks.'"

"Very interesting. But to a civilian it sounds like racial discrimination," said Angela.

"Far from it. It's just more military jargon to keep those not in the know guessing," answered Mike.

"Guessing about what?" Angela pressed.

"Think about it. I've been home two days and already had two racial confrontations. We're living in troubling times—racial problems, a sexual revolution, mass demonstrations, not to mention a foreign war," Mike said, visibly troubled.

"After Martin Luther King's assassination, race relations in the Corps deteriorated. It is better for Marines to call each other *chucks* or *splibs* than *crackers* or *niggers*. Someone outside the Corps listening to the troop would have no idea what the Marines were talking about," Mike continued. "They would not guess there were any internal problems, name-calling, or physical confrontations. Better having civilians guess than know. Our Marine image must stay pristine. It is sacrosanct. Perception is important in the wake of the My Lai atrocity. Marine Corps needs to be the standard-bearer, the best of the best."

Angela rolled her eyes. *Enough about the Marine Corps.* She asked what Mike wanted to do after dinner.

A hot shower and bed was his quick answer. He was not going to meet the general for dinner. Angela's father might be pissed about his no-show, but Mike was not in the general's chain of command, so there would be no consequences. In addition, he wasn't about to argue his assessment of Nam or be quizzed about the early morning altercation. He had a mission to complete and no one was going to stop him.

Angela smiled and nodded.

Back at the apartment Angela informed Mike it would take a few moments for the shower's water to heat. The hot water came from the main house. Because the three guys who lived there were gone, they would have plenty of very hot water. The two musicians were on a road trip, and the third occupant was in Berkeley at some student rally.

■■■■■

Mike stood under the shower and let the hot water pound his face. He had turned the faucet to the max to get the water as hot as possible. The small bathroom filled with steam. The water caressed his muscled body. As he relaxed, he started to daydream. He wondered if he was on a fool's errand. What relief was he bringing to the Diamonds? Could he help them accept Danny's death?

Mike was startled back to reality when cool hands caressed his back.

"I thought I'd get in the shower before we ran out of hot water," said Angela. Her arms reached around his chest. She pulled him to her. With her chest pressed into his back, she explored his torso.

"Now I understand the *force in readiness* concept," said Angela as she gently held him.

Mike turned. He took her face in his hands and passionately kissed her. They stumbled out of the shower, barely making it to her bed. Still wet, their entangled bodies began to move. Their union validated Mike. He was alive. He had survived. Maybe he could love again.

"It's been a while," said Mike after a quick surge of passion.

"I enjoyed it," said Angela.

He was still inside her when his passion started to rise again.

"That feels wonderful," said Angela.

Ever so slowly, they started to move. This time Angela whimpered in ecstasy. They held each other, relishing the sexual afterglow. Angela kissed his scarred nipple and asked if he would like a beer.

Angela got out of bed and walked to the kitchen. Mike was admiring her full figure when he heard a loud crash outside the AC unit window. Mike quickly jumped to his feet to investigate.

Angela met him in the kitchen. "It's my neighbor's cat. He likes to get on the air conditioner. Sometimes when the unit goes on it startles him and he makes a hell of a racket."

"You turned off the air conditioner earlier," said Mike.

Angela lowered the cold beer bottle and touched Mike in the crotch.

"Jesus H., that's cold," said Mike as he quickly stepped back.

"Well, Marine, would you rather worry about the cat outside or the pussy inside? I can tell you the inside feline needs more attention. Matter of fact, she's demanding more."

Mike smiled and swept her off her feet, carrying her back to bed.

They fell into a deep sleep sometime in the early morning, both exhausted from a marathon of sexual indulgence.

Mike opened his eyes as the morning sun streamed into the bedroom. He looked over his shoulder into the beautiful face of Angela. She had curled into his body with her arm across his stomach, leg intertwined with his. He started to move and felt a slight pressure on his manhood.

She whispered into his ear, "Where do you think you're going?"

"The sun is up, I'm up, everybody up," he said.

She smiled but would not let go. Slowly rolling on top of him, she said, "I've got other plans."

Later, after a morning shower and quick cup of coffee, they drove to Diamond Cycles. With a passionate kiss goodbye, Angela dropped Mike off in front of the motorcycle shop.

"See you later, Marine," yelled Angela as she drove off. Mike was glad no one was on the sidewalk to hear her. Somehow, he felt embarrassed.

■ ▮▮▮▮

The sign on the door indicated the shop was closed. Mike decided to check the back of the building for a garage door. He walked down the block to an adjacent building cut-through that would lead to the back alley. The steel garage door was open, and lying in the center of the threshold was Chuck. The dog immediately bounded toward the intruder. Mike held his ground. Chuck stopped two feet from Mike, cocked his head, and started to wag his tail like a puppy.

"Good morning, Chuck," said Mike as he carefully extended his hand palm up. After one sniff, Chuck started to lick Mike's hand.

"That's a good boy. Where is Eddy?"

Inside the garage, Mike found Eddy polishing a custom Harley painted candy-apple red. The chrome parts shined as bright as the SoCal sun.

"Good morning," said Mike. Eddy almost jumped out of his skin.

"So much for a faithful watchdog," said Eddy, looking with disdain at the so-called guard dog.

Chuck just stood next to Mike licking his hand.

Turning to the bike Eddy asked, "What do you think of the Harley?"

"She's beautiful, an extraordinary piece of form and function—moving art at its finest."

"Art and power," said Eddy. "This Hog is completely custom. She's got a thirty-eight chrome V-twin OHV Knucklehead 989cc bored and stroked to 1200cc plus. I talked to George at S & S cycle and he built a special carb to make this baby fly. The frame is a 1949 FL, raked, with big Springer front end, and long, straight, tuned dual exhaust pipes. The pipe is custom by R & R. They will add 10 percent to your horsepower. The gas tank is an oversize custom Tombstone with an added tachometer. The lights are from a 1932 Cadillac V-12 roadster; big bad chrome jobs. I set the two Caddy lights staggered on top of each other for better night riding. They extend a foot in front of the springs.

"The added touch is a chrome '49 Beehive taillight, just the right style. The small sissy bar has sergeant chevrons and crossed rifles as braces. The seat is original leather Big Bobber. You can ride five hundred miles and not have a sore ass. Added a Pillion solo pad for a buddy seat. The tires are Pirelli, slim eighteen on the front and fatty sixteen on the back. Marine Corps red with gold metal flakes paint job on the front and rear fenders is spectacular. Pinstriping is dead on, no pun intended. Final addition was my special flaming white ice paint that surrounds the Eagle, Globe, and Anchor emblem on both sides of the gas tank. In addition, this baby has some security features that will prevent any jacking. She's a show winner."

Mike looked over the machine for several minutes. He noted the detail and artisanship. The air intake cover was chrome with a raised three-dimensional diamond. The gas tank's Eagle, Globe and Anchor insignias were so realistic they looked like photographs. The white flames that surrounded the emblems gave them the illusion of movement. The bike glistened in the morning light. It felt alive under his touch. Then there was the script; in small, sweeping cursive on the tank next to the gas cap was, *Oh Danny Boy 1968.* Mike traced the lettering with his finger.

"I built it for Danny," Eddy said sadly.

Mike just nodded. They both stared at the machine for some time.

"I got a pot of coffee on. Let's go upstairs and talk. Ma stayed with her sister for the night. She won't be back here till early evening. Come on, Chuck, let's see what Smokey's up to. He's our house cat," said Eddy.

They went upstairs and sat at the kitchen table. The area still smelled of burnt cookies. For several minutes, they watch Smokey and Chuck play.

"Tell me what kind of Marine my son was." Eddy's voice trailed off.

Mike told him what a fine man and great Marine his son was. They talked quite a while about Danny before Eddy asked how Danny died.

Mike vividly remembered the day.

There was nothing unusual about the patrol. It was like hundreds of others. The day was hot and extremely humid, typical Nam in the rice paddies. The platoon had been slogging in the putrid, green, slimy paddy water all morning. They became used to the stench of human waste that fertilized the paddies. The stagnant waters were breeding ground for every imaginable insect. The leeches were the worst. But the constant buzz of a thousand insects and the horrible smell were just part of the day-to-day drudgery. The Marines wiped their faces with the green towels hanging around their necks and struggled forward.

"I wouldn't let my troops walk the paddy dikes," Mike said. "That's where the VC planted their booby traps. The easy trails were the most dangerous, I preached. As the platoon moved towards the isolated vill, the point man alerted to something in the adjacent tree line. I halted the column, got squads two and three on line, and spread out. We waited for something to happen. We waited and waited in the blistering sun. I became impatient. I told Danny to wait with the radio with the first squad while I went to the point. Trudging through the paddy muck towards the front, I heard a massive explosion. The shock wave threw me into the fetid water face-first. Regaining my footing, I looked to the rear. There was smoke and debris in the air. Some of the troops frantically yelled, 'Corpsmen up.' I tried to run back. My boots sucked mud. It was slow going."

Mike vividly recounted the large crater in the dike that appeared in the area of the explosion. It filled with brownish-red paddy water. He yelled for Danny to get on the hook and call for a medevac. When no one answered, he became angry.

"Luckily, the troops had spread out, so we didn't have other casualties." Mike didn't tell Eddy that the squad spent the rest of the morning collecting Danny's body parts. A bloody helmet, something that resembled an arm, a bare leg, just parts and pieces were found. The remains reverently placed on a spread poncho liner. The scene looked like a meat locker where a mad butcher worked.

Mike took a couple of deep breaths to regain his composure and simply said in a very quiet voice, "Danny tripped a large antipersonnel mine."

Together they looked at the top of the kitchen table. Neither said a word. Both had tears streaming down their faces. The anguish and sorrow were palpable. Reliving the explosion was like chewing broken glass mixed with gunpowder for Mike.

Eddy pulled a blue shop rag from his back pocket, wiped his eyes and handed it to Mike.

"Thank you. Danny was a good Marine and a great friend," said Mike.

"He was a better son," said Eddy.

The after-action report concluded Danny had taken the PRC 25 radio off his back and placed it on the paddy dike. The report speculated Danny was trying to keep the radio dry when he tripped the booby-trapped artillery round. The crater indicated the round was from a 155 mm howitzer high explosive round.

"I wondered why the Corps insisted on a closed casket," said Eddy. "Ma won't accept the fact that Danny's gone because she didn't see him in the coffin. She thinks it all is a mistake. Especially after we got a congratulatory letter from the commandant on his promotion to sergeant three days after we were notified of his death. She's sure Danny is going to walk through the front door any day." Eddy took a long pause and continued. "The Corps gave us several names of VA grief counselors. I'm not sure if we're ready to go quite yet."

"I'm not sure it's something you should put off. The sooner you contact help, the sooner she'll get better."

"How do you get better after losing your only son?"

Mike looked at the floor. He had no answer.

They talked some more. Eddy asked if Danny suffered. Mike

reassured him he did not. Eddy said he had to open the shop for business. Downstairs, Eddy went into a small office off the work area. When he came out, he had an envelope.

"This is for you. Danny would want you to have it," said Eddy as he handed the manila nine-by-twelve envelope to Mike.

Mike opened the envelope. Inside were three sheets of stiff paper. One was the State of California registration for a 1967 Harley-Davidson 1208 cc Motorcycle; the second, a clear title for the HD. The last sheet was a bill of sale indicating the owner of the custom HD was Mike Ruhawk and the seller Edwin D. Diamond. Mike looked at Eddy uncomprehendingly.

"The candy apple–red shovelhead Harley is yours," said Eddy.

Mike looked twice at the papers. "Eddy, I can't—"

Eddy cut him off, and in a forceful whisper he said, "Stop! You don't want to say anything but thank you."

Mike paused to gather his composure. "Thank you. Every day I ride the bike I'll think of our loss. He was special."

Eddy turned his head and sniffled. "Now we got to get you some leathers so you can be a real Harley biker." Without any more words, Eddy quickly moved to the front of the store, wiping his eyes on his sleeve.

After trying on several motorcycle jackets and boots, Mike placed a large, traditional black leather jacket, black leather riding gloves, calf-high leather boots, and an extra-wide studded black leather belt on the metal counter. The boots were steel toed with reinforced heels and side-to-side straps over the ankle, heel to heel; true biker boots. The black leather jacket had zippered pockets, zipper cuffs, and a large leatherneck collar.

"That should do it," said Eddy. "I've got a custom-painted helmet to match the bike for you in the back and a patch. The bike is free, but you gotta pay for the merchandise. Your total comes to $209. I can put that on an account for you or—"

"I'll pay cash," said Mike.

"In that case I'll throw in the HD wallet with a chain. Your money will be safe when you ride." Eddy rang up the total on the NCR resister. Mike counted out the cash. All he had were crisp new twenty-dollar bills.

"A pleasure doing business with you," said Eddy. They both smiled.

Mike asked if there was a shoe repair shop in the area. His leather jacket needed a little altering. Eddy said there was one down the street. Mike gathered up his purchases.

"Before you go, let me get Danny's colors." Eddy went into his office and came back with a large embroidered patch. The patch was a huge eagle with its wings spread. In its talons was a banner that read *Semper Fi*. The colors were vibrant: gold, silver, red, yellow, and blue.

"Please sew this on the back of the jacket. It would be a great tribute to Danny and all Marines," said Eddie.

Mike could only mutter, "I'll be back in a few." He held his emotions in check. There would be another time to let the dam break.

■ ▮▮▮▮

The shoe shop was a short walk away. Mike enjoyed the smell and feel of the new leathers.

After dropping off his apparel, he returned to the motorcycle shop. Eddy put him to work doing inventory. The shelves needed restocking and parts needed ordering. They worked through lunch, enjoying each other's company. Later, Eddy appeared with ham sandwiches and colas. The bread was homemade, the colas cold and the company perfect. They ate and talked business.

Eddy and Danny had big plans for the store. More HD apparel and maybe a lunch counter. The specialty of the house would be Harley Cheeseburgers and Chopper Fries. Abruptly, Eddy ended the conversation and said he had some mechanical work he had to complete. He returned to the motorcycle on the workbench and worked silently.

While Eddy worked on one of the cycles, Mike asked if he could use some of the milling machinery. With Eddy's permission, Mike did some metalwork. His finished projects were two interesting cycle-chain buckles for his motorcycle boots. Eddy gave a knowing smile at Mike's handywork. He said he had never seen anything like the buckles. They were certainly clever.

When Eddy was ready to close shop, he went over Danny's bike with Mike. After a familiarization lecture, Eddy kick-started the engine, the bike roared, and Mike quickly hopped on. Getting the thumbs-up from Eddy, Mike pushed back the kickstand and put the bike into gear. He gave the bike a little throttle and moved down the alley.

Once on the street he opened up the gas. The Harley sprang to life. A huge smile spread across Mike's face as he shifted gears. The sensation of speed was addictive. He felt the G-force as he accelerated. Everything came alive—the fragrances of budding flowers, the temperature drop of driving from a sunny street to a shady avenue, the smell of hot asphalt, the perfume of a female driver at a stoplight. All his thoughts focused on the ride, the bike, and the moment.

Mike returned to the garage after a long, exhilarating ride.

"Eddy, this is one sweet machine. The ride is as smooth as silk. The power is almost frightening. I love it," said Mike as he shut down the bike and dismounted.

Eddy stood in the doorway smiling.

"I got one more thing for ya," said Eddy. He disappeared into his office and returned with a pair of well-used black saddlebags.

"These bags were made for me by Bernie. He owns the shoe shop you took your leathers to. He rides Harleys. They're patterned after World War II Army Harley bags. I used them for many, many years. Traveled all over with them. Now they'll be used by another traveler. Enough room for almost anything. Enjoy them and the ride." Eddy handed the worn bags to Mike.

"You've been more than generous," said Mike as he gave Eddy a bear hug. The moment caught both off guard. The hug was a father-son embrace. After several hearty pats on the back, they shook hands.

"I'll be back tomorrow to say my goodbye to you and Sally. I have to get on the road. Some more stops to make. More Marines to—" Mike said no more. He got on his custom motorcycle, started the engine, and said, "Till tomorrow."

Eddy watched Mike motor down the alley as he slowly closed the heavy steel garage door. Chuck lay down at Eddy's feet, whining softly, trying to convey his sorrow. The dog understood Mike was leaving just like Danny. The door chains rattled in their gears, and the metal panels squealed in protest as the overhead door slammed into the concrete.

▰▪▪▪▪

Angela pulled into her apartment driveway to discover a very large, bright-red motorcycle parked next to the front door. Only last week she had mused her life was uneventful. She just went to school, took exams, talked to her mother, and then did the whole thing over and over, again and again. Now, in one day, this complicated man rocked her world. She felt confused, vulnerable, elated, and desired. Now a biker had pulled into her drive. What next? A juggler in a clown costume?

Angela had brought dinner, Chinese carryout. She struggled to open the apartment door balancing several small white paperboard containers. Mike open the door from the inside and grabbed the boxes that were about to fall. He held the door open. Angela entered the living room. The room was an organized mess. There were piles of clothes on the chair, camping gear on the floor, hold-down straps on the kitchen counter, and a leather jacket on the couch. Mike moved the straps off the counter with his forearm and placed the carryout on the wood top.

"What's the occasion, junk on the bunk inspection?"

Mike immediately started to tidy up the room so they could sit. "I'll have this picked up ricky-tick; just sorting things out so I can ship my uniforms and other stuff to Quantico."

"OK. Where's the biker?"

"You're looking at him."

"That's your motorcycle?"

"Yes, ma'am. I'm the proud owner of a Diamond Custom Cycle."

"What are you going to do with it?"

"I'm going to ride the Harley to Virginia with a few stops between."

"I can't—" Angela stammered, then suddenly dashed to the bathroom, dropping her Chinese in the sink with a loud thud. Mike went to the sink to salvage the wire cartons. The aroma of sweet and sour pork flooded the room. As he spooned the contents back into the white box, he heard Angela crying in the bathroom.

Mike waited for Angela to come out of the bathroom. He cleaned up the living room. His uniforms and some personal items filled a large cardboard box. Everything else he carefully packed into the saddlebags. Slowly the bathroom door opened. Angela had washed her face and combed her hair. She looked composed.

"When are you leaving?" Angela asked.

"Tomorrow morning."

"So, we have tonight."

"Yes."

"Is there anywhere you would like to go tonight? Sightsee, clubbing, movie, bar," said Angela sarcastically.

"No. I would like to stay here with you."

"You want another night of sex?"

"Angela, that is uncalled—"

She cut him off in mid-sentence. "It's just the truth. I'm a one-night stand, a chippie."

Mike got up and moved to hold her. She backed away. He held out his arms. Angela looked at him and started to sob. He pulled her to him. She resisted for just a second, then fell against his chest.

"I hate you," she moaned.

Mike gently stroked her hair and held her tightly.

Time passed. Mike said, "You hungry?"

"Emotionally stuffed but starving for food."

"Let's reheat the Chinese and eat. Then we can talk."

The phone rang while they were eating. Angela answered. She listened and said, "Oh my God" several times, then burst into tears. She hung up the phone as if the device were burning hot. Her father told her the North Vietnamese had just listed her brother as a POW.

The mood instantly changed from disappointment to joyous optimism. All Angela could say was "He's alive."

It was getting late. Mike cleaned up the kitchen while Angela showered. He put his saddlebags on top of the counter, ready to go. He sat on the couch and slowly enjoyed his beer. It was going to be difficult to leave, but he had his mission. They died, he lived. He had to honor their deaths.

Mike got up to get another beer out of the fridge when Angela emerged from the bathroom. She was gorgeous. She struck a very sexy pose in her white, stretch baby-doll nightgown.

"I think we've done enough talking," said Angela. "I have accepted the fact I am a brazen jezebel. I'm yours for the taking."

She moved into Mike's open arms.

The moment was broken by a loud thump against the garage wall, followed by a scream, then a flood of profanity.

"What the hell was that?" said Angela.

"Call the police," Mike said as he ran out of the apartment.

The police took about five minutes to get there and over two hours to leave. Angela put on a robe and stayed inside. Mike stayed outside until the police left.

"OK, what the hell was that all about?" asked Angela as Mike entered the apartment.

"The other night you said the neighbor's cat had caused all the commotion outside the window. I checked the air conditioning unit when I got back from Eddy's. Then I decided a little home improvement was needed. Found everything in your kitchen's junk drawer—hammer, nails, etcetera."

"What did you do?"

"I made a punji board."

"A what?"

"The VC are very crafty. They dig a hole and put sharpened bamboo stakes in the bottom. They push them into the ground with a sharpened point up. Sometimes they spread human feces on them. Then, they camouflage the hole. The idea is that a Marine will step on the camouflage cover, fall through, and imperil his foot on the stakes. It's called a *punji* pit and works surprisingly well."

"And?"

"Looking at the small area between your neighbor's fence and the window, I noticed the top of the chain link fence flattened. The grass was stomped down between the fence and the side of the garage. I speculated you had a peeping tom. I vaulted the fence and stood where the pervert would stand. If you bend down you'll see a space between the air conditioning unit and the windowsill. It gives you a view of part of the bathroom and full view of the bedroom. I improvised, made a punji board spiked with eight-penny nails. Our peeper was a little early tonight, but the police hauled him away. He had a few holes in his sneakers and foot. Boy, could he scream, wanted an ambulance. Said he was going to sue. Wanted my name— his lawyer would get my sorry ass thrown in jail."

"What did you do?"

"I complied, even spelled Diamond for the police. I'm sure Eddy will laugh his ass off when the cops pull in asking for Danny. Tomorrow I'll tell Eddy what to expect. When the police follow up with you just tell them the truth. You've never met anyone by the name of Danny Diamond, and you don't know anything about what happened tonight. Ignorance is bliss."

"You're amazing." Angela smiled, shaking her head.

"Yes, I am," said Mike.

"Now, where were we?" said Angela as she dropped her gown.

CHAPTER 3

THANK YOU

ANGELA STOOD WRAPPED ONLY in the flimsy white silk robe, her body backlit in the apartment doorway. Mike looked over his shoulder at the Roman goddess and felt blood rush to his loins. He had to leave to dampen his carnal lust.

Mike started the motorcycle engine, pushed back the kickstand, shifted, and gave the bike gas. Mike stopped at the end of the drive and looked back. The apartment door had closed, the porch light turned off. Twisting the throttle, the red bike roared down the residential street. The V-twin motor throbbed off the single-story homes in the predawn. Mike pulled onto Highway 110 and headed south to pick up 91 East to La Palma. Traffic was LA-level congested. The normally thirty-minute drive took over an hour. As Mike rode, he thought of Angela. He would have preferred to take his leave with her and develop their relationship. *Maybe she's the one.* But he was a Marine officer on a mission. Duty, honor, and commitment weren't just words. Any personal relationship would have to wait until his mission was completed. He kept repeating that to himself until he turned into the alley behind Diamond Motorcycles. Mike parked his bike and opened the garage door. The sweet smell of chocolate chip cookies and coffee greeted him.

"Hello," yelled Mike.

"Hello to you. I'll be down before the shovelhead is cold," said Eddy. Chuck bounded down the stairs and jumped, putting both paws on Mike's shoulders. The dog licked his face.

"I'm glad to see you, too," said Mike.

Eddy came down the stairs wearing his black leather jacket, carrying a brown grocery bag and two cups of coffee in heavy white ceramic mugs scrounged from Eddy's last Navy deployment.

"Ma made us some travelin' goodies, so let's go," said Eddy as he handed Mike a cup of joe.

"Where to?" questioned Mike.

"Ya said you were leaving today. I'm gonna ride with you. Haven't been on the road for a while. So, mount up, Marine, and let's ride."

"I have to say goodbye to Sally," said Mike.

Eddy paused. "Best to just head out now. She's cooking more cookies and burning a lot. Don't want to disturb her 'cause she'll burn them all."

Eddy chugged his coffee, then moved his panhead Harley out of the garage. It was like Mike's except the front forks had more of a rake and the front wheel extended about an additional foot from the frame. It was one of the original 1950s choppers. Mike looked over the bike while scratching Chuck's head.

"Where we off to, skipper?" asked Eddy.

"Silver City outside of Reno."

"The best way is 395 North. It'll get us out of LA. I'll ride with you to Red Mountain; should be a good ride. Before we take off let me look at your rig."

Eddy examined the bike attachments while Mike sipped his coffee. Mike's sleeping bag, saddlebags, and small red bug-out bag were strapped to the bike. Eddy went back into the shop and came out with elastic tie-downs. The bands were made from auto tire inner tubes cut crosswise.

"Throw away your straps; need rubber or the bike's vibration will loosen everything and your load will be highway trash," said Eddy.

Mike switched the cloth straps for the inner-tube tie bands. They were ready to roll. The only difficulty to starting was getting Chuck into the garage. He didn't want Mike or Eddy to leave. As they pulled out of the alley, Chuck began a mournful howl.

It took some time to clear LA traffic. Once they passed the Hesperia area, the traffic became manageable. They took State I-395 and skirted the western edge of the Mojave Desert. The air was fresh and light, free of contaminants. The morning sun shined in a clear, deep-blue California sky. Lush LA green gave way to arid brown desert. Light changed colors as it reflected off the bare landscape in the thin desert air. The ground's tans and light browns became the vermilion reds and burnt oranges of early morning. Later in the afternoon, the haze would change the ground palette to dark russet. The wind blew fine particles of grit across the highway. A faint smell of mesquite and sage clung to the dust.

Traffic thinned as they approached Kramer Junction. Edwards Air Force Base was to the west. Several jets roared overhead, drowning out the rumble of the two Harleys. Eddy pulled into a rustic rest stop south of Red Mountain. He gave Mike the brown bag of chocolate chip cookies. The two hugged, tears welling. Without saying a word, Eddy turned his bike and headed back to LA. Mike watched him ride off and felt remorse in his chest, like a son losing his father. He watched as Eddy faded in the distance. Mike remounted his bike, started the engine, and headed north.

Mike calculated he had about 250 miles to go and needed gas. He was hungry. It was late morning and all he had for breakfast was a cup of coffee. Bishop City seemed like a good place to stop for gas and food. He took the exit and found a gas station. While fueling up two men on Harleys pulled up in the pump station next to him.

"Nice ride," one of the men said.

Mike ignored them.

"No need to be an asswipe. Just admiring your ride," the man pressed.

"Thanks, man," Mike said. "Any decent place to eat here?"

The two men laughed. "If you're picky, no. Try the diner off the next exit. Been eatin' there for years and never choked or puked from the food."

Mike nodded to the men and rode off.

The eatery was empty except for a plump woman behind the quick-order counter.

"Sit anywhere," said the waitress.

Mike found a booth next to the front window. He wanted to keep his eyes on his bike.

"I'll have a tuna sandwich on toasted whole wheat, tomatoes, lettuce, and mayo, side of cold slaw, and a large Coke with lots of ice, please."

While Mike ate, four bikers pulled up and entered the diner. All looked like mountain man—unkempt, wild hair, and long, straggly mustaches. The leader had the letters *F* and *U* tattooed on his arm. *Fu* and his followers each wore a jean vest with a large purple patch on the back. Inside the patch shield read, *Comanchero MC.* A bottom rocker patch read, *Reno, Nevada.* Embroidered in the center of his patch was a satanic yellow eagle with its talons raised, ready to strike.

"Where ya from?" Fu asked.

Mike said nothing.

"Not a tough question," said Fu.

Mike looked out the window, seemingly bored.

"The dorkie silent type, ey?" The others laughed. "Here is the situation," Fu said. "You're on our turf; you're flying no colors. Ya gots to pay a toll to pass through." Fu paused and looked at the others, then said, "Two hundred bucks and you can keep ridin'. If ya don't have the cash, we take the bike as collateral. When you get the cash, we'll give you the bike." They all laughed at the inside joke. Even if he paid, they were going to take his chopper.

Mike looked at the bikers, thought a moment, and said, "OK. I'll pony up the money." He stood quickly and left a twenty-dollar bill on the table for the waitress.

"The money is in the saddlebags on my bike."

Fu and his entourage followed Mike outside.

As he bent down to reach inside his saddlebags, he unsnapped his boot buckle.

"Where's the money, asshole," said Fu.

Mike stood. "After much deep thought, I've decided not to pay the toll."

"Say what?" said a confused Fu.

"The way I see it you have two choices. One, get on your bikes and ride, or two, I call an ambulance for y'all in about five."

The other three bikers had joined Fu and now laughingly pounded each other's backs.

"Well, well, we gots one crazy mo-dicker here," Fu said. "He has no idea who he's messin' with."

"In my book, the odds are just right. I'll cripple two of you so you'll never walk again without a wheeled walker. The third I'll hit so hard he'll be out for the night with some brain damage. Not that anyone will be able to tell. And the fourth will just grab his balls and run home like a little girl to mommy."

The four just looked at each other, amazed.

"Which one of you wants to step up," said Mike, knowing he was going to put Fu's teeth down his throat in the count of five. He started to silently count. *One, two, three . . .*

At that moment the two bikers Mike encountered at the gas station pulled up.

"Yo, my brothers. Peace be with you," said one of the riders.

"Stay out of this, Pope," said Fu.

"Today is for peace, not war," continued the man dressed in red leathers, punctuating his statement with a huge smile. Like Fu, Pope and his co-rider wore the colors of the Comanchero gang, but their bottom rockers indicated they were from the Bakersfield, California, club.

"This is our mark," Fu said. "This dude rode out of LA. He's our property."

"Fu, you know north of Bakersfield 58 is our turf. So, let's not have a dispute within our family. This renegade is my mark now."

Everyone heard the low rumble from the road. Two by two, eight more bikers pulled into the parking lot. The bikes quickly formed a circle around Mike, Fu, and his three subordinates. All the new bikers had their leathers on showing club colors, the same red leathers as Pope.

"The best plan for you is to mount up and ride out. My homeboys haven't had a good stomping in a couple days," Pope said. All his Comancheros revved their engines in agreement. Fu did a quick assessment of the situation, mounted his bike and hand-signaled the three others to do the same. Fu gave Pope the middle finger and sped off with his three pals.

Mike stood next to his bike wondering what was coming next. Pope strolled over to Mike and looked him up and down. Then he examined the bike.

"My brothers, park your bikes and get some grub. I'm buying."

The Comancheros shut their machines down. They all went inside laughing about the standoff. Mike and Pope faced each other.

"This is a Doc Diamond cycle, right?" asked Pope.

"Yes," Mike said stoically.

"I've always admired his work. The double diamond on the air cover is classic. His paint job is one of a kind. Love the flaming ice. I see the Marine Corps chop on the tank. His son in the green machine, I hear he got wasted in the Nam?"

"He did," answered Mike.

"So, who the fuck are you?"

"A friend. We served together," said Mike. A silence followed.

"I like your style, friend. I thought about letting Fu have a piece of you. It would have been fun to watch. I saw you palm the buckle off your boot. Can I see it?"

Mike handed the buckle to Pope without hesitation.

"Very cool." He tried the four linked rings on his fingers. Each ring attached to the other like a bicycle chain. At the base of each link was a brass bar to add weight and bulk. Pope slammed the links into his other hand. "Nice!"

The boot buckles were Mike's custom brass knuckles, a sure jawbreaker in hand-to-hand combat.

"I think you could have gotten two, but Fu is good with a knife."

In response, Mike simply reached into his boot and pulled out a thin Philippine balisong folding knife concealed in a pocket between the looped pull straps for his right boot. The surgical knife was manufactured for Mike in Taiwan by a Chinese blade artisan. The beautifully crafted knife had two half handles that folded over to protect the razor-sharp, stainless-steel, double-sided blade. The blade and handles pivoted to form one sturdy knife. In the hands of a trained fighter, this weapon could be devastating. Mike fanned out the five-and-a-half-inch pointed blade. With a flick of his wrist, the knife flashed in the sunlight. Then he did a spinning routine with the butterfly knife. The blade appeared and disappeared into the handle. His hand twirled up and down. The blade flashed and whistled like fluttering bird's wings, then disappeared into the knife's handle only to reappear an instant later. After several more twirls, the deadly weapon vanished into his boot.

"Impressive. Are you any good with that pig sticker?" asked Pope.

Mike just smiled.

"OK! Here is what I'm going to do for you. I'll provide safe passage for you while you're on our road. Think of it as goodwill for all the Marines who are headhunting in Nam."

Mike nodded.

"I know you're very thankful for me saving your ass and feel indebted, so it would be righteous for you to buy grub for everyone. Now, put away your toys and join us for some good cheer," said Pope, grinning as he gave Mike back his buckle buster.

Mike snapped the brass knuckle/boot buckle back in place and ensured both weapons were secure. Then he entered the diner with Pope. They were greeted like conquering heroes with hoots and cheers. Everyone was having a good time. Even the cook and waitress were laughing.

Mike discovered many of the riders had served in the military. Some were felons, others just run-of-the-mill bike enthusiasts. They all knew Doc Diamond. Eddy got the nickname *Doc* in the Hollister motorcycle rampage of 1947. He had been a Navy corpsman in World War II and patched up some bikers and bikes after the drunken fiasco in the small California town. The riders were sensationalized in newspapers and magazines like *Life* as disenfranchised war veterans who knew no laws and could not socialize after the horrors experienced during the war. It made good press, sold magazines, created the outlaw biker image, and was a complete fabrication.

Mike saw these bikers for what they were—individuals with like interests who had difficulty with society and authority. They had their own culture, different rules and standards. America was full of organizations like this. Most conformed to the laws of the land; some did not. Mike was unsure what laws the Comancheros followed.

The Comancheros were intrigued with Vietnam and the war, enthusiastic about the Marine Corps, and questioned the war's weapons and tactics. Mike enjoyed their banter, but he had to get to Silver City. The early dinner lasted several hours, and the total bill was $128, Mike paid.

In the parking lot, the bikers split into several packs. Mike stayed with Pope and a rider named Skink. They would ride with Mike to Silver City. The trio rode through Inyo National Forest. The ride was spectacular. The sun was setting in Yosemite National Park. The shades of color varied from raw vermilion to cerulean blue as they rode uphill. The warmth of the desert-dry ninety degrees gave way to the cool, moist seventies of the mountains. The breeze was rich with the smell of redwoods. The pure wilderness and chill felt amazing. Mike was cool for the first time in months.

They stopped in the parking lot of the Nevada State Railroad Museum. The railyard was full of old steam locomotives and rail cars from the Virginia and Truckee Railroads. In a different time, Mike would have spent a whole day soaking up some of his heritage.

Pope gave Mike his phone number in case he needed their assistance. Mike thanked them, and the two Comancheros saluted with a snap of a finger to the brow and rode away. Mike watched them go, realizing he never learned Pope's proper name. *So it goes when you ride alone,* thought Mike. He powered up and rode toward Silver City. Mike exited into a residential area and easily found the house of the late Second Lieutenant Arnold MacDowell.

Mac was commander of Captain Mike Ruhawk's Third Platoon in Hue. He was killed on Ly Thoung Kiet Street by machine gun fire on February 3, 1968, a day that continued to haunt Mike. As all good Marine officers did, Mac led from the front. He was with his first squad as they dashed across the deserted street. The small group was about halfway across when machine gun fire erupted. The heavy 108 mm rounds tore up the paved street and splintered the brick sidewalk. The force of the 600 bullets a minute devasted Mac's detail, leaving bodies pulverized, limbs ripped from torsos—six men dead within four seconds. It took two days of fighting before a well-aimed 106 recoilless rifle round silenced the NVA machine gun. Only then could Mac's body be recovered.

The MacDowells' white, two-story colonial house was dark. There were no cars in the drive when Mike arrived. Mike thought this was for the best. He was tired and needed a shower. His back ached from riding all day. An oily film covered his face.

Reversing course, Mike motored to a nearby rustic motel off the highway. He took his leather jacket off and placed it on the cycle seat. He wanted to be somewhat presentable when entering the office. A haggard, balding, and morbidly obese man wearing a food-stained wifebeater undershirt sat behind the reception counter on a barstool. He was smoking a cheap cigar that smelled of black cherry mixed with cow dung.

"Hello," said Mike.

The attendant was reading a romance novel and didn't look up and said, "Ten bucks for the room, five bucks for linens and towels, forty for the week; cash in advance, no visitors, no liquor, no drugs, no guns, no fights, vacate by ten. Front office closes at midnight."

Mike just shook his head. "You give military discounts?"

"Nope," the man grunted.

Mike reached into his pocket and laid out two tens. The man reached under the counter, retrieving thin bed sheets, a threadbare pillowcase, and two small, gray towels. He placed them on the worn wooden counter. Then, he reached for the nearest key hanging on a board behind him.

"A room in the back would be great."

The man turned to say something. Mike placed two fives on the counter. The attendant snatched the cash and pulled a key from the lower corner of the board.

"Number thirty, last cabin on the right in the back next to the dead elm tree."

The room was just that, a room. Maybe twelve feet square with a single metal-framed bed that could have been from a mental institution. There was a rust-stained pedestal sink. The yellowed sink bowl was probably resurrected from a turn-of-the-century hotel. A white, chipped porcelain bathtub with cast iron claw-feet sat in the corner. The shower was a single long, iron pipe affixed to the wall with a giant, corroded showerhead set over the tub. A dented chrome ring circling the showerhead held a thin plastic shower curtain. The toilet had a worn, smooth wooden seat. The tank for the toilet was attached to the wall, five feet above the pot, with a long pull chain for flushing.

Surprisingly the room was spotlessly clean. Mike put the sheets, towel, saddlebags, sleeping bag, and bug-out bag on the bed. He turned on the shower, stripped, and got soap out of his bag. The water was scalding. He dialed back the hot water and stepped into the tub. Mike loved hot showers and couldn't get enough. Each time he soaped his body he thought of the times in Nam when he dreamed of a shower. They patrolled for days and days with no opportunity to bathe.

After the luxurious shower, Mike dressed in a pair of red nylon USMC jogging shorts and a gray USMC T-shirt to match. He made the bed. On top of the bed, he unrolled his green, down-filled military surplus sleeping bag and blew up his small travel air pillow, then put it in the thin pillowcase. He sat on the bed and opened his saddlebags, pulling out a water bottle, the brown bag of chocolate chip cookies, and a Louis L'Amour novel, *The Cherokee Trail*. Mike was hooked on L'Amour adventures in Nam. He settled back in bed to the protest of a sagging mattress and squeaking springs. He munched a few cookies, drank some water, and read. Finally, Mike got sleepy and turned off the overhead light. Lying back in the dark, he remembered the Western novels he'd read in the Nam.

■■ ▮▮▮▮▮

Mike was a respected combat officer. He had the ribbons and awards to prove the point. He was exceptionally cool under fire and made all the correct tactical decisions. His commanding officers praised his skills. What his superiors were not aware of was that Mike had the uncanny ability to block out fear until a firefight was over. Panic and dread hit him hours after a battle. When the last medevac chopper had left and all the resupply birds had returned to their bases, Mike would fall apart. He didn't curl up into a ball like a newborn babe nor shake like a panic-stricken kitten. Instead, he got severe diarrhea, doubling over in pain.

Mike was constantly afraid he would crap his pants in battle. The fear of this embarrassment was greater than the fear of being injured or killed. Therefore, it was always paramount that he had toilet paper in his pack.

Military combat rations, better known as C-rats, contained canned food and ancillaries. The ancillaries were salt, pepper, sugar, powdered creamer, instant coffee, a hot chocolate powder pack, a foil-wrapped chocolate disk, round crackers, a package of four cigarettes, a pack of matches, gum, a white plastic spoon, a P38 can opener, and a small packet of toilet paper. There was never enough TP for Mike. When the after-action diarrhea hit he sometimes tore pages out of a book to supplement his TP ration. Soon every Marine in the platoon was writing home asking for paperbacks for their fearless leader. Many times, as Mike squatted next to a trail or paddy dike, his troops would march by and leave paperback books for him. No one was embarrassed or amused when they saw their leader squatting. They were thankful to have him and in awe of his combat leadership.

Sometimes, Mike had time to read while squatting. He became hooked on Western novels and always carried one or two. Mike chuckled to himself remembering what one of his corporals had said.

"Skipper, you always wipe your ass with the most exciting chapters."

A siren squealed, awaking Mike, who leaped out of bed. He threw open the hollow-core entrance door, and his hand smacked the light switch for the outside light as he ran into the yard. Mike's bike lay on its side, its siren screeching. The headlights and taillight flashed. Mike reached over and flicked a toggle switch under the seat. The lights and siren ceased. Someone had moved his bike. Mike looked in every direction for a perpetrator. He saw no one.

For security, Mike pushed the motorcycle into the cabin. It was a tight fit. After checking the bike for damage, he locked the door, turned off the cabin lights, and went back to bed. He wondered who would mess with his bike. Then, he remembered what Eddy said and silently thanked him for his foresight.

"This is a great bike, a showstopper for sure," Eddy had said. "The shovelhead is boss, and every biker wants one. Somebody will try to jack it up before you get home. Guaranteed! I put in a couple deterrents to stop the dirtbags. One," said Eddy as he reached under the gas tank, "is a second gas line cutoff. Just turn the valve and the gas line is closed. If someone tries to start this baby, it'll cough and then stall. Second, the lights and old police siren are set on a mercury switch. When the bike is on its stand, toggle the switch under the seat. If anything moves the bike, the mercury tilts and triggers the alarm. The sound and lights should scare the shit out of them and give you time to break some arms." Eddy set up the bike and tested the alarm. The sound was deafening in the enclosed garage.

Eddy was the best.

Mike's last thought before falling back to sleep was the need to examine his bike in the morning to ensure it was roadworthy.

Mike's mental alarm clock woke him. He looked at his wristwatch. In the dawn's light, the Tourneau read 0532. He stretched, then rolled out of the sack, stripped, and took a scalding shower. He dressed in jockeys, new denims, a white, short-sleeve collared shirt, and his new cowboy boots. He packed everything else and inspected his motorcycle. There was a small scratch on the front fender and a rectangular object behind the transmission attached to the frame. It was black and about the size of a matchbox. A powerful magnet held it tight against the frame. Mike pulled it off the bike. He examined the small box. It looked solid. The only thing he could imagine was a tracking device. Who would want to know where he was? Better yet, why? Maybe it was about the bike. *Hi-tech for motorcycle thieves,* he thought.

Mike loaded the gear on his bike and rolled out the door. He started his engine, mounted the bike, and cocked his arm to toss the magnetic device into the woods. Then he smiled and pocketed the small box. It was early and he wanted breakfast. *First things first!* Mike rode to a pancake house, ate a large breakfast, and washed it down with multiple cups of coffee. Now, he was ready to meet Second Lieutenant Arnold MacDowell's widow.

Marine Corps officers were few in number. Fewer yet were officers who shared combat. Company-grade officers formed strong bonds within their own units. Mike had shared many C-rat meals with Mac. They often talked about the loneliness of command. They were responsible for everything their Marines did and didn't do, on and off the battlefield. Some officers saw the responsibility as a burden. Others like Mike embraced the responsibility as a challenge. Mac was a great sounding board because he shared the same decisions and responsibilities. Sometimes, they talked about their families.

Mac had married a high school sweetheart after completing OCS. In self-deprecating humor, he said Helen was one of his older brother's rejects. She was the beautiful prom queen who ended up with the homely Marine. The joke always got laughs. They dated on and off through college. When Mac went in the Corps, they decided to marry. After TBS training, Mac deployed to Nam for his thirteen-month tour. He took R & R as soon as he could. They met in Hawaii for a belated honeymoon. Nine days after splashing on Honolulu beaches, Mac shipped home in a shiny metal government coffin.

Mike pulled to the curb at 401 Lakewood Drive, the home of Mrs. Maryann MacDowell. There were two vehicles in the drive, a new wood-paneled Ford station wagon, and a black four-door Ford Fairlane with the Lyon County Sheriff Department logo on the doors. Mike parked and walked to the front door. He pressed a brass door buzzer and heard the chime inside. The door opened and a thirty-something-year-old man with a diapered baby in his arms answered.

"May I help you?" asked the short, slim balding man dressed in dark slacks and a tan, collared dress shirt.

"Yes sir. Is Maryann MacDowell home?"

"She's busy right now. Can I help?" said the man.

"Your little one is a handful," said Mike.

"Junior is hell on wheels," said the man, grinning as he struggled with the baby.

"How old is he?"

"The munchkin just turned a year last week. Listen, we're kind of busy and we're not buyin' anything."

"I'm not here to sell you anything. I'm here to see to Maryann."

"I'm her husband. Anything you want to say to her you can say to me."

"It's important I speak to her."

"Listen, buddy, I don't know you from Adam. If you want to speak to someone, talk to me or get lost."

"My name is Mike Ruhawk. I was Mac's commanding officer in Vietnam. I came here to give my condolences to Maryann."

The man stepped outside and closed the door softly. He put the baby on his shoulder and patted the infant's back. "The Marines! God almighty, you can't leave well enough alone. My idealistic brother had to enlist. He had to do his duty for God and country. Married Maryann never thinking of the consequences, then she has to go through all the bullshit, being alone and pregnant in a place that hates the war. Now, the great cult leader comes to hold her hand . . . the gall! Leave us alone. I'm going back into my house. If you're not off my property by the time I close this door I'm calling my boss, who just happens to be the county sheriff. He'll put your ass in jail for trespassing with criminal intent to do bodily harm. Now get the fuck out of here."

The man abruptly turned and closed the door in Mike's face. The lock made a loud click. The baby began to cry. Through the door, Mike could hear a woman say, "Who was that, hon?"

"Just some salesman. Nothing for you to worry about; he's leaving."

Mike got on his bike, looked at the front door, and sighed. The similarities between Mac and his brother were not immediately apparent until the brother started to speak. Their voices sounded the same. If he had closed his eyes, it could have been Mac talking. Mike rode off disheartened. He returned to the pancake house to consider his next step. Something was troubling him about his attempted visit to Maryann MacDowell.

Sitting at the same table as before, he thought about what had happened. Over a cup of coffee, he realized the gravity of the MacDowells' situation. Maryann must have been pregnant when she went to Hawaii. Mac had been in Nam about eight months when he took his R & R. The baby's birthday was in the month Mac was to return home. All Marine tours were thirteen months. The math was all wrong.

Mac never said anything about his wife being pregnant before or after Waikiki. Surely, he would have said something about a future baby, a son. Maybe Maryann didn't tell him. But why not? Now the older brother—Maryann's new husband—blocked a visit from one of Mac's friends. Could the baby be the biological son of the brother? Mac had told Mike on many occasions how happy he was that his brother was helping his wife while he was in Nam. How close had Mac's brother become to his former girlfriend?

Mike had trouble getting his mind around that idea. He took his memo pad out of his pocket and reworked the math again with pencil on paper. Nine months was nine months, no matter how you worked the date.

Mike put away his pad, finished his coffee, and paid his bill. He went to his bike and grabbed his saddlebags. Reentering the restaurant, he went to the men's room. There he changed his special-occasion clothes for riding apparel—worn jeans, T-shirt, biker boots, and leathers. His next stop was Burns, Oregon. He hoped the visits would get easier. Before he started his bike, he planted the tracking device on a car in the next parking space.

Mike bungee-corded his gear to the bike, put on his Ray Ban pilot sunglasses with the wire ear wraparounds, and started his V-twin. As he left the parking lot, he looked at the license plate of the adjacent car. The tracker was affixed to a Texas car. He chuckled. "Adios, motherfucker." Mike decided to stay on I-395 instead of the faster 80, 95, 78 routes. The drive through the National Forest of Plumas, Modoc, and Fremont would be picturesque.

As he drove out of the Reno area, he had mixed feelings. He felt more like an intruder than someone who could help bring closure. Was he on a fool's errand? Just because he was the Marine's commander, did that entitle him to intrude into that Marine's family? Was this more a him thing than a Marine thing?

As Mike drove, he contemplated his journey. Was he trying to shed his guilt like some slimy reptile? Could his mission be totally self-serving?

■■ ▮▮▮▮

The day was new and full of hope as Mike headed due north. The eastern sun was on his right with the light reflected off the Cascade Mountains to his left. Here was the true purple mountain majesty. The plains to the west filled with light-green and tan scrub growth, highlighted by wind-twisted dwarf trees. The vertical mountain slopes filled with century-old Ponderosa pine trees. The landscape's browns and greens contrasted sharply with the white-capped peaks, every mile a painter's dream. The scenery dazzled the beholder. Here in nature's splendor, it was easier to believe in a benevolent God.

The ride gave him a sense of freedom—motoring on the open road, feeling the wind in his face, smelling the earth, seeing a kaleidoscope of colors, and believing that no obstacle was insurmountable. The air smelled of fresh-cut grass and old-growth juniper. The changing colors add to the euphoria. All the demons of Nam faded. Mike felt whole. He felt alive. He believed there was a purpose to his life. All his senses told him to keep motoring on and never stop. *Enjoy the freedom. Screw this misbegotten self-mission.* Yet, in the back of his mind, he felt compelled to relive each death. It was like an addiction, a primal validation. Each visit made him feel more alive. Yet each visit made him feel guiltier about being alive. He was caught in an emotional riptide. The harder he swam toward his fallen Marines, the farther he was pulling from the safety of the living Corps. He drove toward the dead hoping to understand why he lived, and they did not.

Mike was south of Lakeview, Oregon, about halfway into his six to seven-hour ride, when a black-and-white state police cruiser flashed past him in the opposite direction. The sedan was going a hundred-plus. With lights flashing and sirens squealing, the car faded in the distance. Out of habit, Mike checked his speedometer. He was going sixty-seven in a posted fifty-five zone. He dialed it back to a comfortable sixty. In Lakeview, he pulled into a gas station to fill up. Mike went inside to pay the gas, use the restroom, and buy a bottle of cream soda. When he returned to his bike, there was an Oregon state trooper standing next to the Harley. The trooper was dressed in gray with a black Sam Brown belt, black knee-high boots, and a gray Smoky the Bear hat. He was tall and well proportioned with a smooth oval face.

"Can I help you?" Mike said to the trooper.

"This your motor-sickle?" questioned the trooper in a thick Western twang.

"Yes sir."

"Let me see your driver's license and registration," demanded the trooper.

"Yes sir, and your probable cause is?" questioned Mike.

"You a lawyer or something?" retorted the trooper.

"Or something," said Mike. He stood his ground, putting one hand on his hip, and raised the soda bottle to his lips.

"The PC is the motor-sickle helmet law. Oregon law requires all motor-sicklests wear protective helmets."

"Yes sir, but I'm not riding. I'm off my bike standing here talking to you. My helmet is on my bike."

The trooper stepped away from Mike and unsnapped the retaining flap on his service pistol.

"I observed you riding your bike without a helmet on. Now put your driver's license and registration on the bike's seat, then back away or you will be arrested," said the trooper as he put his hand on his gun.

Mike slowly took the documents out of his wallet and complied. The trooper picked up the papers without taking his eyes off Mike.

"Do not get on your motor-sickle. Do not leave the area. Stay where I can see you," said the trooper.

"OK," said Mike. He sat on the gas station building's curb and slowly drank his soda. He gazed off into the distant hills, ignoring the trooper.

The state cop went to his vehicle. Mike watched him out of the corner of his eye speak into a handheld microphone attached to his car radio. Within minutes, a second and third state trooper pulled into the gas station. The trooper who stopped Mike returned with Mike's license and registration.

"You have an Ohio driver license with motorcycle endorsement and California registration. Do you have a bill of sale for this motor-sickle?"

"Yes, sir," answered Mike, not moving.

"I want to see it," said the trooper.

"That was presented when the bike was registered."

"You're in Oregon now and I want to see your bill of sale."

"OK." Mike put his empty bottle on the curb, stood, moved to his bike, and began to reach into his saddlebag.

"Keep your hands where I can see them. Do not reach into your bags," said the trooper in a loud voice.

Mike put his hands to his sides.

"We are going to search you and your bike. If you present any problems, we will cuff you and take you to jail. Do you understand?" asked the first trooper.

"Yes sir, I understand, sir."

"Slowly take off your jacket and place it on the ground," said the trooper.

Mike took off his leather jacket and put it on the ground. The second trooper gave Mike a quick pat down. He passed over the boot knife and brass knuckle buckles, not realizing what they were. Then he picked up the coat and went through the pockets. He looked at the first trooper and shook his head.

"Unroll the sleeping bag, empty the gym bag and saddlebags, then step back," said the first trooper.

Again, Mike complied. The second trooper carefully searched the contents of each article. He sniffed the fluids in the water bottle and thermos, patted the sleeping bag flat, checked the pockets of each pair of jeans, checked his cowboy boots, unrolled the socks, shook out the shirts and each pair of jockeys. He fanned through the paperbacks and checked Mike's bug-out bag. He found nothing incriminating. A large white envelope was in the bottom of the saddlebags. The second trooper handed it to the first. The envelope was white with the Department of Defense Bureau of Naval Personnel Washington DC20370 Official Business stamp in the upper left corner and, printed in large black block letters across the front, *Official Record* with the Department of Defense logo. The trooper opened the envelope and pulled out several sheets of paper.

The trooper took his time reading the documents. One of the documents was the bill of sale for the Harley-Davidson, another was insurance validation for the bike, and the balance was government documents.

"Your Marine travel documents indicate your destination is Quantico, Virginia. You taking the scenic route?" asked the trooper as he put the documents back in the envelope.

"Yes, sir."

"Pack your stuff," said the trooper, handing Mike his papers.

While Mike picked up his gear, the three troopers huddled and the two who came as backup drove off. Mike clipped the D ring to the rear fender strut, securing his bedroll to the bike as the first trooper approached.

"Can I buy you another soda?" said the first state trooper in a conciliatory manner.

"Pardon me?" said a surprised Mike.

"Sorry for getting off on the wrong foot. I would like to buy a returning vet a soda or cup of coffee."

"That would be outstanding," said Mike.

Sitting on an outside bench under a shade tree next to the gas station, the trooper apologized. There had been a lot of biker gang violence on the West Coast, mostly concerning drugs and guns transported across state lines, the trooper explained. When the trooper passed Mike earlier, he wasn't sure if he saw gang colors on Mike's jacket or not.

"The embroidered eagle on your jacket was a blur with my pedal to the medal. I passed you going ninety plus," said the trooper. When Mike pulled the probable cause bullshit, the trooper overreacted.

Mike told him he had a tough job, few police, and too many criminals. Mike also admitted he had somewhat of a chip on his shoulder. He was having trouble with civilians. Moreover, he was angry but not sure why. The trooper admitted he had the same problem when he returned from Nam. He served with the 1st Air Cav. in the highlands in '65 as helicopter door gunner. Married when he got home, he had trouble with friends and family. No one seemed to understand how he felt. After his divorce, he found a home with the state police. He got anger management training as part of the law enforcement curriculum.

The trooper asked where Mike was headed.

"North to Burns," said Mike.

"I'll radio ahead so you don't get hassled," said the trooper. Mike thanked him.

Outside the gas station, the trooper gave Mike his card and said if he had trouble in Oregon to show the card to the police. He said it was like a Monopoly get-out-of-jail pass. Mike looked at the card: *Sergeant Steve Sullivan, Oregon State Police, Post 71 Clearview, Oregon.*

"Thank you, Sergeant," said Mike.

"My friends call me Sully. Remember to put on your helmet."

"Thank you, Sully," said Mike. They shook hands. Sully got in his cruiser and drove away with a wave. Mike waved back and started the Harley.

CHAPTER 4

WHITE DOVE

THE INTERSTATE HIGHWAY TO Burns was a lonely stretch of two-lane asphalt. The barren bluffs of the high desert surrounding the great Northwestern basin made the vista seem endless. The great expanse of green prairie grass gave the feeling of infinity. Watching the gentle waving of the long pale grass could be hypnotizing. Mike's thoughts drifted back to his first meeting with Johnny "White Feather" Williams. Johnny's family was his next scheduled visit.

Then a second lieutenant, Mike Ruhawk was meeting his Marine Force Recon team at Camp Reasoner in DaNang for the first time. He had trained hard for the command. The Marines sent the gung-ho Marine officer to Army Ranger School, Army Airborne School, Marine Combat Diver's Course, and Marine Escape and Evasion School. He was as ready as any butter bar going into combat could be. His team filed into the small 1st Reconnaissance Battalion CP building near LZ Finch. The recon team called themselves the Animals. Mike fit in perfectly with a last name of Ruhawk. The team immediately christened him Hawk.

Platoon Sergeant Mal LaPue from Louisiana was called Skunk because of a white streak in his hair. Joe Ritchie from Illinois was called Lizard because his face was heavily pockmarked from smallpox. Bill McCormick from Iowa was Tortoise because he moved in slow motion even while running. And Johnny "White Feather" Williams, the full-blooded Paiute Native American from Oregon, was called Pony. The team joked that when Johnny turned twenty-one, they would call him Stallion, but no one ever did. Johnny died before his twentieth birthday.

Mike rolled into Burns, Oregon, at about 1600 hours. The main street was Monroe Avenue. The buildings on either side were wood framed and brick with a definable Western look. This could have been a typical cattle town in the early 1900s. Mike drove down Monroe slowly to get a feel for how a newcomer would be welcomed. No one noticed him. A young teenage girl on the sidewalk in pink hot pants and an electric-purple tie-dye halter top waved to him. Mike waved back to the giggles of her girlfriends.

Mike motored through town until he came to the intersection of two state roads. On the corner was the quintessential budget court motel. In the middle of the court was a huge flashing neon sign: *Wagon Wheel Inn.* In a separate box below the red neon Wagon Wheel sign, a yellow sign flashed *Vacancies.*

Mike's tires crunched on white gravel. Conestoga wagon wheels imbedded in the gravel designated the parking spaces. He parked between the wheels and went inside the office. Yellow roses in pots surrounded the red office door. Cracker barrels, saddles, farm tools, and cowhides decorated the outside and inside of the motel lobby.

"Howdy pilgrim," said the man behind the counter. He was dressed in a ten-gallon white Stetson, a brown leather vest over a white-on-white dress shirt, tight-fitting blue jeans, and heavily tooled brown cowboy boots. He looked like a battered stunt double for an elderly John Wayne.

"Howdy," said Mike.

"Lookin' for a place to drop your bedroll?" said the cowboy.

"Yes sir, I am."

"We have several vacancies. All rooms have TVs, air conditioning, and views of the great Western plains. Across the road is a working longhorn cattle ranch. Tours are available. My brother owns the ranch. Down the road is a great family restaurant called Kelly's Kitchen. I eat there every night. Kelly's my daughter. If you're looking for some good times, there is the River Roadhouse down Highway 205. Tonight, there's dancin' to the GOTB, short for Good Old Times Band. They play country western and rockabilly. My cousin runs the place. We give discount coupons for Kelly's appetizers and the Roadhouse cover charge. Now, can I get a room for you?"

"Yes sir, you may, and I'd like the coupons too. How much a night?" Mike asked.

"Twenty-nine a night, and if'n you plan to stay multiple nights, it would be twenty-five."

"One night would be great. Do you give military discounts?"

"The Wagon Wheel Inn supports our men and woman in uniform. With proper ID our rate is twenty-five a night," said the cowboy, standing a little taller.

Mike presented his military ID and put two twenties on the counter. The cowboy gave him a key, a map of Burns with the café and roadhouse circled, discount coupons, and change.

"Thank you, Captain, for your service and business. If you want any extra towels, please come to the office. Is there anything else I can help you with?" The cowboy manager grinned, showing a set of brilliant white teeth as large as piano keys.

"Yes sir, there is. Can you give me directions to the main post office?"

"It's on Jefferson Street. I'll circle it for you on the map."

"While you're doing that, would you circle the Indian reservation for me?"

The cowboy's eyes narrowed. "That's not a good place for tourists, if'n ya get my drift, paleface."

Mike looked at him for a very long moment. "I get your drift."

"Now, enjoy our Western hospitality." The cowboy grinned.

"Thank you," said Mike and took his key.

The Wagon Wheel Inn was horseshoe shaped. There were twelve units to a leg for a total of thirty-six, plus the office and lobby. Each curve of the *U* was separated from the other rooms by a breezeway. This provided an area for ice machines and vending machines for each leg. Mike's room was on the end of the first leg next to the breezeway.

The room was clean and fresh, the king-size bed constructed from large striped pine logs adding to the room's frontier look. The bedspread was a faux patchwork quilt. The lone chair matched the bed frame with the addition of cowhide cushions. The dresser was distressed clear pine. On the pale-blue walls were Fredric Remington reproductions of cowboys chased by Indians. The all-white bathroom had a tub and shower with a shower curtain decorated with a cowboy swimming in a huge water tank. The toilet seat was wrapped in paper tape with *sanitized* printed across the front. The bars of soap were wrapped in cowhide-pattern paper.

First-class Western, for sure. Mike grinned.

Mike put all his gear in the chair, stripped, and headed to the shower. After toweling off, he shaved, then dressed in his cowboy outfit and added the denim jacket.

Mike found the post office. He talked to the postal clerk about the physical address for P.O. Box 89. The clerk informed him that the box was the Indian reservation's catch-all bin. Each day, a representative from the reservation came in and picked up all the mail. The rez was an independent nation, "don't ya know." If Mike needed to find an individual, he should talk to that "Injun," the clerk said. "That Injun buck comes in about eleven, don't ya know."

Mike's next stop was Kelly's Kitchen. It was already 1800 hours and Mike was hungry. The eatery was a square box wedged between a farmer's bank and Woolworth's 5 & 10. The facade looked like an old Western saloon. It even had swinging doors at the entrance. The inside was bright. The smells were mouthwatering. There were about fifteen round tables seating six, strategically placed to give max serving room. Against the wall were tables that seated four. All the tables were covered in red checkerboard oilcloth.

The place was busy. After a short wait, a very attractive young woman with a long blond ponytail and curvy shape seated Mike next to the outer wall. He asked her about the specialty of the house.

"Fire-grilled Texas longhorn T-bone steak, Idaho baked potato with all the fixins, California buttered green beans, homemade honey bread, and all the coffee ya can drink."

"Sounds great! Can I get a tossed salad with thousand island dressing added to that?"

"That would be my pleasure," she flirted. "How would like your steak cooked?"

"Medium with a little pink, please."

"I like mine the same way . . . large and pink," she said. Then she batted her eyes and walked away. Mike enjoyed her exaggerated wiggle.

The service was fast and the meal excellent. Every bite was a savory pleasure. Mike finished and asked for the check and another cup of coffee. Mike gave the young waitress a twenty and the discount coupon. The gal smiled warmly and took the bill, coupon, and money to the cashier, near the front door. The cashier came to Mike's table. She was a pleasant-looking woman in her late thirties with great breasts who clearly liked her own cooking. She wore a white, ruffled sleeveless blouse and gingham skirt.

"Hello, I'm Kelly Johansen," said the woman.

Mike rose and introduced himself.

"Please sit down. Do you mind if I join you?" asked Kelly.

"That would be my pleasure." Mike smiled.

"Thank you. You're staying at my father's place?"

"Yes, and he was nice enough to give me the coupon."

"The coupon is for an appetizer. Since you did not have an appetizer, I would like to apply the discount to your salad. Is that OK with you?"

"That's great. May I buy you a cup of coffee?"

"That would be nice."

Kelly turned her head and waved at Mike's waitress to come to the table. "Nancy, would you please get me a cup of coffee and refill Mike's cup? Please bring him a piece of Momma's fresh-baked apple pie." Looking at Mike she added, "It's on the house. Please ask Jane to staff the register. Thank you."

Nancy did as she was asked, but disappointment showed on her face. Kelly had cut the stud from the herd, and Nancy thought she should have had first pick.

"Thanks," said Mike.

"You'll thank me again after you've tasted her pie. It wins first place every year at the state fair," said Kelly.

Mike learned from Kelly that Burns was originally a lumber town before it became a cow town. Now it was an overnight stop for people going to Baker City and Ontario to the east or Bend to the west.

"Some people stay here and boat on Lake Malheur to the south," said Kelly.

Mike inquired about the roadhouse between mouthfuls of pie. Kelly informed him it was a hoot of a good time. It being Saturday, they would have a live band and the place would be jumping. Their conversation was interrupted by a disturbance at another table. Six construction workers dressed in Carhartt overalls, covered in sawdust and concrete dust, were hassling Nancy.

"Come on, sweetmeat, just a little peck," said one of the men at the table as he pinched Nancy's butt.

"Ouch. Keep your hands to yourself, Roy," said Nancy. The other men just laughed.

Another man at the table grabbed Nancy's wrist and pulled her toward him.

Mike quickly got up, walked to the construction workers, and clutched the wrist-holder's neck in his hand. The laughter ceased.

"Howdy," said Mike. "You boys look like you been working hard today." While he was talking, he squeezed with his fingers, applying vice-like pressure to the man's neck.

The man let go of Nancy's wrist. She immediately pulled back from the table. Mike leaned over the man, who was now holding Mike's arm, and quietly said, "It would be to your benefit if you took your hand off my arm. If you decide not to, I will apply more pressure." The man held on. Mike applied pressure using his thumb like a spike, driving it into the carotid artery. The man whimpered in pain and quickly withdrew his hand. Mike eased the pressure.

"Now, as I was saying, because you all work hard, I'm sure you appreciate when other people work hard. Nancy has a tough job trying to keep everybody happy. So, if you all give her the respect that you would want on your job, we'll all have a nice dinner."

One of the men jumped to his feet. "Mind your own fucking business."

"When I see someone trying to take advantage of another person it becomes my business," said Mike.

"Who ya think you are, some pious do-gooder?" said the standing man. The other construction workers at the table started to get up.

"All I know is I can put a hurt on y'all and not break a sweat," said Mike.

"Sit down, Billy, and shut up," said Kelly, standing next to Mike. "If you or one of your friends touches any of my gals again, I'll take you in the back and horsewhip all of you sorry asses."

"We don't have to take this shit from you or anyone else," said Billy. "Come on, boys, there are better places to eat." They all got up and left. At the door, Billy turned and pointed at Mike and said in a loud, menacing voice, "I'll remember you."

Kelly face turned red as she looked to Mike. "I apologize for their behavior."

"You shouldn't be the one that apologizes."

"Yes, I should. Billy's my baby brother," said Kelly.

Mike could feel Kelly's embarrassment. He laughed to himself. *Guess it's true that you can pick your nose but you can't pick your relatives.*

Mike left the balance of the twenty for Nancy's tip, took a last swig of coffee, and thanked Kelly for the pie. It sure was award winning. He promised to look for Kelly at the roadhouse. He was going back to the motel to clean up.

During their chat, Kelly told Mike how to find the Paiute Indian Reservation. He decided to go there first. The rural road Kelly described led to the center of the reservation. The community was about fifteen minutes from Burns and a hundred years of hardscrabble further.

The Paiutes of Oregon were hunter-gathers. For thousands of years small groups would gather berries, nuts, seeds, and hunt for deer, birds, and fish. They roamed the Cascade mountain range, Payette Valley, and the Blue Mountains. These groups settled near Lake Malheur and formed a tribe. Then the white man came. Now the once noble "savages" were banished to a small, economically barren area north of town.

Mike felt that history as he drove by dilapidated trailers, tin shacks, and weather-beaten houses on the verge of collapse. Old rust-ravaged cars, broken refrigerators, and smashed farm equipment were the monuments to a once-proud people. There seemed no compelling need to number houses. Everyone on the reservation knew each other. The non-Indian community had difficulty understanding the lack of organization and tribal mentality. The Indians dealt with the white man who separated them by years of indifference and segregation with apparent apathy. The area seemed devastated by neglect and lack of opportunity.

Disturbed by the sights, Mike abruptly decided to delay his visit and did a U-turn on a dirt road and drove back to Burns. The sun was setting over the Cascades. Darkness engulfed the Harney Basin. The illumination of the Caddy headlights on his Harley was refreshing compared to the dark depression of the reservation.

Mike wanted to feel good about something. A little socializing and some good country western music should elevate his mood. So, he drove south to the River Roadhouse.

The roadhouse sat near the lake town of Narrows, Oregon, a good thirty miles south of Burns in the middle of the great plain. Mike could see the lights from ten miles away. A super-large wooden sign illuminated with spotlights marked the establishment. It advertised ice-cold beer, dancing, and live music. There were no other buildings for miles.

Mike pulled into the dirt parking lot. The lot was as big as some shopping mall parking lots in Ohio. Near the front doors was a designated area for motorcycles. There were about a dozen assorted bikes. Mike parked and shut down his twin. He put the Harley on its stand and set the security switches.

The roadhouse was built like a gigantic barn with a metal gambrel roof. A long porch ran the length of the front. Short telephone poles supported the overhanging roof. Standing next to the entrance doors were two large cowboys. They were big, each with at least forty pounds on Mike and dressed in full cowboy regalia. Both had pearl-handled revolvers strapped to their sides. Mike wondered if the guns were real. Besides taking a cover charge, they were the designated bouncers. The cover was five bucks. Mike presented his coupon and was admitted for no charge.

The place was jumping. Mike speculated there were over a hundred gyrating bodies on the dance floor and more at the bar. To the far right were tables, the center was the dance area, and the far left was a raised stage for the band. The floor was rough-cut wood planks beaten smooth by stomping boots. The vaulted ceiling was exposed and filled with large wooden trusses, spinning fans, and spotlights. Along the back wall was a long mahogany bar. Behind the bar was an ornate Victorian mirror, which gave the illusion of a huge dance floor. Liquor bottles of every type were stairstepped below the mirror, adding a potpourri of color. The feel was that of an old Western dancehall. Mike moved through the noisy, standing-room-only crowd to the bar.

"What do you have on tap?" Mike yelled over the noise of the crowd.

"The special of the night is Coors. One dollar for a large schooner," said the bartender, who was dressed as if it were 1890. He had on a puffy white shirt with arm garters, a plaid vest, and checked trousers held up by red suspenders.

"I'll have the schooner of Coors. I'm putting two twenties down on the bar. One of the twenties for beer; the other is for you to make sure I never have an empty glass. Can you do that?"

"Consider it done," said the smiling bartender.

Mike turned to the crowd. Everyone was dressed in cowboy and cowgirl attire, forming lines on the dance floor, kicking their legs and shuffling about while hooting and hollering. Their booted feet stamped loudly on the wooden floor.

Let the good times roll, thought Mike.

The band began to play Johnny Preston's rendition of "Running Bear." The crowd started to chant "white dove, white dove, white dove, white dove." The people on the dance floor formed a circle. A long-legged young woman dressed in fancy white leather boots, a short, skintight white leather skirt, and a white buckskin push-up bra with fringe stepped into the center of the circle. The roving spotlight caught her in its beam. The other overhead lights dimmed. The crowd grew quiet. She put a white feather in her headband, adjusting it straight and tall. She raised her silver-bangled wrist and let out a loud whoop, shook her bracelets, and dropped her hand. The music thundered. A throbbing beat began. The crowd went berserk and began to sing.

> *Running Bear loved little White Dove*
> *With a love big as the sky*
> *Running Bear loved little White Dove*
> *With a love that couldn't die.*

White Dove started to gyrate. She jumped, twirled, and thrust to the sound of the music. The dance was exciting, sensual, and provocative. Several men jumped in to join her, but none could keep up the feverish pace. The band played on and on, adding extra refrains. By the time the last note sounded, the band and crowd were exhausted. As quickly as the girl appeared, she disappeared into the cheering audience. The spotlight went out and the house lights came up to full power. The majority of the crowd quickly moved to tables and bar. Orders cascaded over the harassed bartenders. The band took a break. The tempo of the crowd slowed as patrons guzzled their beer.

Mike enjoyed the show and needed a beer to quench his lustful thirst. He had difficulty getting the bartender's attention. Yelling over the others to be heard, "One more for the road," he shouted.

"Hello," said someone behind Mike. He turned. It was White Dove.

"Well, hello," said Mike, enchanted by the female in white, who posed provocatively in front of him.

"Would you buy a thirsty girl a beer?" she said seductively.

"That's the least I can do for the performance you put on," said Mike.

"The locals get a kick out of it. Ya know, an Indian gal doing her ritual dance."

"If that dance is a part of a ritual, I want to join the tribe. You are something to behold."

"Thanks! You're not from around here, are you?"

"What gave me away? My short hair or—" Before Mike could finish talking, White Dove's head snapped back. Someone had grabbed her braided hair and brutally jerked.

"You stood me up. Now you're whorin' around. You're one stupid bitch squaw." It was Billy, the same guy who harassed the waitress at the restaurant. He now stood between Mike and White Dove.

"Well, well, if it ain't the faggot from Kelly's," said Billy.

"You have a problem with women," said Mike, still with his hands on the bar.

Billy ignored him, reached into his pocket and threw a ten on the bar. "That's for any booze this half-breed slut hustled."

Mike looked at the floor. "Billy, I think you dropped a twenty when you were flashing cash."

Billy bent down to pick up the bill, his fist still intertwined in White Dove's hair. When he touched the twenty, Mike's knee smashed him in the nose. Billy crashed to the floor, blood flowing from his nostrils.

"Let me help you up," said Mike. He grabbed Billy's dirty, tangled hair and crushed his fist into Billy's jaw. He was out cold. White Dove froze in disbelief.

"Sleep tight," said Mike, patting the top of Billy's head.

Mike picked up his twenty, put it back on the counter for the bartender and said one of his patrons had slipped on the floor and knocked himself out on the brass footrail. "Someone should call a paramedic."

A group formed around the sprawled bleeding man as Mike slipped through the crowd toward the exit. Just as he stepped outside, he felt a tug on his arm.

"You can't just leave me here," said White Dove.

Mike looked at her, turned, and without a word strode toward his Harley. She ran after him.

"Jesus, Mary and Joseph, you're a biker," she said.

Mike flipped the switches and started his bike.

"Please, listen to me. When Billy wakes up, he'll be like a rutting buffalo. He'll lash out at anything. I can't stay here. I've got to leave town now!"

"Not my circus, not my monkey. I've got to be at the Paiute reservation in the morning."

"Damn it. I could have handled Billy. You should've stayed out of it."

"Gotta go," said Mike and backed out of his parking space.

"OK, OK, listen. I know everybody on the rez. Maybe you could use some help."

Maybe, Mike thought. *The sooner I get out of town, the better.* "OK, hop on and hold tight."

As they sped away an ambulance approached with its lights flashing and sirens blaring.

White Dove directed him to a small, wood-frame house in town. She went in and came right back out with a large yellow banana-shaped tote bag hanging from her arm. Mike got the impression she had been planning to split for some time.

The next stop was the Wagon Wheel Inn. She suggested parking behind the motel. Once inside the room, Mike pulled the curtains closed and turned on the light. White Dove was already in the bathroom and had locked the door. Mike heard the water from the shower splashing in the tub. He turned on the TV. The nightly national news had images from Vietnam. He turned off the TV, needing no reminder.

White Dove came out of the bathroom rubbing her hair with a towel, wearing tight navy-blue short shorts and a large pink sleeveless T-shirt. Mike appraised her body. Her legs were stunning. She could have been a Rockette on Broadway. The thin shirt revealed her endowment. Her face was exotic with large, dark-brown eyes, high cheekbones, a thin straight nose, pouting lips, and waist-length jet-black hair. Mike fell in lust.

"How was the shower?" asked Mike, trying to hide his lustfulness.

"The hot water was wonderful. I'm sure I left enough for you."

"Thank you. Ya know, we haven't been introduced. My name is Mike Ruhawk."

"Pleased to meet you. I'm Terry 'White Dove' Smith." They shook hands.

"When do you plan to leave Burns?" she asked.

"As soon as I conduct my business at the reservation, hopefully tomorrow," said Mike.

"What do you have to do?"

"I'm looking for the family of Johnny 'White Feather' Williams."

Terry started to shake, then cry. Mike helped her sit on the bed. She put her head into her hands and sobbed.

"Johnny and I grew up together. We had the same dream. Leave Burns and starting a new life outside the reservation. He found the Marines. After his enlistment, he said he could go anywhere and not be just an Injun. He only has a grandmother here. Mother ran off with a used car salesman and his father drank himself to death. After the Marines informed Grandma Williams that Johnny had been killed, the tribe honored him six days in the ceremonial lodge. His spirit is now with the Great Sky Warrior." She paused. "Why do you want to talk to Grandmother?'

"I was Johnny's commanding officer in Nam. He gave his life so our recon team could live."

"Grandmother Williams would consider your visit a great honor. Warriors always honor fallen brothers. The Great Sky God speaks to Mother Earth and gives many privileges to those who fight for our land. It would give me much pleasure to introduce you to Grandmother Williams."

They agreed to visit first thing in the morning. Afterward, Mike would be happy to take White Dove as far east as Iowa. He had another family to visit there. She was overjoyed. At present, Mike needed a shower and rack time for some Zs. He was bone-ass tired.

Mike took his running shorts and went into the bathroom,

closing the door. Terry turned on the TV, sat on the end of the bed, and combed her hair. Mike's shower was long and hot. He dried off, put on his shorts, and entered the bedroom. Terry was in bed sound asleep. Mike turned off the TV and lights. He slid into the king-size bed thinking of the gorgeous women next to him.

The deep rumble of a high-performance engine woke Mike. He could feel his rigid member against Terry's buttocks. They had spooned sometime during the night. Mike put his hand over Terry's mouth and whispered, "Quiet." Carefully, he got out of bed and went to the front window. Two men exited a jacked-up pickup. The wheels were off-road large. The huge front grill had a winch that looked like it could move oil derricks. The motel's floodlights created shadows obscuring their faces. One looked like he was wearing a mask. As they got closer to his room, Mike realized the mask was gauze and white surgical tape. The bandage covered the man's nose. *Billy Johansen.*

Mike went to the door and heard the two whispering.

"Shit, his custom Harley ain't here," said the other man.

"You sure he's here?" said Billy.

"The Mickey Dee twins said White Dove and that dipstick got on that Marine cycle. The same one I saw parked here today."

"Who the hell are the Mickey Dee twins?"

"Ya know, Johnny Burger and Harold Bunn, the bouncers at the roadhouse. Like the McDonald's hamburger, they being so beefy and all."

"That's funny," Billy said, sounding more like a cat coughing up a hairball.

"Let's kick in the door."

"You dumb ass. My father will kill us," said Billy.

"Well, fuck! What do wanna do, BJ?"

"We'll try the rez. If she ain't at her grandma's house, we'll go back home and wait. The squaw cunt always comes crawling back."

They turned, got back into their off-road pickup, and sped off.

"All safe," Mike said.

Terry came up behind Mike and pressed into him.

"I'm impressed by your man-part. When I watched you silhouetted in window, I had to make sure I wasn't dreaming."

Mike turned to face her.

"My God, Kemosabe, you built like Silver," giggled Terry.

"Well, what are you going to do about it?"

It was still o'dark thirty when Terry shook Mike awake.

"Time to get up, 'Long' Ranger. We gots to get to the rez before sunup. Gotta get out of Burns before eight."

Mike rubbed his eyes. "Why?"

"Because Billy gets his ass in motion around eight. You're the Marine. Isn't one of your slogans 'know your enemy.' So, I'm up; now get your ass up. Time to break camp and move out."

Mike laughed. She sounded like a drill sergeant. He tried to pull her back to bed.

"No more poontang till we're safely out of town."

Mike jumped to attention. All of him stood upright. "Sir, yes sir."

"Put that wild thing away and get dressed now," said Terry, smiling.

Early morning twilight had just broken over the Sawtooth Mountain Range when Mike and Terry pulled onto a gravel driveway with more weeds than rock.

"Try to pull in near the house. It'll be hard to see the cycle if someone's lookin' for it," said Terry.

The house was a one-room adobe structure with a flat, corrugated-steel roof. An old battered screen door hung at an odd angle. A dirty blanket acted as the front door.

A very old woman came to the opening. She had a large, triangular-patterned Indian blanket draped over her hunched shoulders. Her hair was snow white, braided, and hung on either side of a stoic face. The face looked weathered, the color of aged ivory, but smooth as if made of the finest porcelain. She wore a loose, faded sack dress and worn, fuzzy house slippers with plastic puppy eyes.

"Hello, Grandmother," said Terry.

"Good morning, White Dove. Good morning, friends," said Grandmother. "Please come to home. I made sassafras root tea for visit."

Mike and Terry looked at each other, wondering how she knew they were coming. Inside the only light came from an old potbelly stove.

"If you need light, lantern on table," said the little woman.

Terry lit the green railroad lantern with a wooden match from the accompanying Mason jar. Warm saffron light made the one room glow. Terry looked at Mike and motioned to her eyes with her fingers. Mike cocked his head, wondering what she meant.

"White Dove will tell you I'm blind. No matter; I see what you cannot," said Grandmother. "Please sit. I much to say." Terry and Mike sat in cane chairs that appeared as old as the owner. When they settled in, Grandmother began to speak.

"I'm spirit guide for Wadatika people of high desert. I have visions of what's to come. Last night, I saw snow-white dove and red-tailed hawk soaring clear blue morning sky. Each carry one big eagle's feather in beak." The octogenarian paused. "They flew higher and higher, then swooped down to Mother Earth, landing on green man cactus. Each put a feather in the top flower. Storm came, much lightning, big wind. Each went on its own journey. One flew to sun. One flew to stars. I woke, heard bad truck sounds on road. I knew you soon come."

"Grandmother, my friend has come a long way to honor you and Johnny White Feather. He is one of Johnny's warrior friends."

"Johnny had many warrior friends. He wrote about great warrior leader Hawk. You are Hawk."

"Yes, he is, Grandmother."

"Give me your hand, Warrior Hawk."

Mike placed his hand in hers. Her hands were smooth and supple. If Mike hadn't known better, he would have thought a child was holding his hands. Grandmother started to sway and hum. She held his hand for a very long time. Mike became unnerved, as the handhold was intimate in a very strange way. He looked to Terry for help.

Terry had her eyes closed, swaying and humming in rhythm with Grandmother.

Grandmother abruptly dropped Mike's hand and said, "Tea now." She got up and went to the potbelly stove and took the dented copper kettle off the top. On a rough wooden plank table were three brown earthenware mugs. Grandmother went to the table, reached for the mugs, and poured the scalding sassafras tea. It looked like she could see the mugs. The tip of her index finger draped over the mug's rim so she knew when to stop. She filled each steaming mug to the brim, then put the kettle back on the stove.

"Take cup. Follow."

Mike handed a steaming hot mug to Terry and took the other. They followed Grandmother out the open back screen door onto a narrow, well-used dirt path leading to a cleared plateau about fifty yards from the house. She sat on one of several laundry-basket-size flat rocks and faced the bright early morning sun.

"Sit. Welcome the new sun. I thank Sky Father for day. I pray he warms Mother Earth. Each day has many gifts. Johnny's gift was honoring traditions, honoring tribe, honoring family. He would be leader. He saw different vision, went to fight. Now you honor him, you honor family, you honor tribe.

"I hope the spirit of White Feather rest now," the grandmother continued. "Cloud Chief know not why White Feather fought in another land—not tribal land. Many tribes, many warriors fight for lands that are not theirs. Many, many, many years after fight ends, White Feather will be honored by Cloud Chief. Mother Earth cries a long time before desert blooms. Drink tea and go. Finish your vision quest."

Mike and Terry did as told, both kissing Grandmother on her cheek. She lifted her face to the warm sun and smiled, no words spoken.

Mike and Terry rode through the rolling Blue Mountains to Baker City. The early morning light revealed spruce, pine, and fir on the slopes. Some of the landscape looked harsh and barren, a testimony to the lava fields of a prehistoric age. The flat basins and rugged tree-shrouded hillsides provided pasture for prairie antelope, mule deer, and elk.

It was about nine when they gassed up and found a restaurant that served truck drivers on I-84. This corridor connected Portland and Seattle in the west to Salt Lake City in the southeast. Mike's destination was Muscatine, Iowa. Looking at the map while eating breakfast, Mike saw that he could drive fast and hard through the Rockies and plains and make the trip in two days, or one if he rode non-stop for twenty hours. As he folded his map, Terry made a request that surprised and bewildered the unflappable Marine captain.

"Mike, could we stop in Boise for a couple of hours?" she asked.

"What's in Boise?"

"Well, not really Boise."

"OK, where?"

"Kuna."

"Kuna?"

"Kuna is just south of Boise," said Terry.

"What's in Kuna?"

"A prison."

"Why in the world do you want to stop at a prison?"

"I want to visit my husband."

"Husband!" Mike said, bewildered.

"Yes. Henry 'White Cloud' Williams is my husband and one of Johnny's older cousins."

Mike looked at her and thought, *She never said she was married. She has no wedding band. What the hell is going on?*

"I understand this may be confusing," said Terry.

"That's an understatement!" exclaimed Mike, trying to control his temper.

"Johnny and I had different plans for leaving Burns. His way out was the Marines. My way out was marrying Henry. A Paiute shaman married us about four years ago. We were going to move to Boise. It's about the midway point between Salt Lake and the Northwest coast. He had a cattle-hauling business, three big tractor-trailer rigs. They were fully booked. Then a drunk ran a red light, and Henry hit the car with his truck, killing the driver. Driver was white with wife and three kids. Henry had a case of beer on his front seat. He lost everything and went to jail for manslaughter. He got fifteen. After appeal, the sentence was reduced to five. He has been in Kuna four years. I haven't seen him in over two years."

Mike glared. "When we met in the roadhouse, did you have this planned?"

"I'd never seen you before. You were new and I hoped we could get it on . . . then get a ride out of town. I had no idea that BJ would appear or that you were going to the reservation."

"Well, the plan worked. You're out of Burns. The question is what now?"

"If you want to dump me here I understand. I'm sure I can get a ride to Boise with a trucker. No hard feelings?"

"Damn it! That would be the smart thing to do." Mike paused and took a deep breath to control himself. Taking her to Boise would not be out of his way if he rearranged the order of his visits.

"OK. I'll take you to Boise, if you answer one question."

"Shoot, Kemosabe," said Terry, smiling with relief.

"Why do all your Indian names have *White* in them?"

Terry laughed. "Sometimes white men ask the strangest questions. All Burns's Paiutes are related. White is a family name. We just put an animal name after it to mock the palefaces' ignorance of our culture. You all think it's something Indian. We're just messin' with you."

Mike smiled. "You just earned a *got ya* . . . OK, so here is what we're going to do. I need another helmet. You can use mine. I don't know what the helmet laws are in the next several states, and we do not want to be stopped by cops. I'll rearrange my gear on the bike. The buddy bump on the rear fender is going to get real hard. Be prepared for a hard ride. You need to get into a pair of jeans and a long-sleeve shirt. The granny dress and a sleeveless blouse won't cut it when we're pushing seventy. You can wear my jean jacket. Go change in the head."

"Head?" asked Terry.

"Yes, head. Marine for bathroom."

▰▋▋▋▋

Mike leaned against the bike after rearranging his bedroll and bug-out bag. Terry came out of the truck stop in form-fitting, low-riding black jeans that sculpted her legs and butt, held up by a large, brown, leather-tooled belt and silver oval rodeo championship buckle. She wore a man's green striped cowboy shirt with the tails knotted in front, showing a flat midriff. Her long hair was braided and pinned to her head with a large turquoise stone brooch. Black cowgirl boots with metal heel taps and toe taps clicked on the concrete as she walked to the bike. The banana tote bag hung over one shoulder. She had his jean jacket over the other shoulder, strutting with a don't-give-a-damn attitude. Several men stood in the doorway ogling.

I-84 followed the old Oregon Trail along the Snake River Valley. The high country of the Pacific Northwest with the Rocky Mountains backdrop gave way to the Snake River Plain. Boise seemed to pop up in a spot you'd least expect to find a city, like an island in a sea of tall trees.

They arrived a little after noon. There was hardly any traffic in the metro area. Mike could not figure out why until he remembered it was Sunday. They pulled into another gas station where Terry phoned the prison to inquire about visiting hours.

Terry got back on the bike and said she had until four. Mike looked at his watch. It was a little after one civilian time.

The correctional facility looked like an industrial park from a distance. There were numerous outbuildings with narrow windows, all of unpainted cement-block construction. Then there were the towers and barbwire. The prison sat on a plain. Absent of any vegetation, it was an austere and uninviting place. The feeling around the whole area was one of hopelessness.

Mike dropped Terry at the visitor's gate. They agreed that he would return at four. If she wasn't there waiting, it would indicate she had made other plans. Mike would continue without her. Terry gave Mike a kiss on his lips, thanked him, then turned and walked to the wire-enclosed gate with her banana bag over her shoulder. Mike muttered, "Good luck" and rode away.

Mike drove to the Snake River Birds of Prey National Conservation Park. He coursed the scenic trail until he found an area with a panoramic view of the river valley. Parking next to a concrete picnic bench, he shut down the Harley. The silence was comforting. After taking off his helmet and leathers, he walked to the edge of the bluff. A wide valley opened below him. The hills were shades of dark orange and purple. The river was a twisted ribbon of glistening, iridescent cobalt blue. He heard the screech of wild birds. Shielding his eyes from the sun, he looked up and watched two Cooper hawks soaring on the thermals. Their flight seemed like a sophisticated dance until they suddenly plunged out of sight into the valley. Mike wondered if they caught their prey or just enjoyed the flight. He walked back to his bike to grab his sleeping bag. He laid it out on the prefabbed picnic tabletop. A stunted, climate-beaten Ponderosa pine tree provided shade. He kicked off his boots, rolled his jacket up for a headrest, and lay down. A three-hour nap would help him feel better about where he had been and where he was going.

At precisely 1600, Mike pulled in front of the visitors' gate at Kuna. Several people were coming out of the facility. Many were women, presumably wives and girlfriends of inmates. Some had small children. Terry was not one of them. He watched and waited, then became resigned she would not appear. The feeling of loss gnawed at his chest. Just as he started the bike to leave, Terry appeared.

"Miss me?" she said in a syrupy sweet voice.

"Where the hell did you come from?"

"Indians are sneaky."

"You weren't at the gate. I was ready to leave."

"I've been waiting in the bus shelter on this side of the street. You drove right by me."

"Well, hell, get on, let's go."

"I haven't eaten since breakfast. Let's find a place to eat."

The day was exceptionally clear; not a cloud in the sky. The air was warm and dry, a good day to be on the road. They stopped at a hamburger shack near I-84. They stretched their legs after getting off the bike and then ordered at the outside walk-up window. They took their thick, juicy hamburgers, shoestring fries, and milkshakes to an outside table. Both ate as if starved. Mike finished, wiped the ketchup from his mouth with the thin paper napkin.

"I am ready to listen if you're ready to talk."

Terry looked off in the distance. "Henry is happy. I know that might sound strange, but he said he's found his life's purpose."

"Sounds like he's found religion," said Mike.

"Maybe." She paused. "He has been corresponding with another Indian in the US Economic Opportunity Office. The guy's name is Russell Means. He's starting a group called the American Indian Movement. Russell wants Henry to become part of his grand governing council as the logistic manager."

"Logistic manager," questioned Mike. "From inside prison?"

"He expects to be out soon. He has a parole hearing coming up and thinks his chances are good. Once he's out Russell will get him set up. His job begins immediately. From what Henry said, this AIM group is going to hold tribal meetings all over the country. Places like San Francisco, Minneapolis, Washington DC, and Wounded Knee. 'AIM' wants the US government to respect their civil rights and honor their historical treaties."

"Good luck with that," said Mike.

"They want an Indian that can set everything up before the council arrives. With Henry's trucking background, he's a perfect fit."

"Great for Henry, but what of you?"

"Henry says he still loves me and wants to be with me. He understands I do what I do to survive in a white man's world. He wants me to stay with his sister until he's released: maybe ten months with good behavior. Until then, no more white men, time to be true Indian, follow the Wadatika sprit."

"OK, where is his sister?"

"She has a trailer in Sturgis."

"Here we go again; where is Sturgis?"

"Sturgis, South Dakota. Ya know, the great Harley-Davidson rally."

"No, never heard of the place."

"What kind of a biker are you?"

"I'm a Marine who just happens to ride a Harley-Davidson."

"Oh. I thought you were a twisted biker who happens to be a jarhead," said Terry with a mischievous grin.

"Mean in the Green Machines, but as a civilian I'm a soup sandwich kind of guy. Ya know, I somehow feel responsible for you. I guess I can take you to Sturgis. Then I have to continue my mission."

Terry leaned across the table and kissed him on the lips. "Thank you."

Mike pulled a map out of his jacket and laid it out on the table. He figured travel time should be between three to four hours.

"Here's the plan. We'll ride to Idaho Falls, stop for the night, get an early start tomorrow, and drive through to Sturgis. OK?"

"Tonight we can stop at the Fort Hill Indian Reservation. We can get food and lodging for free and it's just south of the Falls."

"Indian reservation? You're sure there will be no trouble?"

"As a kid, the whole White family tribe followed the Indian rodeo through the Northwest during the summer. Each rez has a rodeo. We made lots of friends. There is always a place to stay for Indians on a rez."

"I'm not Indian."

"You're my captive paleface, known as 'Mike Big Spear.' Have no fear. White Dove will protect you from the savage red man. I will personally see to your punishment."

Mike leaned over the table and kissed her on the forehead. "I will look forward to prolonged torture by said Indian woman."

They cleaned off the table, used the restrooms, and got back on the bike. The sun was to Mike's back. The ride from Hammett to Fort Hall was glorious. The traffic was minimal. The Harley hummed. Mike felt like the king of the road.

▰▮▮▮▮

Mike had grown up riding off-road bikes—Hondas, Ducatis, BSAs, Yamahas, and Triumphs from 75cc to 750cc. The first time he got a road bike was in college. He saved for two years, working any type of job, from washing dishes in the college cafeteria to cleaning portable outhouses at night. He bought a sparkling new pearl-white/azure-blue 1960 Triumph Bonneville 650cc with his savings. She was his joy. He rode all over Ohio on that Bonnie. Now he was riding the custom Harley Softail on a smooth, asphalt-paved four-lane highway and enjoying the experience even more. The machine was perfect and the ride sensational. The girl who had her arms wrapped around him was gorgeous. Mike put aside White Dove's manipulation; maybe it was an ends-justify-the-means situation. God only knew he had used that logic in Nam. For now, he was in the moment and felt every movement she made.

The Snake River Plain offered wide expanses of prairie framed by breathtaking mountains. Peak after glistening peak was silhouetted on the skyline. The highway paralleled a slow-moving clear river. In the distance, several large pale-azure lakes sparkled in the late afternoon light. Wildflowers bloomed in a palette of crazed colors. This could be where Jackson Pollock got his inspiration. The air smelled of newly cut sweetgrass with a hint of mint. He was living and enjoying the feeling. Liberated from all apprehension, Mike felt reborn.

A tap on Mike's shoulder pulled him back to the real world. Terry indicated the upcoming traffic interchange was their exit. She directed Mike on several secondary roads, some paved, and some dirt. After numerous turns, they approached a cluster of nondescript shanties. They stood like white lifeboats on a calm sea of tall sun-dried grass. Terry directed Mike to stop in front of a closed building that stretched awkwardly from a central hall. A crude sign indicated the wooden one-story was the Lincoln Creek Day School. Terry got off the bike and walked to one of the shanties across the dirt-rutted road from the school. She knocked, then entered the small house unannounced. After a few moments, Terry reappeared with a smile.

"We lucked out. There's a tribal meeting tonight at the rez Catholic Church. It's potluck. All you can eat with a donation to the school building fund. Minimum of five bucks donation, beer included."

"Sounds good to me. What time?"

"Kickoff at seven, eats at eight, dancing till the band passes out."

"Where do you want to go until then?" asked Mike.

"After today's ride, I think we deserve a few ice-cold beers and a bath."

"That's one of the best ideas you've had. Show me the way."

Terry directed him to a small, isolated trading post with two glass-cylinder gas pumps, circa 1920s. The gas pumps looked like giant tombstones in front of the station. There was no indication of civilization for miles in any direction, only scrub brush and light-yellowish-brown dirt as far as the eye could see. This was the wide-open spaces of the West. Mike filled his tank while Terry bought a six-pack of long-neck bottled beer. Terry popped two tops with her belt buckle and handed one to Mike.

"As I paid for the gas and beer, the cashier asked if I was going to the school fundraiser tonight at Saint Kateri Tekakwitha. It sounds like the whole tribe is coming."

"Sounds outstanding!"

"Let's down a cold one and hit the trail," said White Dove.

"Thank you for the gas, beer, and party. And the insight into one of life's mysteries. Why cowboys and cowgirls wear those large belt buckles."

"If you stick with me, cowboy, you will learn many mysteries of the wild frontier, Injun style."

Mike nodded and they clicked bottles. After quickly downing the chilly beer, they remounted. The road led to an unmarked trail filled with sagebrush. Mike had to navigate the stones and scrub growth to stay on the weeded trail. After heart-stopping twists and turns along steep bluffs, they came to a small stream. The stream originated in a blind canyon a hundred yards away.

"This is the place. Park next to the small dogwood. The hot spring pools are up in the rocks," said Terry excitedly. She quickly scrambled off the bike and scampered up the rocks like a graceful animal carrying two bottles of beer, laughing as she ran. The flat, smooth rocks formed steps in the arroyo. After carefully shutting down the bike and setting the kickstand, Mike dutifully followed.

He tracked her by the discarded clothing—jacket here, shirt over there; boots flung aside, jeans on a rock, and panties hanging from a small cactus. Mike soon found Terry in a pool of sparkling water, on her back. The pool was part of a natural grotto shaped like a huge Italian wine bottle with a small waterfall at the skinny neck and overflow basin at the fat base.

Terry blissfully floated in the warm water, her eyes closed, beer balanced on her stomach. Her hands gently moved water over her body. Mike sat on his haunches and watched the Indian maiden. She glistened in the diffuse light of the canyon. *She is stunning,* he thought. His libido was going crazy; he ached for her.

Finally, she opened her eyes. "Are you getting in or are you a creepy watcher?"

"For now, I'm enjoying nature's beauty and all the glory she holds."

Terry splashed water on Mike as an invitation to join her. He slowly took off his clothes and put them in a neat pile. Then he slipped into the mineral-rich hot water.

"My God! This feels good."

"The best is yet to come," said Terry, handing him her beer. Mike took a deep chug.

They floated side by side. The hot mineral water relaxed every muscle. The heat penetrated deeply into their bodies. For the first time, Mike's war wounds, both mental and physical, seemed to slide out of his body and into the water.

"I have to show you something very special. You'll be the only white man to enter. Follow me," Terry said with a hint of unspoken promise.

She got out of the pool and climbed up the flat rocks. Mike followed, mesmerized by her shimmering form. Water drops sparkled on her firm breasts. Her hair hung like long braided ropes down her back. Her hips swayed provocatively. As she climbed the boulders, her form somehow became multidimensional. Mike had a difficult time focusing on the rock steps; he felt intoxicated. They came to a second, large wide waterfall above the bottle pool.

"Stand here. When I call come to me," said White Dove.

Terry parted the falling water like a curtain and disappeared. Mike stood transfixed. A faint yellow-gold light began to glow from behind the falls. The flickering rays grew stronger. It was like looking through a rain-splashed window during a heavy rainstorm. Shapes formed and reformed. Then a strange voice echoed from the rocks.

"Come . . . come to me . . . come, my great warrior." The sound resonated in the small canyon as if multiple people were calling. Mike walked into the falls. The warm water cascaded over him, but he didn't feel a drop. There was a cave behind the falls the size of a railroad boxcar. In the center of the room was a chair carved out of natural butter-colored sandstone. There sat Terry. Directly in front of her was a small fire in an ancient stone firepit. The light from the flames danced on the walls, revealing animal pictographs. The flickering flames gave the images life. The stylized figures were running, jumping, and dancing. Mike watched the shapes, mesmerized by the action. They moved about as if caught on an early black-and-white film.

Terry moaned. She had one leg draped over an armrest, the other stretched out in front of her; one arm hanging on the opposite armrest, the other across her chest with her hand cupping her breast like an offering. Her head was back, hair covering half her face, her mouth open, and her eyes closed. A soft moan came from her lips, her breathing heavy.

She sat open, exposed, and inviting, looking like a sex-starved animal. Somewhere, far away, Mike heard a deerskin drum beat a loud heart rhythm. He began to sway to the rhythm. On the wall next to him were numerous petroglyphs of human hands. Mike felt compelled to put his hand into one of the carved impressions. Immediately his senses became inflamed. Suddenly, he could hear the individual drops of water falling from the rocks, smelled the overpowering scent of a herd of rutting deer, and unexpectedly tasted the sweet lips of every lover he'd known. Then the cave exploded into a kaleidoscope of twinkling colors. Mike raised his head and a primordial howl left his chest and echoed in the rock cave. His body quivered. His vision narrowed, senses inflamed. He attacked.

Afterward, they floated in the hot spring's pool. Mike felt drained. Nothing like the cave experience had ever happened to him. He became a prehistoric predator. He attacked Terry savagely. She submitted. Now looking at her, he felt ashamed. She had bruises on her arms, stomach, and legs. Bite marks on her neck, breasts, buttocks, and genitals. She even had some hair missing from her head.

As if reading his mind she said, "Not your fault. I dropped a couple of tabs of acid into the beer. Thought we could use a fun-loving LSD trip; never imagined it would turn you into a wild beast."

"I'm sorry, I just . . ." His voice trailed off on the wind.

"If there's someone to be sorry, it's me. I took advantage of your goodwill and trust. You're my last white lover before I embrace the Wadatika sprit. I wanted to do something I would remember. You, I will remember, big blue-eyed brave."

Mike had nothing to say. His mind whirled. If he could assault Terry like some psycho, what else was he capable of? Had he a savage heart? Mike got out of the pool, dried himself with his shirt, and put on his clothes. Without a word, he walked back to the bike. Terry soon followed.

"I would like to sleep here if that's all right with you," Mike said meekly.

"Indians like to sleep under the stars. This would be great."

The Catholic Church was a typical Western Indian mission building—cheap and functional. The structure was artfully built from reclaimed wood. The shiplap siding was painted white and peeling from years of hot summers and frigid winters. The humble building sat on a bluff overlooking the Blackfoot River. The area was barren except near the river where small scrub trees and berry bushes grew. The parking area held numerous pickups and old cars in various conditions of repair. None were new. The mission's front doors were open, throwing a column of honey-yellow-amber light into the ebbing sunset of reds and pinks.

It was a festive event. Multiple tables lined the recreation hall. They were long, crudely constructed two-by-four and plywood tops on sawhorses with brown wrapping paper taped to the ends. Each table held a variety of cooked dishes. The smells made Mike salivate. He looked over the food and his stomach growled. Choices ranged from baked apples with cinnamon to grilled spotted trout fresh from the river, and everything in between. American-Indian and Mexican-American cuisine were the dominant foods.

Mike gladly put a twenty into the donation jar. Terry started to mix with the crowd. She was greeted as a long-lost sister. Mike was introduced as a friend and was accepted without question. While Terry kibitzed with her friends, Mike went to the keg of beer.

He took two plastic Solo cups from a small table near the keg and drew beers. Two men drew beer right behind him. They were big, bulky-looking men bronzed by the sun. Both had long braided ponytails. They were neatly dressed in clean jeans, polished cowboy boots, and pressed cowboy shirts buttoned at the top.

One of the men said, "Sweet-lookin' bike ya riding."

"Thank you."

"Ya got Cally plates on it. That the way ya heading?" said the other man.

"No sir, going to Sturgis," said Mike.

"Big Harley rally this time of year in Sturgis."

"That's what I hear."

"When you get to Sturgis, say hello to Dawn for us. Just tell her the Saluda brothers hope to see her real soon," said the older of the two men.

"I'll be sure to do that."

"See ya around," said the younger brother. They walked away.

When Mike had a chance to get Terry alone, he handed her a beer and asked, "Who's Dawn in Sturgis?"

Terry told him that Dawn was Henry's sister. "She runs a tattoo shop in Sturgis during bike week."

"Who are the Saluda brothers?"

"Oh, there're like big brothers. They've been looking after me and

Dawn since we were kids. We all hung out together when the rodeo came to the rez. Ya want me to introduce you?"

Mike replied that he had met them. "Real nice guys."

"Ya, but they can be dog-ass mean, especially if they had too much firewater."

After dinner, with the tables cleared, a three-piece Mexican band played some soft romantic music. Mike loved dancing slow with Terry. They had rhythm and danced all night. When the band packed their instruments, Terry and Mike said their goodbyes and rode back to the hot springs.

The inky black sky was filled with billions of twinkling stars. Mike felt like he could reach up and touch their brilliance. Sitting low was the Big Dipper. It reminded Mike of another constellation, the Southern Cross. It lit the dark night in Nam. As he watched the heavens above, Terry built a small campfire out of mesquite twigs. The dry wood snapped and popped, sending hot embers into the night. They both lay back on Mike's military surplus sleeping bag. Neither spoke. Time seemed to slow, both caught in their own worlds. Each realized this was but a moment, a passing of fiery comets on very different paths.

Mike reached into his saddlebags to get his thermos. He poured two cups of hot coffee into paper cups from the mission. He dug out the crumpled brown paper bag of chocolate chip cookies from inside the saddlebags. The cookies were a smashed mess of gooey chocolate. Mike tore the bag and placed it in front of Terry as an offering. She smiled and accepted the unusual gift. They sat next to the campfire and savored the hot coffee and messy cookies. Both enjoyed the quiet.

In the high country, temperatures reached the low forties at night—even in the summer. Mike convinced Terry the only way to stay warm was to sleep nude. Terry laughed and said she had never heard the hypothermia line before. She intended to share Mike's bed. This would be their last night together.

As savage as their lovemaking was in the afternoon, the evening was tender and gentle. They fell asleep in each other's arms.

■ ▪▪▪▪

The morning dew was heavy on the sleeping bag. Neither Mike nor Terry wanted to crawl out of the warm sack. Mike felt melancholy, wondering about his choices in life. *How do you know the decisions you make today are correct? How do those decisions affect your future? If you turn right, the bullet misses you; turn left and you're dead. Is there a greater plan, or are we just random particles bouncing around in a chaotic universe?*

His thoughts were interrupted when Terry slid on top of him. Mike was tempted to say he loved her. He knew it wasn't true, but he wanted to say it. Maybe to prove he could love someone. Maybe to lessen his feeling of guilt, who knew? Mike was thankful for Terry. For the moment, he stopped thinking and just felt.

They got dressed after bathing in the hot springs. They packed the bike and roared out of Fort Hall. Just north of Idaho Falls, they stopped at another truck stop for breakfast. Over coffee, Mike planned the route. They'd go to Yellowstone, then to Cody, and then take I-90 east to Gillette. Mike looked forward to the splendor of the Tetons and Rocky Mountains.

Yellowstone National Park was a natural wonder to behold. When they crossed the state line into Wyoming, the traffic started to slow. Mike saw every imaginable vehicle, including house trailers, motor coaches, and buses. Intermixed with large vehicles were station wagons, vans, pickups with slide-on campers, and motorcycles. They ranged from dirt bikes to big touring bikes with trailers. He felt like a float in a motorized Fourth of July parade. It was difficult to see the natural beauty of majestic rock promontories, misting great falls, century-old Ponderosa pines, geothermic geysers, and slow-winding rivers while concentrating on the congested motorcade. Mike would have liked to stop and appreciate the country he fought for.

The drive out of the mountains of Yellowstone to the grassy plain of Cody was uneventful. Mike noticed more motorcycles going east. The rally at Sturgis was still a week off, but he believed these bikers were headed that way. They got some refreshments in a little gas station in Cody. Mike could envision the town at the turn of the century when herds of cattle filled the pens waiting for auction and rail shipment to market. Hundreds of years before cattle, buffalo roamed the vast vista to the south. Stories were told of herds of bison so large that the ground was covered in a dark-brown blanket of furry hides as far as one could see. The plain continued uninterrupted to the horizon.

Mike studied the map and realized after Sturgis they could quickly detour and drive by Mount Rushmore. That would be a sight to see. He voiced his plans to White Dove.

"If you really want to see a wonder, see Mato Tipila," said White Dove.

"And what the hell is that?" asked Mike.

"It's a very sacred place for Indians, a place white men haven't defiled, a place of the gods."

"OK, where is it?" asked a frustrated Mike.

"It's near Sundance in Wyoming," said Terry.

After topping of the gas tank, they continued to Sheridan. Geographically, the city was on the eastern side of the Bighorn Mountain Range. They stopped for a vending machine sandwich in a rest area north of Sheridan. There, they picked up Interstate 90 East. After passing Gillette, they took the detour to see Mato Tipila. It would only add about a half hour to the total travel time. Mike thought he could appease White Dove and still see Mount Rushmore later.

Mato Tipila, aka Devil's Tower, was a solid igneous rock jutting more than 1,200 feet into the air. It dwarfed the surrounding terrain. It was a virtual statue to the great Northwest, a monument to nature's realm, which was far greater than man's. White Dove was right. He was impressed with the pristine nature. This was a grand statement. Better than anything man could do. This was something no government policy could corrupt.

They crossed into South Dakota near Belle Fourche, winding their way back onto I-90. After a total of over 600 miles and ten hours of riding, they arrived in Sturgis.

The town of 4,000 residents swelled to 250,000 during the summer's Bike Week. Each year the attendance grew exponentially. The hordes of visitors swamped the town with drugs, booze, thefts, assault, and debauchery. It was a pagan festival without rules.

Mike and Terry joined the throng of other bikers riding into what was dubbed the "New Wild West." They saw thousands of motorcycles parked two rows in the center island and lining both sides of the entire main street, no open space between bikes. Every make and model of Harley imaginable, and some unimaginable. All were on display. It was a motorcycle carnival fueled by a crowd ready to party.

The sidewalks filled with people wearing biker regalia. The majority wore some type of black leathers. Both men and woman displayed tattoos. Every part of the body seemed to be exposed and showed a different tat. Women flaunted themselves as if the rally were a Roman orgy. The crowd pulsated with energy. A mixture of smells permeated the air: Deep-fried potatoes, baked bread, burned caramel, boiled sauerkraut, grilled burgers, and hotdogs wafted out of overcrowded restaurants. The numerous bars blared a variety of music into the street, from disco to hard metal. Sometimes the revving of loud motorcycle engines masked the tunes.

Mike and Terry cruised down the street, absorbing the sights and sounds. Terry directed Mike to go east until reaching the intersection of 206 and 131st Avenue. Parked on the corner was a large, bright aluminum Airstream travel trailer. Painted on the side in six-foot black letters was *Tomahawk Tattoos,* and underneath in frontier scroll *The best ink in the West.*

Mike pulled into a makeshift parking lot behind the trailer, squeezing next to one of several custom Harleys. Adjacent to the trailer was a large red-and-white-striped carnival tent. Three sides were open, revealing four old-fashioned barber chairs. Hovering over each chair was a tattoo artist working on a customer. Behind the chairs, pinned on the tent flap, were sheets of papers showing designs, drawings, pictures, cartoons, symbols, logos, and tribal markings. In front of the barber chairs were several rows of wooden benches made from logs and milled lumber. Customers sat waiting their turn.

A woman at a small folding card table yelled, "Twenty-nine." One of the men got up and approached the table. He exchanged a piece of paper and money and she directed him to a recently emptied chair. The money woman had a multicolored headband pulled tight on her forehead. She wore a floral, puffy blouse, blue jeans, and red-white-and-blue cowgirl boots. Terry walked to the woman at the folding table, her head down busily writing in a small journal.

"Please take a number. It will be about forty-five to an hour wait."

"What kind of place you runnin', Injun?" said Terry mischievously.

The woman raised her head as if slapped, then did a double take only to scream in delight.

"*Ter-ry!*" she exclaimed loudly.

"*Daw-ney!*" Terry yelled.

Both jumped about holding hands, hugging with joy. They stumbled and toppled the table.

"Have you seen Henry? How did you get here? Have you talked to Grandmother? Have you eaten? How long are you staying?" Dawn asked in rapid fire.

"Slow down, girlfriend," said Terry. "Let me introduce you to Mike. He's my protector, ride, and friend."

"Pleased to meet you," said Mike.

"The same," said Dawn, warily.

"He's cool. He knows about Henry," said Terry.

Dawn smiled and reached out her hand. Mike took it in both of his.

After the intro, Dawn turned her duties over to one of the artisans at the chair. They picked up the spilled tickets, money, and table.

Dawn, Terry, and Mike went into the air-conditioned trailer next to the tent. Dawn made fresh lemonade and poured a glass for each, leaving the iced pitcher on the table. Mike complimented her on her business. She explained the operation was self-contained. The trailer was her base of operations. It provided lodging, stove, water, and septic. She had a diesel generator set up on her pickup truck to power the trailer and equipment.

Dawn had been coming to the rally for years. Over 70 percent of her yearly revenue was generated during rally week. The only problems were with the town of Sturgis. They kept increasing the temporary business tax, business permit costs, and health inspection cost. All had to be paid before the opening of business.

Mike listened intently. She sounded like a very good business executive.

"The town looked a little crazy as we drove through," said Terry.

"Bike week officially starts this weekend, so the crowd is just getting warmed up."

"Do you have any problems with the bikers?" asked Mike.

"Very few. Most are here to have a good time. So far, my problems aren't with the bikers."

"Who causes the problems?" asked Terry.

"There is a so-called city association that demands money for business insurance," said Dawn.

As if on cue, there was a knock on the trailer door. It was one of the tattoo artists saying several men wanted to talk to her. Dawn looked out the door.

She turned back and said to Terry and Mike, "Speak of the devil."

"Do you mind if I tag along?" said Mike.

"Be my guest," said Dawn.

Terry decided to stay in the cool comfort of the trailer and finish her lemonade.

Dawn and Mike approached the three men. One was dressed in a loud, green patterned business suit, a lavender dress shirt with an obnoxious, iridescent lime-green tie, and a black leather vest. He looked like a fifty-year-old overstuffed sweet potato with short stumpy legs. The other two men had on white hard hats, white muscle shirts, purple gym shorts, and ankle-high tan work boots, no socks. They were gym-pumped muscular, at least four inches taller and fifty pounds heavier than Mike. One body builder carried triangular signs printed with *SBI Protected,* the other a long hickory-handled sledgehammer.

"Hello, Miss Williams. Your business is thriving," said the suited, overweight pin-headed man as he scanned the area. "The Sturgis Business Insurance Company is here to help you survive the tremulous Bike Rally week. As I explained before, we protect against theft, fire, property damage, and personal injury for you and your employees. Have you considered my proposal?"

"The cost was three hundred a chair, total of twelve hundred dollars a day or thirty-six hundred for three days, half payable now. Is that correct?"

"Yes, that is correct."

"You wanted the payment in cash and there's no written contract to sign . . . for my convenience, correct?"

"Yes, that is correct," said the sanguinary grinning man.

"Would you please come with me to my office? It's behind the tent. I believe we should conduct our business in private," said Dawn. The group followed her behind the tent, stopping next to the truck. The generator on the truck hummed loudly.

Dawn stepped forward. She was inches from the suited man's flushed face.

"I may be a woman, an Indian, but this isn't my first rodeo. Extortion is illegal. Get your fat ass and the meat-headed kids off my property before I call the sheriff."

"Miss Williams, please reconsider. It will take some time for my brother, the sheriff, to get here. In that time, many things could happen. Like your generator breaking down."

The muscled man swung the sledgehammer, crushing the electrical junction box for the generator. Sparks flew and smoke billowed from a small electric fire. As the man started a second swing, Mike parried and grasped the handle, stepping inside the swinging arc to redirect. The hammer's gleaming iron head smacked the second muscled man in the thigh. The man went down like a fallen dinosaur, screaming in pain. Mike jerked the hammer's handle into the swinger's gut. The man grunted, then bent over. Mike pulled the hammer out of the man's hands and in one fluid motion swung the hammer, hitting the second body builder's foot. The muscle-bound man wailed in pain, falling to the dirt, grasping his injured foot. The fat man looked in amazement as his enforcers lay rolling in the dust with faces twisted in agonized misery.

"I believe one of your employees did at least a thousand dollars in damage. Pay the lady," Mike said in a quite matter-of-fact voice while twirling the sledge as if it were a baton.

The fat man struggled to get his wallet out of his jacket pocket. He counted out ten new one-hundred-dollar bills and handed them to Dawn.

"Sometimes bullies like you have a difficult time understanding how the world really works." Mike took the man's wallet and looked at the driver's license.

"Now I know where you live, Mister George B. Watts. If anything happens to my friends, I will cripple you for life, fuck up your family, burn down your house and anything else I can to ruin your miserable life. I have extensive training and years of experience doing that very thing to people who are smarter, better equipped, and who will fight and die for their cause. So, believe me when I tell you I will do what

I say. Some advice for the future—remember that there is always a meaner dog in the yard."

Mister Watt's posture became defiant and smug. He even smiled. Obviously, he did not believe Mike. Maybe he still thought he had the upper hand and his brother's badge would ensure his future.

"I think you need a reminder of my commitment," said Mike. In a flash, Mike used the handle of the hammer to break the fat man's humerus bone of one arm and the radius bone of the other arm. The man stood stunned before crying out. He looked bewildered. His arms hung shattered and useless at his sides.

Calmly Mike turned to Dawn. "I think you should call an ambulance."

"My God! What have you done?" said Dawn.

"I've cleaned up some of the rubbish in Sturgis. You won't have any more problems with these boys. If there is a problem, the Saluda brothers should be here any day. Now, I have to talk to Terry." He handed Dawn the sledgehammer. She held it like it was a poison reptile. Dawn looked at the hammer, then stared at the three men, two on the ground, whimpering, and the other staring at his arms and babbling.

***

Mike knew he needed to get out of town quickly; and he knew saying goodbye to Terry would be tough. Mike told her if things got difficult with the local sheriff to call Sergeant Steve Sullivan, the Oregon highway patrolman he had met. Sully was top drawer and could help. Most states had reciprocating police agreements.

Terry suggested Mike head north to the Cheyenne River Reservation. There was a little town called Bridger in the rez where he could spend the night without fear of arrest or reprisal. Mike assured her that he put the fear of God into the insurance scammers. He doubted if they would do anything but whine in the hospital.

The two embraced, then kissed. Terry tried to hold on to Mike as he gently pushed her away, got on his bike and rode out of town.

As Mike sped away, he tried to rationalize his actions. He could not. His reactions were instinctual. What was right was right. He acted to meet a threat. However, he was not in a combat zone. There were laws. He needed to get a grip or something bad was bound happen. He had to change. *Think,* he told himself. *Think, think before you act.*

CHAPTER 5

TALE OF TWO MILLERS

MIKE FLIPPED ON HIS headlights and drove through Bridger. He thought it would be better to drive to Pierre. There, he followed the sign for the regional airport, where there were numerous places to rest. He thought about checking into a motel but decided against it, not knowing the reach of the Sturgis sheriff. Near the runway, he found a rutted access road leading to the airport maintenance compound. He drove down the dirt road until he came to some metal sheds. Mike chose a spot next to a road grader and camped for the night. His shoulders hurt. His ass was numb and feet felt like lead. The sleeping bag on soft grass would be welcoming. The sound of aircraft landing and taking off was comforting, just like sleeping next to the metal mesh runway at An Hoa Combat Base in Nam. He fell asleep thinking how difficult personal relationships could become.

The rain woke Mike, striking the side of his face. Within moments, he was soaked. Mike looked at his watch; 0400. He crawled out of his sodden sleeping bag fully clothed. Pouring the water out of his boots, he struggled to tug them on. Next, he packed the soaked gear and got back on the route heading east. Raindrops stung his face. They hit with the force of soft buckshot. Soon his clothes were so wet he started to shiver. He rode in the rain for over two hours. The highway sign stated *Huron 10 miles.*

On the main street of Huron, he found a twenty-four-hour coin-operated laundry mart. Mike's face broke into a strange smile—shelter. He parked his bike in front of the shop. The store was empty. Several oversized washing machines and dryers lined the walls. Mike dragged his wet gear inside, bought detergent from a vending machine, and did his wash. Scanning the storefronts across the street, Mike noticed a hole-in-the-wall café. Mike put his empty saddlebags over his shoulder, grabbed his gym bag, and dashed across the rain-swept street. A welcoming woman at the café door handed him a cotton hand towel and a plastic-encased menu.

"Take any dry seat ya want. I'll see if I can find you a towel from the back. Ya look like a drowned polecat."

Mike thanked her and sat in a chair by the window. Before he could wipe his face, the door greeter put a mug of steaming hot coffee and a large yellow towel on the table.

"What da ya want for breakfast, traveler?"

"Thanks for the coffee and towel; I'll have the breakfast special."

The woman yelled to the cook, "One blue plate stacked."

The cook repeated the order, adding, "On the grill."

"Be back at ya." She met the next customer at the door with a dry hand towel.

The restaurant was small and warm. There were only about ten chrome Formica-topped tables and a lunch counter that could seat twelve. The decor was utilitarian, plain, and simple. The only things on the aged tan walls were posters of trains—old steam locomotives hauling freight through the high passes of the western mountains. The posters were vivid in bold colors reflecting the stark beauty of the high Sierras.

Mike chowed down on two fried eggs, four pancakes, six strips of bacon, four linked sausages, hash browns, thick creamed chipped beef on rolls, fresh fruit, and a stack of buttered whole-wheat toast. He washed the meal down with a large glass of orange juice, milk, and multiple cups of coffee.

"Good grub, ay?" said the lady as she cleaned the table.

"Best meal I've had since I left Kadena," said Mike. "Would you mind if I left my stuff here while I put my clothes in the dryer across the street?"

"No problem-o. Just return the towel when you're done."

"Thank you." Mike got up from the table, out the door, and dashed across the street through a cloudburst of falling rain.

He put his clothes in the dryers. By the time he was finished the rain had stopped. Casually he walked back to the restaurant, enjoying the clean early morning air. The sun crept over the horizon as he crossed the main street. The town smelled freshly scrubbed. The new day looked like it would be clear and sunny.

Opening the restaurant's door Mike noticed a bald, thin man with a large bushy mustache sitting at his table. The older man was dressed in faded blue jeans, scuffed brown cowboy boots, a clean white short-sleeve T-shirt, and a grease-spattered white apron. He sat enjoying a cup of coffee, lost in thought.

"Hi," said Mike as he approached the table.

"Semper Fi," said the man, putting the coffee mug down.

"Semper Fi," said Mike as he sat down.

"My older brother was in the Corps," said the man at Mike's table. "Bought the farm on some crappy hill in Korea. Couldn't help hear you say Kadena, then saw your motor-sickle with the Marine emblem on the gas tank. Are you active or are you out?"

"Active on leave."

"Where ya headed?"

"East, going to Madison, Wisconsin."

"Fastest way is south on I-281, then to I-90 East through Minnesota. Then take 90/94 south into Madison. Eight hours on a good day, nine if ya have any problems."

"Thanks."

The man reached into his pocket and put an old skeleton key on the table. "There is a storage building behind the laundry mart. The key is for the apartment above it. It's vacant. Has a bed and good shower. You look like you could use some soap and some shuteye."

"That I could, thank you."

"Thank you, and breakfast is on me. Semper Fi, Marine," said the man. He pushed himself away from the table, got up, and went back to the kitchen. The gal that was handing out the towels came to his table from the kitchen. She had a puzzled expression.

"Sam said to give you a heads-up. There are bath towels in the closet. He told me to shit-can the check. If that ain't odd, he has tears in his eyes. I've never seen him cry. What the hell did you say to him?"

"Semper Fi and thank you," said Mike. He put a twenty on the table and politely stood, took his saddlebags, and left.

<hr>

The white cinder block building was dry and clean. The diner owner used the first floor as a garage to store dry goods for the restaurant and supplies for the laundromat. In the corner of the garage was a tool chest with red shop towels on top. Mike rolled his bike into the open space between cases of soap detergent and tins of lard. He took some time to wipe down his bike. Next time he would give it a detailing. He closed the wood-paneled garage doors. There were clothes hooks next to a staircase leading to the second floor. Mike stripped off his soaked leather jacket, jeans, and boots. He hung his sopping apparel on the hooks. Slowly, he walked up the stairs in his tighty-whities carrying his dry clothes in his sleeping bag. The apartment was a walk-up one-bedroom kitchenette with a bathroom. He took a long hot shower, dried off, and shaved. Afterward, he packed his clean dry clothes, crawled in the sack and passed out.

Mike woke at 1800. He had been out almost ten hours. He tidied up the apartment, went to the garage and carefully arranged his gear. His leather jacket was damp but wearable. Boots were still wet. He started the Hog, pushed it out of the garage, closed the door, and rode around the block, stopping at the restaurant. He asked a girl at the register for Sam and was told he wouldn't be back until the morning.

Mike took out his green pocket memo pad and wrote *Semper Fi.* He tore the page from the pad, folded it around the key, and gave the note to the girl, thanked her and left.

It felt good to get back on the road. The sun was in his face as he rode due east along the southern border of Minnesota. The light had a yellow tinge as if shining through a colored filter. The countryside glistened. This was lush farmland with wide expanses of corn, wheat, rye, and soy. He caught brief glimpses of well-manicured farms in groves of juniper trees. Occasionally a small town appeared near the interstate. Often the only sign of inhabitants was a white church steeple nestled in a grove of red oak. By the time Mike got to Worthington, the sun had set. He pulled off I-90, got gas, used the restroom, drank a terrible cup of coffee, and purchased a bag of peppermints.

Night driving was boring. He thought about what lay ahead and longed for support. Then he remembered his company's first sergeant. The "first shirt" was old Corps, twenty-six-plus years in the Green Machine. Top could be counted on to come up with some down-on-the-farm bromide for any situation. Mike wondered what he would say to this misadventure. Something like *My uncle George always rushed in where his shit-eatin' dog wouldn't go.* Mike missed his Marines and the Corps. He needed the stability now. He felt alone. He wanted his family. People he could trust and depend on, someone to cover his back, his Marines. They were his rock.

Sometime after 0200, he pulled into a truck stop near Onalaska, Wisconsin, just north of La Crosse. He needed gas, food, and a walk. His back ached. His stomach was on fire. The truck stop had a twenty-four-hour greasy spoon. Mike ordered a BLT and large glass of milk. Both slid down his throat and hit with a burp. He paid and left. He stayed on I-90 until it intersected with 94 South, which would take him to Madison, where he had an appointment with Corporal Marion Miller's family.

Corporal Miller was a difficult Marine to lead. He was smart and perceptive. He came from a wealthy family, educated in a prep school, and had a degree in psychology from Princeton. Miller turned down the opportunity to go to Officer Candidate School so he could, as he often said, "immerse myself in the culture of the Corps." He had told Mike he should have gone to OCS. Mike never could figure out if Miller was doing research for a thesis paper or trying to usurp his leadership. Miller was always playing an angle, his needs before the unit's. Marion truly believed he was smarter than everyone else. *In the end, it doesn't matter how smart you are. A chicom grenade kills you just the same,* thought Mike.

Mike had some trouble finding the house in the University Heights section of Madison. It was still dark, and the streetlights provided little illumination. So, he found a coffee shop. The patrons in the arts and craft decorated shop were mostly businesspeople and students. Many stole sidelong looks at Mike in his leather biker garb as the shop seats quickly filled. Mike slowly sipped a hot latte, watching the hurried pedestrians pile in. A young man with a shaggy beard and shoulder-length hair, wearing a short-sleeve University of Wisconsin shirt, dirty ripped jeans held up by a macramé belt, and leather string sandals asked if a seat next to Mike's was available.

"Dude, you here for the protest?" asked the bearded man.

"What protest?" answered Mike.

"Against the war, dude. Ya know, Vee-At-Nam."

"Oh."

"We're going to shut down the campus, dude. People are coming from all over the country. This will send a message to *the Man*."

"And what might that message be?"

"The war is morally wrong, dude. It's genocide. Stop the war now, dude."

"What about stopping communism?"

"Dude, that's a dying dog. TV will kill it quicker than a silver bullet."

"Really, I can't wait," said Mike sarcastically.

"Gotta go. See ya on campus, dude." The protester got up and put on the tan jacket he was carrying. When he turned to leave, Mike noticed a flag stitched to the back of his canvas jacket was red-and-blue striped with a yellow star in the center; the flag of the Viet Cong. Mike stared at it in utter disbelief.

He wondered what was happening to his country. Protest he understood. But to display the flag of the enemy was treasonous. *How could the authorities let someone do that?* One of the great American freedoms was free speech. However, free speech was not free. Some dirt-encrusted Marine in a shithole paid the price. *Stand and fight, not scream and run,* Mike thought. He then thought about Jane Fonda, one of his teenage objects of sexual fantasies. *Why the hell isn't she rotting in jail for aiding and abetting the enemy?* The government had pictures and recordings of her in Hanoi joking with the NVA, telling the world that the USA was committing war crimes by bombing hospitals and schools in North Vietnam. He would never spend a buck to see the traitorous bitch again.

Mike had respect for Joan Baez's husband, David Harris. He said he was against the war and went to jail for his convictions. Harris loved his country and was willing to pay any price so his voice was heard. Mike thought it despicable that some US citizens went to Canada to avoid the draft. He thought if they truly love their country, they would have stayed and become conscientious objectors or jailed dissidents, like Harris. Maybe if all the protesters went to Canada, the US could end the war. At the very best, the agitators would be gone never to come back. The one thing he knew for sure was there were no easy answers to a war that was tearing the nation apart.

He became angry sitting and waiting. It was time to get on the road. The wall clock indicated it was past eight—time to meet the family of Corporal Marion M. Miller. At the coffee house, Mike washed his face and changed clothes. He felt presentable.

■ ▪▪▪▪

Mike parked in front of a white Victorian mansion in the Queen Ann style located in University Park. The huge, white, colonnade-porched house was stunning, with multiple hip roofs with leaded-glass-windowed dormers, corner towers, and overhanging eaves. The landscape was half flowering garden and half manicured lawn. All was enclosed by a white picket fence. The size and beauty was spectacular. Mike had never seen anything like it, a true Norman Rockwell scene.

Mike knocked on the oversized front door of the mansion. After several knocks, he used the giant, brass, lion's-heads ring knocker. The sound echoed inside the house. On the other side of the door, he heard "All right already." The door opened slowly.

Mike was welcomed by, "Oh my God!"

Mike stared at the person, equally stunned. Sitting in a wheelchair, dressed in a blue bathrobe and blue satin pajamas, holding the door open partway, was Corporal Marion Miller.

"Marion, who's at the door?" asked a soft motherly voice from the hallway.

"It's"—the man struggled for words—"it's my platoon commander," said Marion with a trembling voice.

An elegantly coiffed women in her fifties dressed in a light-green silk pantsuit opened the door. "Hello, I'm Marion's mother, Judith Miller."

"Hello, I'm Mike Ruhawk."

"You know Marion from the Marine Corps?"

"Yes ma'am. I was his CO in Vietnam."

"Please come in." Judith looked at Marion with scorn. "Where are your manners, Marion?"

"Yes, Mother. Where are my manners?"

"Concetta," Judith called to Marion's caretaker. "Help Marion and his guest into the library."

"Mother, I can do it myself," Marion said.

"I'm just trying to help," said Judith condescendingly.

Marion used his hands, or more accurately part of one hand and the stump of the other, to wheel himself into a dark walnut–paneled library. The room was immense with an oversized limestone fireplace. A framed family crest hung above the hearth. The sunlight streamed through a massive stained-glass bay window, flooding the room with color. A huge, thick, azure Persian rug with a red flower motif lay on the parquet floor. Two wall bookcases full of leather-bound books stretched from the floor to the ten-foot ceiling. The room was like something out of the Biltmore mansion. Marion's mother motioned for Mike to sit in a burgundy leather wingback chair next to the bay window. Marion parked his wheelchair across from Mike.

"Long time no see," said Marion.

"Almost four years."

"Time flies when you're having fun. For me, it seems like eons ago."

Marion's mother pulled a matching wingback chair to sit with her son and visitor and lit a cigarette.

"Mother, could we please have some privacy?"

"Marion, I want to welcome your friend into my house."

"Mother, please leave!"

"Marion—"

"Get the fuck out, now," exploded Marion.

"Don't use that vulgar Marine language when you speak to me, young man."

"Fuck you! Get out."

"Your father will speak to you when he gets home," said Judith as she stormed from the room, her face red with embarrassment.

Marion yelled, "Oh my, I can't wait until dear Daddy gets home so we can talk about his difficult day at the mill, or his fucking golf score. Better yet maybe we can discuss which bimbo he's banging. Please close the doors, Mommy dearest."

Mike sat stunned.

"Well, Lieutenant Ruhawk, what brings you to good old Madison, Wisconsin, and the joy-filled Miller household?" Marion said as he turned off the rage and turned on civility.

Mike looked at Marion for a few moments, wondering at the depth of volatility before him.

"The proverbial cat got your tongue, Lieutenant?" smirked Marion.

"It's Captain Ruhawk," said Mike, his eyes riveted on Marion.

"But of course it's captain. You are ever so confident, competent, and chock-full of the Corps ethos crap. I would have thought you would be a major by now. But time in grade can be stifling," said Marion with another childish snicker.

"What happened?" demanded Mike. "I thought you bought it."

"Where to start? My choice of the Marine Corps, the rigors of Parris Island, squad leader Vietnam, grenade explosion, bodily injuries, multiple hospitals, mystery of the two Millers, welcome home surprise, or home sweet home in Madison? Your choice, *skipper*."

"Explosion forward."

"The explosion was horrific. I just remember flying through the air, the helo ride, and waking up in the NSA hospital in DaNang. The Navy surgeons decided to keep me in some kind of induced coma because of my brain injury. My records indicated I went to Japan for the plunge into Dante's never-ending levels of hell. Developed gas gangrene. A Navy butcher took my left leg at the knee. Next, they shipped me to San Diego where they tried to repair what was left of the leg and started to carve up the right leg, then, moving on to San Antonio for more butchery. There I met my misinformed other family. When I finally came to my senses, these strange people were blabbering all around me. The process confirmed my opinions of the Naval establishment and the Marine Corps in particular. *FUBAR.* Fucked up beyond all reason."

Mike said nothing as Marion continued.

"All the military records indicated I was dead. The revelation that I was a still-breathing crippled mess was discovered months after the medevac. Everyone thought I was dead. My parents even had a closed-casket burial for me. The old-money, country-club, self-righteous, empowered, privileged class were distraught over the loss of Marion Miller. I became a symbol of the godless war when they thought I was dead, and even more so now that I am a mutilated cripple."

"My god, Marion. I don't know what to say," Mike whispered.

"I'll tell you what to say, Captain. The Navy got it wrong. Imagine that. The investigation that followed theorized the two Millers were on the same medevac when delivered to NSA DaNang. Somewhere in transit, the fuck-up occurred and the two Millers went their separate ways, one to Graves Registration, the other to triage. The Marine Corps recommended the closed casket and my family readily agreed. The San Antonio Miller family was waiting with open arms and a loving heart to nurse their war-ravished Miller back to health. But lo, it was me who they greeted with wails of sorrow. The unbearable tragedy is both families would be devastated when the fuck-up was un-fucked.

"So, here I am, paralyzed from the waist down with a catheter in my useless dick, colostomy full of shit between my thighs, two stumps for legs, three fingers on one hand, meatball on the other, titanium plate in my head, condemned to a wheeled coffin, prone to verbal outbursts dotted with four-letter words. My shrink says I have injury-induced Tourette's. Sometimes all I can say is *fuck.* I lost the ability to remember anything with numbers, like my service number, date of birth, social security number, telephone numbers, addresses, birthdates, money, sports scores. Now I'm just wishing and waiting to meet the grim reaper. Probably looks like some long-dead Marine general with his head up his ass. Every day I ask God why he let me live and the other Miller die. Other than that, I'm happier than a pig in shit . . . Now, answer my question. Why the fuck are you here, mon capitaine?"

"I came to offer my condolences to the family of one of my fallen Marines."

"And I thought this story could not get any better. How fucking rich. You have no idea how much I despise you. You are everything I am not; physically, mentally, and now morally. I know I am more intelligent than you, was better looking, and in my prime could whip your sorry ass while napping. Yet, here I am, bound to this chair, unable to add two and two. Moreover, you stand before me, one dumb Marine lifer. You are clueless. You have no idea about life or death. You were ignorant of how the platoon worked. Your sergeants ran the platoon. Staff Sergeant Wolchezski was the power behind the command. He knew his shit."

Mike looked at Marion with a puzzled expression.

"Ski busted me selling weed. He planned to file charges when we got back to An Hoa. I tried to frag him. The gook chicom grenade blew the shit out of me. The poetic justice is inescapable. Here you are adding insult to insult. If there is a God, he must be laughing his ass off. Fuck you, Captain Perfect, you self-righteous asshole. Get the fuck out! Get out! Fuck! Fuck! Get the fuck . . ."

At the end of his outburst, Marion started to laugh. Then he became hysterical. He cried, he ranted about the fucking Corps, his fucking family, his fucking crippled world. He screamed at Mike again to get the fuck out. He called his mother a "cock-sucking whore," called his caregiver a "sniveling cunt," and ran his wheelchair into the mahogany-wainscoting-covered walls. Repeatedly he screamed every known profanity. His mother and Concetta came running into the room. Both began to comfort Marion as he verbally abused them. Marion's arms flew around his head as if a swarm of hornets were attacking him. Then he started spewing "fuck" over and over. Calmly, his mother asked Concetta to call the doctor. Mike looked at Mrs. Miller, the devastation and misery only a mother could feel deeply etched in the once beautiful face.

Mike, bewildered and shaken, quietly backed out of the house. He thought, *Another twisted soul birthed in the labyrinth of rice paddies called Nam.* He sat on his bike to gain some composure. All he could hear was Marion screaming obscenities. *What has this war brought home? Will there be any end to the misery? If you sow the wind, do you really reap the whirlwind?* "God help me," he whispered.

"Excuse me. Excuse me," said a young man walking down the driveway from the Miller house. He was dressed in plaid golf shorts and a white V-neck sports sweater.

Mike looked up.

"Hi, I'm Marion's younger brother, Richard. Please call me Dick."

"How can I help you, Dick?" asked the mentally exhausted Mike.

"I was in the dining room and overheard your conversation."

"Eavesdropping isn't polite," said Mike as if he were talking to an adolescent.

"I just want to ask you something."

"OK, what's on your mind?" Mike wondered what more grief this family could conjure.

"Are you headed to Chicago by chance?"

"Possibly!"

"Can I have a ride?"

"You want a ride to Chicago? On the back of a motorcycle? You want me to take you to Chicago? Did your mother give you permission to go to Chicago?"

Dick said he didn't need it. He was twenty-one and could go wherever he wanted. He pulled his wallet from his back pocket and produced his driver's license as proof of age. The situation was awkward. Mike explained he didn't need any more problems. Dick pleaded. He had friends in Chicago. He had to have a break from his family's madness, and his brother's tirades.

"All I want is a ride, please?"

Mike told him he would drive to the corner, turn right, and go halfway down the block. He would give Dick ten minutes to tell his mother he was going to Chicago with a friend. No way was he to inform his parents, Marion, or anyone else that his transportation was Mike.

"Ten minutes only, then I leave," said Mike.

Mike could hear Marion screaming inside the house as he rode off.

CHAPTER 6

CHICAGO

THE CLOSER MIKE AND Dick got to Chicago, the more traffic they encountered. It was like being amidst a swarm of ants.

The ride to the big city had been uneventful, with Dick saying very little. *How could anyone stand being in that house?* Mike thought. Marion's wounds had infected his entire family. The former Marine corporal was a danger to himself and others. *Scars of war are as much mental as physical,* Mike thought.

Mike maneuvered through the congested traffic to an off ramp. He followed Dick's directions to a brownstone house several streets away in the Lincoln Park section of North Chicago. Several young men there greeted Dick with high fives and smiles when he got off the bike. They had a boom box sitting on the building's steps blaring Buffalo Springfield's "For What it's Worth." The lyrics blasted from the speakers. Mike could hear the words over the roar of the bike.

There's something happening here. What it is ain't exactly clear.
There's a man with a gun over there, telling me I got to beware,
I think it's time we stop, children, what's that sound?
Everybody look, what's going down?

Mike looked at the group standing around the boom box and shook his head dismissively; longhairs with bell-bottom trousers and tie-dye shirts hanging out in the street doing nothing. *What a waste.* He hurriedly rode off, wanting to shed the guilt of Marion Miller as fast as he could drive. It was a relief to end that saga. Now Mike had to find the Johnson family of the South Side. The address he had was in the Dolton Area.

Mike had to take a shower and clean up before meeting the Johnsons. He found a motel wedged between a paint store and used car lot. Mike parked next to the industrial-looking office. It was all steel and concrete block. He almost broke his hand trying to push open the glass door to get service. Finally, a solenoid in the door clicked and it swung open. A woman behind a plate-glass partition greeted him. A semicircle was cut out of the glass where it met the counter, just like a ticket booth at a movie theater.

"Help you?" said the receptionist. She had a vermilion dot on her forehead called a bindi.

"A room for the night, please."

"One people?"

"Yes, one person."

"Forty dollar, please."

Mike pulled two twenties from his wallet. "Ground floor please."

"Ground floor, please?"

"Yes, ground floor."

"No understand ground floor."

A child's voice from somewhere in the background said, "First floor, sis."

"First floor, yes."

"Yes."

"Forty dollar, please."

Mike slid the twenties through the hole. A brass key and registration card slid back to him.

"Do you have a garage?"

"No."

"I need a safe place to store my bike."

"Bike store three blocks north, yes."

"I mean a place to put my motorcycle," said Mike.

"Motorcycle store Forty-Seventh Street, yes."

From a door next to the office emerged a tall, thin, olive-skinned, bespectacled boy who looked ten or eleven. He was dressed in new blue jeans, black high-top Converse gym shoes, and a cotton kurta, an embroidered collarless shirt.

"My sister is slowly learning English. How big is your motorcycle?"

"Come on outside and see for yourself."

After looking at the Harley, the boy said, "I have a place where you can park your motorbike. Storage fee is ten dollars."

"I love young entrepreneurs," said Mike with a grin.

"I will clean and polish for another ten dollar."

"Deal!" They shook.

"My name is Rajiv. If you desire girlfriend, boyfriend, liquor, food, any pleasure, you ask for Rajiv. I get for you, yes."

"OK, my name is Mike. How old are you, Rajiv?"

"I will become teenager, thirteen years of age, next week. I am freshman at Riverdale High School. I am honor student, straight As, and track star, and run cross-country. I will win state title next year. I will go to University of Chicago, become number-one brain surgeon. Marry at thirty years of age, have two sons, make lots of money. Now, follow me to toolshed."

"That's wonderful you've got your life planned," said Mike as he followed Rajiv to a toolshed behind the motel.

"I will make space for motorcycle."

"Excellent. Does the shed lock?"

"I have lock; I rent for five dollars, yes."

"Rajiv, you're pushing it."

"Pushing it?"

"Here's the deal, Rajiv. Clean, store, and lock for twenty bucks or no deal."

"Deal? Deal! Twenty dollars for clean, store, and lock," said Rajiv.

Rajiv made room in the shed and helped Mike push the bike into the cavity. He locked the doors with a huge padlock. Rajiv gave Mike the key.

"Please put toolshed key on room key ring. Papa would be very upset with me if key is lost," said Rajiv.

"Roger that," said Mike.

"Roger who?" said Rajiv.

Mike went to his room to shower, shave, and rest. He lay down at eleven and put in a wakeup call for 1800. After he got up, he would call a cab to take him to the Johnsons'.

■—IIII

Staff Sergeant Goodell Johnson's family lived only five miles from the motel. The socio-economic distance was as if they lived on the dark side of the moon. The taxi driver was reluctant to take Mike to the Johnsons' neighborhood. The area was "mucho bad," said the driver. "They will *mantanza diablo blanco* for sure." The conversation ended when Mike flashed a new crisp twenty.

The taxi driver sped away from the small brick ranch house before Mike could close the car door. The backseat door slammed shut when the vehicle screeched around the corner. The area was scruffy, with some lawns in need of mowing. Several houses were boarded up with for-sale signs in their front yards.

The Johnsons' house was well maintained, with a nice, freshly cut green lawn and colorful zinnias blooming in front of a small brick porch. Mike went to the front door and rang the bell. A heavyset black woman wearing a blue plaid dress and white apron opened the door.

"May I help, young man?" asked the woman.

"Yes, I'm looking for Staff Sergeant Goodell Johnson's family."

"I'm his mother, and his father is on the couch."

"My name is Mike Ruhawk. I was Goodell's CO in Vietnam."

140

"Oh my, please come in."

"Thank you." Mike walked into a small living room. The furnishings were modest and clean. The house smelled of tasty foods and freshly baked bread.

"Mister Ruhawk, this is my husband, Joe. Honey bear, he was—"

"I heard. What can we do for you?" said the powerfully built man dressed in a one-piece gray cotton jumpsuit. He was so large he could have played defensive line for the Chicago Bears. When he approached Mike, Joe's body language displayed guarded apprehension.

"Sir, I came to Chicago to offer my deepest condolences for the loss of your son. He was an outstanding Marine NCO. You have every right to be proud of him."

Goody's parents were stunned. Then Joe lost his composure and burst into tears. Margret Johnson hugged her husband, both agonized with grief. Mike hung his head and looked at the hardwood floor. He was out of his element with the intimacy of heartbreak. Their sorrow made him feel intrusive, unworthy, and miserable.

Between sobs Margret said, "Excuse us." They left the room.

Mike sat alone for twenty minutes. The couple finally returned with their dignity and composure intact.

"We were just ready to sit down at the dinner table when you rang the doorbell. Please join us for supper."

"Thank you." Mike felt humbled by the simple offer.

Joe and Mike sat at the dining room table that could easily seat eight.

Margret put platters of breaded pork chops, mashed potatoes, collard greens, and fresh-baked French bread on the table. She went back into the kitchen and returned with a pitcher of sweet iced tea. When she sat, she reached for Mike's hand. He held her hand and Joe's while she said the Lord's Prayer, ending with "God bless all our men and woman who serve our country, and special prayer for Mister Ruhawk and his Marines. God bless."

During the meal, Mike learned Goody was their only child. He had been a high school all-American in basketball and had an athletic scholarship to the University of Illinois. During an afternoon pickup game, he blew out his knee. It was devastating, but Goody never complained. He said God worked in mysterious ways. He joined the Marine Corps the day after he graduated from high school.

He loved the Corps, and so did his parents, both proud Americans despite the overt racism they faced throughout their lives. Joe proudly wore his Eagle, Globe, and Anchor lapel pin on his metro bus driver uniform. Margret wore another pin on her white nursing uniform. Mike reinforced their pride, telling stories of their son's outstanding performance while under his command. "He was one of the best," Mike said of Goody.

Dessert was homemade strawberry ice cream with fresh strawberries. They took their bowls into the living room and sat on the couch. Both wanted to know how their son died. Did he suffer? Was he in pain? They had been told he stepped on a landmine while on patrol. In fact, that was the truth, but death by accident seemed mundane, and Goody and his parents deserved better, Mike reckoned.

Mike told them Goody was a hero, that he rushed into withering small arms fire from entrenched Viet Cong to rescue a fallen Marine. That part was true; he had. Mike embellished, saying Goody was shot while carrying the Marine to safety and then led an assault against the dug-in enemy, weaving through heavy mortar fire to help secure the enemy position. As he consolidated the position, he stepped on an enemy landmine. "He was a true hero," Mike said.

The ice cream melted in their bowls as the Johnsons contemplated what Mike had told them. They had heard how their son was killed before, but never in such detail. Mr. Johnson excused himself. He had to get up early for his four o'clock shift at the transit authority. They shook hands, and parted with a hug and a thank-you. With his head hung low and his back bent, Joe Johnson shuffled to bed.

Margret asked Mike to stay. She had some pictures she wanted him to see. She returned with several photo albums, each album filled with newspaper clippings of her son's outstanding athletic career. Margret carefully paged through the first album, explaining each photo. Mike pondered what might have been had Goody not enlisted, or at the very least survived Vietnam.

It was past nine, time for Mike to leave. He thanked Margret and said he had to get an early start in the morning; there were other families to visit. He asked if he could use the phone to call a cab. She chuckled and said no cabby would come into her neighborhood at night. He could catch a bus on the corner. She would walk with him so there would be no problem. Margret put on her coat and opened the front door. Milling about in her front yard were several teenagers. They wore red-white-and-blue polyester track suits with the hoodies pulled over their heads. One young man stepped forward.

"Hello, Missus Johnson."

"Is that you, Malcolm?"

"Yes'um."

"What's you want?"

"The neighborhood protection committee wants to ensure whitey causing you no harm."

Mike heard muffled snickers from the group. They shuffled their black, high-top sneakers on the concrete sidewalk.

"Malcolm, whenever did I need your help?"

"Times are a changing. We'z gots to stick together."

Margret stepped aside and gestured with her hand. "This here is Goodell's Marine commander. He came here to tell us what a good Marine my son is . . . was. Now you leave him be. He's on his way to catch a bus home."

"Yes'um. Hows about we walk him to the corner. He don't want to run into any bad boys."

Mike heard more cackling and shuffling from the group.

"That would be very nice of you. Just remember, if anything happens, your mama and I will have a little talk."

"Mister Marine will be right as rain with us. Don't worry none."

"Thank you, boys. Have a safe trip home, Mister Ruhawk. Thank you so much for the visit. God bless."

Mike kissed her on the cheek, gave her a big hug, and thanked her for dinner. Then he started down the concrete path. The group formed a protective circle around Mike as they walked to the corner.

"You one lucky peckerwood," said Malcolm.

Mike said nothing and kept on walking.

"We'z the Pee Street Thugs. You'd be bleedin' in a gutter if I ain't told Miss Johnson we'd protect yo white ass."

Someone in the crowed growled menacingly, "Do whitey."

"Shut your piehole, Drib. We keepers of our word, not like them downtown poseurs. Tell us, Mister Marine man, what you doin' at Peak's crib?"

"Peak?" questioned Mike.

"Goody's name on the street. He bein' so tall and all."

"He led an attack, saved a fellow Marine and then stepped on a landmine. He was a real badass," Mike said.

"No shit!"

"No shit. He died with honor."

"Honor. More white sugar for black ants."

"Goody was an outstanding Marine NCO. He would have been one of the best and that's no shit!"

"We had big plans for our homey. He goin' to state and all. Then, he got all righteous and wanted to fight; so's he goes Marine man on us. Now he's just another black brother who got kilt in the po' black boy's war," said Malcolm. He tone was one of loss and disgust.

"Poor black boy's war?" questioned Mike.

"What da ya think Nam is? If'n I'm rich and white, I can buy my way out. Doc drops note on me sayin' my sugar high, bad back, or feet all fucked up. Whiteys with money get any deferments he wants. Or he goes to some fancy religious school and becomes CO. Ya knows—conscientious objector. Poor black boy gets screwed. Just draft mo' brothers. The killing machine needs mo' black juice to keep the wheels rollin'. It don't matter if he the next Messiah. If he darker than white milk, he goes. No problem."

"It isn't a poor black man's war," answered Mike.

"Professor, tell this head-fucked honkie da truth."

An older teen stepped forward. He was sharply dressed with large, silver-rimmed glasses. He was a straight-A student in high school, now in the honors school at the University of Chicago. The gang called him "Professor."

"Black males of all ages are less than 6 percent of the total US population, yet black males between eighteen and twenty-five represent over 14 percent of the US military. Statistically, male Negroes comprise slightly less than 11 percent of the total Marine Corps. Yet, black Marines KIAs in Vietnam 1965 to 1967 is over 23 percent of total killed in action."

"See, Marine man, we can die for whitey, but we can't live with ya."

"All my Marines are treated equally," Mike said.

"That so? Tell Mister Marine about your Thanksgiving in Huntsville," the Professor said to another older teen in the crowd. A Harry Belafonte look-alike stepped forward.

"My family from a teeny, tiny town of Hilltop, Alabama. We goes home every Thanksgivin'. Last year, we'z all gone to Huntsville ta shop. I gots put in da hospital for drinkin' out a ballpark drinkin' fountain. White boys beat da sot out of me with baseball bats. I swear, I never saw da *Whites Only* sign. No matter, I never leave Dolton, never-ever."

"That's civilian bullshit, not Marine," said Mike.

"You really believe the same is not true in your gang?" the Professor piped. "Don't be stupid."

"Ya see, Marine man," said Malcolm, "we lives under the white man's whip. Yo bus comin'. Tonight, you one lucky dude. Next time PST will beat ya like a tin can."

Mike walked to the motel after the bus ride. The street was dark and there was very little traffic. The one working streetlight cast a long shadow. He entered his room, locked the door, and turned off the lights. Mike lay on the bed fully clothed. He wondered why tonight bothered him so much. Were the gang kids and the Professor better informed about racial disparity among troops in Vietnam than he was? To Mike, a Marine was a Marine regardless of race or color. But there did seem to be a disproportionate number of African Americans in combat units. Mike gazed into the ceiling of the darkened room, seeing nothing, hearing nothing, and feeling numb. He quickly dozed off.

Nine hours later Mike jumped out of bed with loud pounding on the door.

"What do you want?" Mike yelled through the door.

"Room service."

"Go away. I'm staying another day."

"Pay noon for day."

"OK, OK!"

Mike felt like a thousand wildebeests had trampled him. A hot shower was his only desire. Shave, clean clothes, and food were his road to salvation. Once he was presentable, he found Rajiv. The bike had been meticulously cleaned and polished. Mike gave Rajiv another twenty for a second day at the motel and twenty for a job well done. The teenager was overjoyed and said he would polish the bike again. Mike wanted to know where he could get a good breakfast. Ever the entrepreneur, Rajiv took Mike to his home. His other sister cooked a fantastic breakfast. He ate like a king. After eating, Mike called a cab. He had a second family to visit, the O'Rourkes from Evergreen Park.

■■▪▪▪▪

PFC Timothy O'Rourke was called "Oak" by his Marine buddies because he was built sturdy and thick like a large oak tree. He led the platoon into an NVA ambush in Ben Du near the river Song

Tinh Yen. Oak's quick reactions to the first burst of gunfire saved his squad and allowed the platoon to flank the NVA. What could have been devastating for the platoon resulted in one KIA and three WIAs for the Marines, and nineteen dead enemy. The tragedy—the one Marine killed was Oak.

Oak's citation read, *For extraordinary acts of valor while under direct enemy fire during ground operations against a superior hostile force in the Republic of Vietnam, Dia Loc Province. Private First Class Timothy O'Rourke distinguished himself by his heroic actions while serving as point rifleman for second squad of second platoon, Company E, Second Battalion, Fifth Marines on 16 June 1968. With total disregard for his own welfare, he closed with and killed eight enemy. After being grievously wounded, he assisted in life saving first aid to another Marine before succumbing to numerous wounds. PFC O'Rourke's bold initiative, superb presence of mind, and steadfast devotion to duty are in keeping with the highest traditions of the Marine Corps and of the United States Naval Service.* Tim O'Rourke was awarded the Silver Star posthumously.

Evergreen Park rested in the center of Chicago's South Side. For generations, the Irish who worked in Chicago occupied this area. The address Mike had was 10102 West 91st Street. The cabby pulled up to the curb next to O'Malley's Pub. The address of the pub matched what Mike had as the home address for Tim O'Rourke.

The bar had a crowd of working men bellying to the bar rail for lunch. Mike found a seat and ordered an Irish ale. He drank the beer slowly, enjoying the ambiance. The interior was paneled in dark cherry with boxed coffered beams overhead. The floor was littered with peanut shells and sawdust. Framed hunting pictures of running hounds and jumping horses hung on the walls. All created the feel of a Dublin pub. The crowd was loud and seemingly full of good cheer. When the lunch hour ended, the pub slowly emptied. Mike and another gentleman were the only ones at the bar by one thirty. Mike asked the barkeep if the proprietor was there.

A florid-faced, round-girthed man in his sixties dressed in a bulky, knit beige cardigan and a plaid tam came to the bar. He could have been an oversized stand-in for a leprechaun during the Saint Patrick's Day Parade.

"Jonathon O'Malley at your service, sir."

"Mister O'Malley, I'm looking for the Timothy O'Rourke family. I think you may be able to help me."

"Maybe, lad. Could you perhaps tell me why?"

"I was his CO in Vietnam and wanted to tell his family what a good Marine he was."

"I believe I can help."

O'Malley explained that Timothy was an orphan. Both his parents and younger sisters were killed in a car accident. The extended O'Rourke family of Evergreen raised him from the age of seven. Timothy's aunt Colleen and uncle Patrick O'Rourke were court guardians, but the real caregivers were the South Side Irish community. Timmy had worked for O'Malley since he was a teen. First, as a barroom sweep, then as a bartender, he always referred to the pub as his home. That was Irish humor. Almost all his relatives worked for the O'Rourkes' company. The family started as gravediggers and expanded in two decades into the largest burial vault manufacturer in the Midwest. Timmy was the next in line to run the family business. He was patriotic and felt Marine training would be helpful when running the O'Rourke firm—more Irish humor.

"We never had time for a proper Irish wake for Timmy. Now is the time, tonight is the night," proclaimed Jonathon O'Malley with the authority of the ad hoc mayor of Evergreen Park. "Enjoy your pint. I have some phone calls to make."

By six thirty, the bar was filled with PFC Timothy O'Rourke's family and friends.

"Bar the door, Patty, the drinks are on the house. All you other bog-trotters go home. This is for the O'Rourke clan and friends only." No one left the pub, causing hoots and catcalls from the gathering.

"Timmy's Marine commander is here and has a few words to say. Pipe down in the back. McGuire, shut your trap. Sally, sit down. Now show some respect if ya know what's good for ya. Stand on the bar, young lad. Pipe down. Listen to the man. Let's get this wake moving. I have to have the bar clean of riffraff and ready to open in the morn," said O'Malley.

"Only for your family," said someone in the crowd. The group erupted into laughter.

"Whoever said that will get not another drop of Guinness from me." The laughter grew louder when one of Johnny's sons raised his hand indicating he was the wiseass.

"Only tellin' the truth, Da," said his son. Soon the group was out of control.

"God almighty, give the Marine a chance."

The group slowly quieted and soon became sullen.

Mike got on the bar. "Friends and family of Timothy O'Rourke, please know he was a good Marine. He served the Corps and country proudly and honorably. He was a warrior. I'm here to tell you he was brave. He acted with courage. His action in Vietnam saved numerous lives while giving his own. No greater deed can one man do than give his life for another. I will never forget Tim O'Rourke. God bless him."

Mike gave some of the specifics of Oak's heroism—several stories, in fact, about him putting his own life at risk to save others or helping frightened or wounded Marines to regain composure. Mike called him a "gentle giant" who treated his fellow Marines as if they were family. "I suspect he got that sense of duty and loyalty from all of you," Mike said, scanning the crowd.

Mike stepped down. The room was graveyard quiet. There wasn't a dry eye in the bar.

Jonathon O'Malley cleared his throat and said, "Praise be to God and the brewmaster." Then he proclaimed, "Drink like there is no tomorrow. Forget the ills of yesterday and remember our boy Timmy as we drown the sorrow of today. Drink up! Drink up!"

The rest of the night was a blur. Mike was introduced to Tim's family and friends, the O'Rourkes, the O'Douls, the Quinns, the Kellys, the Bradys, the O'Learys, the Conroys, the Murrays, and on and on. There were toasts, stories, weeping, laughing, fighting, hugging, backslapping, joke telling, and song singing. One song was sung repeatedly, the obvious favorite of the clan.

From the back of the bar, an angelic tenor started to sing.

Some Guinness was spilled on my bar room floor
when we shut the doors for the night
Out of his hole crept a wee brown mouse
and stood in the pale moonlight.
He lapped up the frothy brew from the wooden floor
and back on his haunches he sat.
And all night long, you could hear him roar,
"Bring on the Goddamn Cat."

Loudly everyone would sing the next refrain together, *"Bring on the Goddamn Cat."* After each refrain, emptied glasses were refilled, and the song started again.

■▮▮▮

Mike felt terrible when he rolled over in bed. He was in his motel room in his underwear and had no idea how he got there. The last thing he remembered was singing about a goddamn cat. Stumbling to the bathroom to get a drink of cold water, Mike found a note next to the sink.

Dearest Mickey,

Thank you for sharing our burden. Your comments are heart felt. We all love

Timmy, miss him every day. He was very special. If he were here, he would say,
"Wherever you go and whatever you do, may the luck of the Irish be there with you."

God Bless,
The O'Rourke clan

The handwritten note was in a flowing script. It was elegant and beautiful. Emotions flooded Mike's heart. He burst into tears. He wept for all his Marines, those living and dead. He wanted to be with them, lead them, cherish them, and keep them safe. Yet, here he was in some roach motel in the Windy City, drowning in misery. He felt like a failure for those he should have saved. They died and he lived.

Mike shook himself like a wet Labrador retriever, his despair shedding like drops of water flung into the air. He had to get a grip. He had a mission, always the mission, and nothing else. Not the time to mourn. When he completed his mission, he could weep all he wanted. Before Mike got into the shower, he phoned Rajiv.

"Two aspirin and a large cup of coffee. Please bring them to my room." Mike was shaving when Rajiv knocked on the door.

"Thank you, Rajiv." He handed him a fiver.

"No money. You been varee, varee good to Rajiv. You depart today?"

"Yes."

"I bring motorcycle to you, OK?"

"That would be outstanding."

Mike gulped the coffee and aspirin. Finished shaving, he then packed his saddlebags. By the time he was ready to walk out the door, Rajiv had the Harley out front.

"My mother made this for you. The drink is what she give father when he stays out late. Mother said make you feel like new man. After you drink you can work all day."

Mike looked into the clear glass. The concoction looked like congealed tomato juice but smelled like curry.

"Drink quickly," advised Rajiv.

Mike said, "What the hell," and downed the drink. At first, everything was fine; then he began to perspire like an adulterer in the confessional. His eyes watered. He got dizzy, then belched and belched again. As if by magic, he felt 100 percent better. His headache evaporated. He felt great.

"Must tell you, no alcoholic drink for one day or terrible sickness will come," said Rajiv.

"Rajiv, please give your mother a kiss for me. You have been number one host. I believe you will be everything you want to be and more. Thank you very much."

After shaking hands, Mike started the Harley and drove off with a wave.

CHAPTER 7

CORPSMAN

MIKE RODE THREE HOURS west through Joliet and LaSalle, to Rock Island. The landscape changed from stunning skyscrape city to dank, smokestack industrial, to gray decaying urban blight, to glittering new suburbs, and finally to flat, deep-brown, furrow farmland. Corn and soybean fields stretched for miles. The images stood in stark contrast to the vastness of the Northwest plain with the backdrop of the Teton Mountains. It was as if Mike had driven to different planets.

Mike was hungry and pulled into a national hamburger franchise off the highway. As Mike ate, he contemplated his next stop—Muscatine. This visit wasn't for a Marine but for a Navy Corpsman.

Outside of the Navy establishment, it was little known that the Navy provided all medical, dental, and religious support for the Marine Corps. The Navy medical personnel attached to Marine units were called corpsmen. Other services called them medics or nurses. These Navy corpsmen, non-doctors, trained much like a civilian paramedic and through rigorous training with the Marines. In most Marine units, the corpsmen were held in high regard as they were lifesavers in combat situations, the first responders when the bullets flew. Petty Officer First Class Eric "Big Red" Emerson was one of the best to ever wear the corpsman's Navy collar caduceus.

Emerson was the senior company corpsman for Echo Company, Second Battalion, 5th Marines. He died in a grenade explosion while treating his CO, Captain Mike Z. Ruhawk, for shrapnel wounds.

Mike felt he owed "Big Red" his life. His image of Emerson's red-bearded face erupting in blood, bone, and brain was the stuff of night horrors. The chicom grenade worked to perfection; it killed and maimed. Mike needed to tell the Emerson family what a great friend and corpsman Eric had been. His family needed to know their son was a professional, a great doc, and trusted friend. Big Red's death had devastated Mike and the company.

■■ ▮▮▮

After lunch, Mike rode his Harley along the Mississippi River to Muscatine, Iowa. The town sat on the high banks of a bend in the Big Muddy. Mark Twain could have written about this area. The setting was like Calaveras County. He expected to see a group of youths gathered on a street corner yelling at jumping frogs. The address Mike had for the Emersons was on Cypress Street in a blue-collar neighborhood of vinyl-sided, two-story houses.

Mike double-checked the house number before he stopped at the curb. The house was a burned skeleton. Blackened timbers jutted into the cloudy morning sky like spears. Thorn bushes had invaded the charred doorways and broken window frames of the first floor. The outline of a charred chair could be seen in the debris covering the front stoop. The lawn was full of crabgrass and dandelions.

Mike turned off his bike and walked to a neighbor's house. He knocked several times; no answer. He tried another neighbor. Still no answer. On the third try, an unshaven blimp of a man came to the screen door dressed in stained panda bear pajamas. The man said the Emersons had moved after the fire, but he had no idea where.

Mike drove around until he found a pay phone with a city directory. He phoned each of the five Emersons listed. None were related to Eric. Mike next rode to the courthouse on the city square. With the help of the property tax office, Mike discovered the charred Cypress Street house was on the auction block because of delinquent back taxes. The county assessor suggested Mike research the fire at the public library. The swirled-pink-granite county library looked a hundred years old, as did the head librarian. After a lengthy search, the librarian found a microfiche of the city's newspaper with a small article about the fire. A faulty kerosene space heater caused the blaze. Fortunately, all family members were at work and school when the tragedy struck. The article offered no other information.

Mike's next stop was the police station. They could offer no assistance. The last stop was the central post office. Mike was told the post office only forwarded mail for six months, and then forwarding address cards were discarded. "They must have moved out of Muscatine," said a postal worker. To find Eric's family would take more time than Mike could afford. He had other families to meet before his leave expired.

It was late afternoon when Mike crossed the metal strut bridge over the Mississippi River, heading east, passing Peoria and driving to Indianapolis. He was so depressed he could not recall traffic, scenery, or events in the four-hour drive. At dusk, he exited at Clermont, on the west side of Indy. Mike stopped at a chophouse and had a generic steak, plain baked potato, and a cold beer. The meal was sustenance, nothing more. Next door was a plain-Jane franchise motel. His plan was to pay, sleep, and go. He got a room for one night, parked, showered, and went to bed. The room darkened and the mental images that haunted him so regularly commenced. The movie titled *Big Red Saves the Skipper* roiled in his mind for hours. The mental movie never varied.

Mike was wounded. Shrapnel had cut his forehead and peppered his left side. Blood poured into his eyes. His filthy jungle utilities absorbed the blood like a new sponge. He leaned against the battered M48 Patton tank feeling dazed. It provided cover from direct weapons. But the NVA mortars had bracketed the wasted city street. Mike was on the tank's phone communicating with the nervous tank gunner, trying to direct fire. The tank slowly moved down the narrow, littered street. The mortar fire stopped and a staccato of AK47 fire began. The rifle rounds sounded like heavy rain on a tin roof as they ricocheted off the armor plating. Mike turned to direct the Marines behind him. There were only two where six started. Several Marines lay wounded on the street. Corpsman Emerson moved from one fallen Marine to another, checking breathing, stopping bleeding, preventing shock, and then moving to the next casualty. Big Red seemed indifferent to the automatic weapon rounds and mortar explosions that surrounded him even though the street was filled with smoke and whirling metal shards of death.

Big Red kneeled next to his CO. In a voice that was calming and reassuring, he explained to Captain Ruhawk how he was going to treat his head wound. As he applied field dressing, the ping of a spoon flying off the body of a grenade sounded like the only noise in the fight. Within milliseconds, the coiled spring sticker would hit the primer and three seconds later detonate the explosive, sending thousands of wire serrations in a kill zone fifteen to twenty meters in diameter. In those few seconds, both Eric and Mike knew they would die. They were looking into each other's eyes wondering what the new universe would reveal. Their world suddenly turned bright red filled with yellow lightning. Big Red's body dissolved into one hundred and eighty-two pounds of raw, ground beef. A gory mist of blood and shards of ivory-colored bone. Mike would have died, but the grenade landed behind Big Red and his body absorbed the majority of the blast. Now, Mike's nightmare always ended with a vision of Big Red's eyes staring back at Mike in abject terror.

Sometime after midnight, Mike fell into a restless sleep. He fought demons conjured up from the muck and stink of a country most people couldn't find on a map. The morning offered no relief for the funk. Mike needed a workout. He was saddle-sore and emotionally damaged. He put on his USMC running shorts, shirt, and sneakers. He did his Marine daily dozen to loosen up, then ran for about a mile along gravel side road. He had to stop because of stomach cramps, which doubled him over. He began to vomit. Everything in his gut spewed onto the pavement. The smell was a sour mix of rotten meat and aged curry. When he was finished, he walked back to his room. Then, he had to hit the bathroom. Soon he felt completely flushed.

He had forgotten Rajiv's warning until another bout of nausea hit him. One thing was certain—he needed a rest. He took a shower, brushed his teeth, and went back to bed.

CHAPTER 8

4-F

THE SOUNDS OF LATE-MORNING truck traffic on the interstate woke Mike at around ten. He felt better and hungry. Thankfully, the motel provided a sample-size bottle of mouthwash. He gargled the whole bottle of minty green fluid. He dressed, packed, left the room, and secured his gear on the bike. It was good to get back on road. Mike felt well enough to have breakfast and continue his journey. Down the pike was a waffle house. His next stop should have been Murray City, Ohio. Instead, on an impulse he decided to visit a special friend from his alma mater, Ohio State University in Columbus, Ohio.

Mike had enjoyed every day as an undergraduate at State. He was an excellent student, good athlete, fun-loving fraternity man, and party boy. His world changed when he met Catherine Anne Burkhart. She was a stunning brunette with long legs and a beautiful smile. They met at an off-campus kegger. She was dating Troy, Mike's rival on the lacrosse field.

Troy was a defenseman and USAA all-American player. Mike and Troy had several clashes on the playing field. The issue was always about Troy's technique with his stick. He was vicious, always striking opponents in the face mask. During college matches, he often was assessed a personal foul and banished to the sideline. His nickname on the team was Slasher.

The night of the party, Mike watched Troy spike Cathy's drink with some type of powder. He followed the couple outside. By the time Troy had gotten Cathy to his car, she had passed out. Mike stopped Troy from putting Cathy in the passenger seat and confronted him. A fight ensued. Mike knocked Troy unconscious and took Cathy to his apartment. The rest of the night, Mike helped Cathy recover. She was deathly ill and could not remember anything about the party. In the morning, Mike took Cathy back to her sorority.

The next day, after morning lacrosse practice, Troy was talking trash in the locker room about Mike and Cathy, bragging to fellow players, "I had her all primed and was taking her back to my pad to show her the real deal."

Mike walked up to the group and said, "Why don't you tell everyone how you enticed her into your car?"

"Well, if it isn't Sir Galahad. You took my meat with a sucker punch."

"You're an asshole who drugs women so you can rape them."

The two shoved each other until an assistant coach broke up the melee and told them to take their problems off campus or they would be off the team.

Troy's parting words were, "See you at tonight's practice."

The evening scrimmage was brutal. Mike was one of the three red-team forward attackers. Troy was one of the three blue-team defenders. Every time Mike got the ball, he was assaulted by Troy. The coach warned Troy about high-sticking and slashing. The game ended in a tie. Mike slowly walked toward the field house, his shoulders bruised and face cut from Troy's merciless beating.

At the gate that separated the field from the athletic complex stood Troy. "You learn your lesson, dickhead, or do you want more?"

"That's cheap play. How you ever made the all-American team amazes me. One of these days a bigger dog will come along and take a chunk out of your ass."

Troy grinned. "Well, you're not that dog."

"What happens on the field is between us. Just stay away from Cathy off the field or you'll see just how big of a dog I can be."

"What are you going to do if I don't?" challenged Troy.

"Let's just say you could have a nasty accident that would end your collegiate lacrosse career," said Mike. Troy laughed and walked away.

Mike and Cathy started to date and soon fell in love. After a year, he proposed. They set the date for the following year after Cathy's graduation. The day after he proposed, Mike got his draft notice. He had to report to the draft board the week after he graduated. Cathy still had her senior year to complete. Mike thought about the situation.

Mike had always been the golden boy, an only child with a doting mother and demanding father. Academics were easy for Mike. He was a 3.50-to-4.0 GPA scholar with little effort. He was a natural athlete who excelled in any sport he chose. With his rugged good looks, he was never without a date. Added to all his natural abilities was a magnetic personality. One girlfriend said he had guileless gravitas. No one knew he felt like he never measured up to his father's standards. He invariably felt the unexplainable need to excel. When he fell in love with Cathy, his world became balanced. His drive was not damped, but now he had someone who could share his successes. A woman who loved him not for what he did but who he was.

His world changed with the draft notice. Should he avoid his military obligation and marry or enlist and do his duty? His mother's mantra of "Do the difficult right over the easy wrong" reverberated in his psyche. His father served proudly in World War II with the Navy, and his grandfather dropped out of Yale to join the Marines in World War I. His country needed him, and he rationalized he owed it for the privileges society provided.

After some time pondering the dilemma, Mike concluded he could achieve a compromise. He would join the Marine Corps because they provided the best training and would demand the very best from him. He would choose the service, not the government. Then he would marry Cathy after initial training, do his duty, and return the happy warrior. His first step was to contact the Marines.

After talking to the recruiter, he realized his training would take almost a year. They could be married after training. The timing was perfect. They would both graduate in the same month, Mike from TBS—The Basic School for Marine Officers—and Cathy from OSU. The wedding would take place at the end of the month. "What could be better?" he asked.

Cathy was upset. She thought the idea was selfish and stupid. She suggested they marry immediately. Mike could get a family deferment or go to grad school for his MBA or law school and bypass the draft. Maybe he could join the Army Reserve, National Guard, Air Force instead. Why in God's name would he join the Marines? For Mike the answer was clear. "The Marines are the best, and if I am going to fight for my country, I want to be trained by the best."

Cathy argued that being "the best" was PR bullshit. Marines, Army, whatever. They carried guns and shot people. "If you go into the Marines, you'll go to Vietnam and die. That would destroy my life. Why can't you think of me for once?"

Then, out of the clear blue, Cathy announced she was a pacifist. Mike was dumbstruck. The subject of war had never been an issue. It was in the news but had no effect on them. Like their friends, they were interested in grades and parties. The anti-war movement was building but had not yet swollen into national sentiment.

It was 1965 and their college friends were having too much fun to look beyond the confines of campus. No one talked about the war. The few campus radicals were seen as troublemakers. All they did was protest every social issue of the day. Like many Americans in the early sixties, to them Vietnam was someone else's problem.

"All wars are wrong, and this French-Indochina war is a crime," Cathy stated.

"What about World War II? Was that a just war?" Mike huffed.

"How can any conflict where millions upon millions die be called just?"

"We were defending ourselves, our way of life, our democracy, and to reestablish peace," Mike countered.

"Noble ideals, but don't try to tell me we are defending our country from the communists in Vietnam. There is a big ocean between them and us. The Vietnamese can't swim that far. They're primitive people. The majority of people in Asia don't have indoor flush toilets. They live in grass huts, for God's sakes," retorted Cathy.

They battled over the issues of Vietnam, duty, commitment and love. The arguments went on without resolve. Their differences were insurmountable. They came to the same conclusion. It was better to separate as friends than battle as lovers. They kissed and parted.

Cathy graduated and went to work for an ad agency in Columbus. Mike received his Marine second lieutenant officer commission after OCS, went to The Basic School, and then to Nam.

Now, after all these years, Mike felt compelled to talk to Cathy again. He wondered how he would be greeted and whether her views of the war had changed. They had not spoken or written since she walked out of his apartment almost five years ago. He had followed her progress through some mutual college friends. Cathy was single and still lived and worked in Columbus.

She had a Milford Avenue address in the Clintonville area of Columbus. He found the white-trimmed brick Cape Cod bungalow without any trouble. The house was set in an established 1940s housing development. The area was trendy for young professionals who wanted to be near downtown. Mike pulled to the curb in front of the house in the late afternoon. He realized Cathy would not be home from work before 1700. He found a small sandwich shop/convenience store down the street. After the chicken salad sandwich, he had a piece of apple pie and several cups of coffee. Mike killed time drinking coffee and reading the newspaper.

At 1730 hours, Mike rode to Cathy's house. There was a bright-blue, two-door Dodge Dart in the driveway. Mike parked behind the car and went to the door. He pressed the brass door buzzer.

"Come in, I'm not ready yet. You're early," a voice called.

Mike opened the screen door and entered the house. It was feminine and cozy inside. There were lots of bright pillows on the furniture and fresh-cut long-stem red roses in a glass vase on a baby grand piano. A note by the vase read, *We make a great team. Love Roger.*

"The wine is in the fridge. Please pour me a glass. I'll be down in a sec." Mike put the note back in the roses and went into the kitchen.

He got the Zinfandel out of the refrigerator, found a wineglass and corkscrew and poured Cathy a glass, set it on the kitchen counter, and waited. He could hear her high heels click down the wooden stairs. She entered the kitchen with her head down, trying to close the clasp on a large jade necklace. She wore a sleeveless, form-fitting, silver sheath dress and jade-colored high heels.

"Can you please help me?"

"My pleasure," said Mike.

Cathy looked up. "Oh my God!"

"Hello," said Mike.

"Oh my God," said Cathy. She threw her arms around Mike's neck. They hugged. She began to cry. Tears rolled down her perfectly powdered cheeks. They held each other tightly. The embrace was lengthy and heartfelt.

"You're gorgeous as a blonde and the dress is a knockout. You're absolutely stunning!"

"I thought you were dead," the muffled voice whispered from the face buried in his neck.

"You should know you can't kill a 'self-absorbed son of a bitch.'" Mike smirked.

"I called you that in the heat of the moment."

"If I could have dreamt of a homecoming, this would be it. You look and feel fantastic," said Mike.

"Damn, I missed you, you SOB," said Cathy, hugging Mike harder.

Mike kissed her soft, inviting lips. It was as if he'd never left Cathy's arms. His passion rose immediately. He felt dizzy. How could he have ever doubted his love for her?

"Am I interrupting something?" said a deep male voice from the outside.

"Oh my God! Roger, come in," stammered Cathy.

A tall, dark-haired man wearing a Brooks Brothers suit, silk striped tie and black wingtips opened the screen door and swaggered into the kitchen. He could have been a male model.. His haircut probably cost a week's paycheck. It was perfectly coiffed. Mike felt outclassed in his biker jeans, red Marine T-shirt, cowboy boots, and worn leather jacket. It was wingtips versus motorcycle boots.

"Hi. I'm Roger Archer." He reached out to shake Mike's hand.

"Hello. Mike Ruhawk," said Mike as he untangled his arms from Cathy.

They clasped hands, both squeezing firmly.

"Great grip. You must work out," Mike said.

"I spend some time in the gym."

"I'm sure you do."

"Are you the Marine that Cathy talks about?"

"I hope so," said Mike.

"Are the Marines as tough as the movies make out?" Roger said.

"Nope," Mike said with a straight face.

"I didn't think so," Roger said.

"The movies make us look like a bunch of limp wrists. Marines are a mean, hard, and cantankerous cluster of badasses, best fighters in the world, bar none. Few make the cut."

"That so?" sneered Roger.

"What military service do you call home?" challenged Mike.

"Herniated lower disk, 4F deferment," answered Roger smugly.

"That so?" said Mike.

Cathy sensed the tension. "Gentlemen, let's have a glass of wine together. Roger, we have plenty of time before the open house."

"Party?" asked Mike.

"Our advertising agency is having an open house and dinner for our newest retail customer," said Roger.

"Roger is the big-hitter account executive. I'm his lead designer," said Cathy, proudly.

"I'm sure you're a dynamic duo."

"We are," Roger said.

The two alpha males sat across from each other with Cathy between them. She explained the ad campaign of a woman clad in sexy lingerie wearing angel wings. The team had proposed the idea to the retailer for his new line of women's undergarments. To Mike, it sounded like a Playboy photo shoot with girls in panties and bras. After the wine, Mike told Cathy he had to go but said he would phone once he got to Quantico. He shook hands with Roger without the macho squeezing and kissed Cathy goodbye. As he walked out the door, he turned to Roger and nonchalantly said, "Hope your back gets better."

Roger stood. "What do you mean by that?"

"Just what I said, 'Hope your back gets better.' Isn't that what you told the draft board, that you had a bad back? Or was it an ingrown toenail?"

"Are you implying my draft status is fraudulent?"

"Make of it what you will," Mike said with a smile.

"Every Marine I've known has been a short-shit with attitude.

You're no different."

"Pardon me," said Mike, turning into the house from the doorway.

"You're a little prick hiding behind a tough guy image of a Marine," said Roger menacingly.

"Because you're a friend of Cathy's, I'll let your draft-dodging ass slide."

"Asshole," said Roger as he stepped forward and swung a roundhouse punch. Mike ducked and pinned Roger's arm against his side, then grabbed his throat. Mike rotated his hip, dropping Roger to the hardwood floor. The breath went out of Roger with a loud oomph.

Cathy's hands flew to her face and she screamed. Mike bent over Roger and whispered, "You are one very lucky draft-dodging puke. With a little pressure, I could crush your larynx. With a simple jab, I could blind you. If I move my arm a little, I could dislocate your shoulder causing you unimaginable pain. But you have a business appointment to keep with my friend and I want you to look pretty. I'm going to help you up, then walk out the door. If you say anything, I'm going to come back and break both your steroid-pumped arms as if they were toothpicks. Then, smash your nose like a pumpkin thrown to the pavement on Halloween night. No party, no more pretty face. If you understand me, and believe me, tap my hand."

Between gulps of air, Roger tapped Mike's hand. Mike helped Roger to his feet. Cathy rushed to Roger's side, helping him sit down. She glared at Mike.

"He'll be fine. A little water would help. I will give you a call soon. Enjoy your evening."

"Has the war made you crazy? You could have killed him. Get out. Get out . . . now! " said a stunned Cathy.

"People keep asking if I'm nuts," said Mike as he walked out the door. He unceremoniously walked down the walkway to his bike. After getting on his motorcycle, he checked his map. He had an appointment to keep in Murray City with the Wisniewski family.

CHAPTER 9

APPALACHIA

MIKE DROVE SOUTHEAST OUT of Columbus to Nelsonville. One of the town's intersecting rural roads would take him to Murray City. That rural hamlet was the gateway to southern coal country. The two-lanes wound through the rolling hills of Appalachia where coal and poverty were king and queen of misery, where electricity and indoor plumbing were considered luxuries, where home-cooked preserves and venison were supper staples and parasitic roundworm and black lung disease were as common as white lightning and barefoot toddlers.

Southeastern Ohio hill people prided themselves on honor and hard work. Families labored in the mines, on small farms, and in light industry that dotted the countryside. Fathers, sons, and grandsons worked and lived side by side. Woman tended the children, cleaned, and cooked. Each thanked God for their daily bread, but forgiving trespasses was a foreign concept. Lingering hatreds grew like the purple loosestrife plants. Those noxious weeds were impossible to eradicate in the hills. Small towns with names like Twin Sisters Knobs, Killbuck, Jerusalem, Round Bottom, and Wolf Creek sprayed, dug, and poisoned the land to stop the spread of the choking, purple flower, but with little success. The plant, like the families, had lived on for generations in the hills. Neither gave an inch. Failures had never deterred the hardscrabble people of Appalachia. They just toiled on relentlessly. As Mike rode, he cringed at the vast areas stripped of vegetation and laid bare, the result of open-pit strip mining by the big coal companies. It reminded Mike of the areas in the Vietnam mountains sprayed with the Agent Orange defoliant.

Sergeant Peter "Ski" Wisniewski was a product of this grim environment. He was raised in the coal-mining town of Indian Tent. Ski would say his hometown "ain't big enough to have no stoplight. That's why we all rode mules." He came from a large Polish family of miners. All six brothers dug coal, as did his father, grandfather, cousins and uncles. The coal companies were generational employers. Ski broke the mold, escaping the drudgery of digging by joining the Marines. He often told his machine gun crew, "It's far, far better to die in the light of the sunny day than under the ground in the dark coal dust of a mine."

Ski was an outstanding example of a Marine NCO, non-commissioned officer. He demanded excellence of himself and his Marines. He always led from the front and treated his Marines as men and brothers. Ski was imposing, at six-four and 200 pounds of muscle, further garnering the respect of his troops.

Mike still had a difficult time accepting the death of this beloved soldier. One of humanity's smallest killers assassinated him.

The 5th Marine's winter campaign was in the NVA Base Camp Area 112. The official USMC name for the op was Taylor Common. The mission was to clear the NVA base camp staging areas of troops and supplies that provided support for attacks on DaNang. What was supposed to be a thirty-day operation lasted over sixty-three days because of inclement weather. The winter monsoons had come early, providing the ideal environment for one of humankind's oldest killers—malaria. Over 18 percent of the casualties during the operation were from cerebral malaria, a deadly form of plasmodium falciparum malaria. The light-orange chloroquine-primaquine-phosphate anti-malaria pills were the only defense against the flying bloodsuckers that spread the infection. Mike ensured all his Marines took their large orange "shit pills," and corpsmen were ordered to watch each Marine to make sure he did. They checked the Marines' mouths and tongues afterward to ensure the pills were ingested. The troops hated the pills because it gave them the brown squirts, hence the name. Some of the Marines invented clever ways to hide their pill, spitting it out after the corpsman checked the next man. Besides the shit pill, there was bug spray to repel the buzzing dive bombers. Even with all the prevention, Marines still got the chills, fever, and crazies. On one occasion, Mike begged the battalion commander to authorize an emergency medevac. He had three Marines that were burning up with malaria. One of the stricken had seizures.

The mountains were covered in dreary gray fog. The saturated ground created a misty shroud that strangled landing zones. The moist air was as thick as a sodden wool blanket. Visibility was less than ten feet. For three days nothing flew. The troops had no food or meds. By the fourth day, there was no need for the emergency evacuation. By the fifth day, fistfights were common over food scraps in trash pits. Thankfully, the sixth day brought sunshine and helicopters. Supplies flew in; wounded, sick, and dead were flown out. Mike stood and saluted the last chopper when it lifted off with the dead malaria-stricken Marines. One of the three bodies was Sergeant Peter Wisniewski.

■▮▮▮▮

Mike was looking for Partridge Trap Road. On the first drive-by, he missed the one-lane dirt road. When he came to a state highway, Mike stopped, realizing he had missed the rural path. He again checked his road map and turned around. After some searching, he found the overturned county road sign in the weeds next to the dirt intersection. He had thought it was a power line access road.

Partridge Trap Road was filled with ruts and overgrown weeds. This made it difficult to distinguish road from the adjacent pasture. Mike followed impressions in the ground. He passed several struggling farms with unattended goats, yard chickens, and small naked children running about. The road followed a natural stream that meandered in a wide valley, abruptly ending in a narrowed "holler" filled with hardwood trees. On a small plateau above the road, Mike saw a wood-plank-sided tin-roof shack. The only access to the building seemed to be a footpath at the end of the dirt lane. Mike parked his bike in a clearing and turned off the V-twin. Soon he heard songbirds serenading their mates. Insects buzzed. Crickets rubbed their legs and jumped from leaf to leaf. Some ground animal scurried about in the underbrush. His Marines would have called this area the "deep dark boonies."

One morning in the deepest, darkest boonies of Nam, Pete Wisniewski explained to his captain where he lived. "I grew up in a holler at da beginning of Rabbit Run Creek. Ya just go to da end of Partridge Trap Road and look up da hill. Our castle sits on a rise, has da prettiest view in Morgan County. On a clear day ya can see all da way to Parkersburg, West 'by God' Virginia."

Mike started to climb the narrow footpath toward the castle. On either side of the trail was dense vegetation, briar bushes, grape vines, and goldenrod. Suddenly, a loud explosion shredded the oak leaves above his head. Mike dove to the ground and rolled off the dirt path. *Shotgun fire!* He felt vulnerable without his M14 rifle. Someone yelled from the path above him.

"What you want?"

"I'm looking for the Wisniewski family."

"Why dat?"

"I'm a friend of Peter Wisniewski."

"He dead."

"I know. I was with him when he died."

There was no response. Mike waited. The only sound was the forest breathing. Mike became restless. He did not want to stand, so he yelled.

"Hello, I'm—"

"Get up," said the person, now behind Mike.

He never heard a thing. He stood slowly and turned and saw a petite woman aiming her double-barreled shotgun at his head. She was dressed in a faded, plain blue cotton dress. Her stringy hair was tied with several twisted white pipe cleaners. She was barefoot.

"You know my boy?"

"Yes ma'am."

"Marine?"

"Yes ma'am."

"Pull yourself up. Dust off. Follow me," she said in a surprisingly strong voice.

The withered woman led Mike up the path to an age-ravished shack with a distressed wooden porch on the verge of collapse. A bluetick coonhound lay in front of the planked door.

"Good boy, Blue," said the woman as she walked into the shack. "Come on in and sit yo'self down. Gots coffee, want some?"

"Yes ma'am. Thank you."

She went to a homemade, rough-sawn, wormy chestnut cupboard and got a teacup. She put the elegant Royal Dalton English cup and saucer on the kitchen table. They emitted a pale-blue glow when the light bounced off the wafer-thin porcelain.

"T'was my great-papa's ma's best china. I saves them for special guests."

"Thank you."

The coffee pot was a very old aluminum percolator with a glass bulb on the top. She lifted it off the wood-burning stove, which looked like a relic from the 1800s. She carefully poured Mike a cup. Then she got a chipped mug and poured herself a cup. The Conservation Corps mug looked like an original 1930 chow-hall issue.

"Take a seat."

Mike pulled one of seven bent-wood chairs from the table and sat.

"I'z gots sweet milk and sugar. Want some?"

"No, thank you. Black is just fine."

The woman pulled up a willow tree stick built chair and sat down next to Mike. As she got comfortable, Mike did a quick survey of the house. It appeared to be a plain wood structure of three rooms—a large front room with a kitchen area, and two back rooms with a central hallway. Beside the cast iron wood stove was a vintage open coil crowned box refrigerator circa 1930s. Other furnishings included a homemade bent-wood rocker with a barrel-slat back, and an overstuffed, cracked brown leather chair. The centerpiece of the room was a large, well-worn crazy quilt–patterned couch with paver bricks for front legs. The dilapidated couch faced a large river-stone fireplace. A small wood fire was banked against the rear of the hearth. Over it hung a blackened cast iron pot. Something in the pot was steaming, adding a cooked vegetable aroma to the room.

"Ya knew my boy, did ya?" said the petite woman. Her loose dentures slurred the words.

"Yes ma'am. He was the machine gun squad leader for my platoon."

"He'z the oldest of my boys, probably the smartest," she said. She paused and took a sip of her coffee. Mike followed suit. To his surprise, the coffee was excellent. He looked into the cup and smiled.

"Good, ain't it? A little hazelnut in the coffee make it tasty, don't it?"

Mike nodded, looking up into the palest green eyes he'd ever seen.

"Why you here?"

"I wanted to tell you what a fine young man you raised. It was my honor to know him. He was an outstanding Marine. He is missed."

She looked Mike in the eyes. He felt as if she were looking into his soul to judge his merit. Slowly, she took several more sips of coffee, her eyes never leaving Mike's face.

Finding him worthy, she said, "I have eight chillin. My two baby girls died, one-year-old and three-year-old. All the boys grew up to be hard men. They all left home. Pete dead, Jerry in jail, Cliff, Gary, Ron, and Jon in the mine. Papa died last year. Black spit gots him. One or more of my boys visit me on weekends. They all check to see if'n I'z alive or dead. They all gots families. They's gots to a'ten them first. I don't mind, I'z gots Blue. He be with me all time. He a good old dog. On Sunday, I walk ta church. God talks to me."

Her eyes turned up and she whispered something only she could hear. Regaining eye contact with Mike she went on. "His home, in the little church on the mount, that be where He speaks. He tellz me Papa, Pete, little May and sister June waitin' for me. He askin' when I wants to see my family and his boy. I tells him I can't go. Blue need me. He understands. He say the table set for all'a us. God say he and his son can wait. He say he gots all the time in this world. I says amen. Want mo' coffee?"

■■ ■ ■ ■ ■

Carolyn Lee Wisniewski talked about her boys growing up in the deep woods of southern Ohio. Some of the stories were funny, some were sad, but all were about family. Her family was her world and she enjoyed it. The whole afternoon was filled with her light. She celebrated God, love, family, and life.

Mike departed in the late afternoon. He drove down the dirt lane wondering how a poor, uneducated, rural mother with three dead children, a son in jail, and a dead husband could be so content. To her, each new day brought joy and beauty. Each moment was cherished as if it were the last. The past was full of amazing tales, but it was the past. The future was in God's hands. *All you have to do is believe and live each day as if it's your last*, Mike thought. *Is life so simple? Or is the mystery of life just another struggle for the living trying to justify their lives?*

Mike's next stop was Kimbolton, Ohio. His destination was the dairy farm of PFC Ted Skull. His fire team called him Bones. The seventeen-year-old was tall, skinny, awkward, and fearless. Another wasted Marine. His killer had been friendly fire.

They were on a routine patrol in the rice paddies near Phu Lac 3, one of the many small vills that surrounded the numerous cultivated fields. Captain Ruhawk was behind the first platoon when a commotion started in the rear of the company formation. Mike halted the company's advance. He called for a radio check. The Second Platoon commander told him that one of his Marines had "Zippoed" a straw-covered hooch. The CO looked to the rear and could see the burning hut, a bright-yellow intensity causing white smoke to drift into the late-afternoon sky.

Mike had not authorized any incendiary teams. They were not on a search and destroy mission. When they encamped for the night, he would have a serious talk with his platoon leaders. Officers must understand there were consequences, that they were responsible for everything their platoon did and didn't do.

The company resumed the patrol. Suddenly, jet afterburners roared. Two Navy F6 Intruders passed directly overhead. The planes were so low Mike could read their tail numbers. He watched in horror as they dropped their load of "napes and snakes" on his Marines. They were 500-pound high-explosive bombs called "daisy cutters" by the pilots and "snakes" by the troops. The ordnance drifted down in slow motion from one of the jets. The other jet jettisoned two aluminum canisters of napalm, aka "nap." Suddenly, the ground erupted, and flames seared Mike's hair. He was dumbfounded, watching in open-mouth fascination as the jets circled around for a second pass. His company gunny sergeant was screaming to put out the air panels, large canvas florescent-orange rectangles that marked friendly positions. There was no time. Like a flying prehistoric predator, the F6s dove out of the clouded sky for the kill. They aligned to drop their next payload. Suddenly, as if pulled by a string, they climbed into the high white cumulus clouds and disappeared from sight.

The Marine Corps's official after-action report found the jet pilots mistook the white smoke from the burning hooch for a "Willy Pete," white phosphorous-marking rockets fired by the A6s supporting the spotter aircraft, an OV-10 Bronco. The A6 pilots were twenty-two clicks, approximately fourteen miles, from the intended target. They saw the billowing smoke and standing Marines and presumed they were NVA. They attacked.

Mike never knew if any judicial action was taken against the pilots. One of his platoons suffered nineteen causalities—eleven with third-degree burns, five with shrapnel wounds, and three KIAs. The other platoons had several WIA but no KIAs. One of the KIAs was PFC Ted Skull. It was Mike's first Marine KIA as a new company commander.

The majority of the company was spared. A large stand of tall, hard green bamboo trees had separated the front of the company column from the rear platoon. The Marines that were with Mike had passed thought the thicket and remained unhurt. Those in the rear were sliced, diced, and charred. What saved the remaining company from a second pass was a frantic radio call from the battalion's FAC, the forward air controller. He had seen the whole friendly fire catastrophe from the battalion's hilltop outpost and called the division's air traffic controller to send an emergency abort order on all attack aircraft in the TO, or territory of operation. Sixty-nine air attacks in the area were immediately stopped.

Mike rode to Cambridge on backcountry roads. He enjoyed the drive through wooded hillsides and deep-green pastures. He passed numerous quaint crossroads towns before nearing Cambridge. The county seat was the only major city before Kimbolton.

It was getting dark and Mike was hungry. He remembered a special restaurant on the west side of Cambridge. He often stopped there when he was working his college summer job. One summer, he helped restore the interior of the Guernsey County Courthouse in Cambridge. Mike worked for a master finish carpenter who contracted with a Columbus architectural firm. The work was challenging. The lessons learned lasted a lifetime. One lesson was "Never try anything difficult on an empty stomach." He needed a good meal and a place to sleep. The restaurant and motel were across the street from one another on Cambridge's main drag.

After his meal, Mike checked in at the Cambridge Travel Lodge, showered, and crashed in a large, king-size bed. He was sound asleep by 1930 hours. He dreamed of dragons spewing fire, babies crying, dogs snapping at naked woman, and endless bright, shiny aluminum coffins stacked one on top of the other. They looked like silver cigarettes stacked on a spent 155mm artillery shell casing. He was startled awake by a ringing phone.

"Good morning, it's six o'clock. The weather forecast calls for sunny skies and temperature in the eighties. Make it an extraordinary Ohio day." Then a click and the recorded wakeup call started again. Mike hung up.

Mike did his morning exercise routine, the Marine daily dozen and his two-mile run. He remembered running this same route six years earlier. He felt great, no cramps. Returning to his room he showered, shaved, dressed, and packed. Down the block was a local country kitchen that served farmer's daybreak specials. Mike ate heartily and then headed toward Kimbolton.

PFC Marshal Skull's family farm was on a gravel road. The Skulls' dairy farm was the best-looking agriculture enterprise Mike had ever seen. The house was a white, square, two-story mortar-and-quarry-stone structure that sat on a small knoll. Behind the house was a large, pristine white dairy barn. To the side was a corrugated-steel-roofed open-sided pole building that housed various kinds of new farm equipment. The farm layout was Marine Corps neat, a place for everything and everything in its place. All the pastures were cultivated and green. Precise rows of knee-high corn filled the back forty.

Mike pulled onto the concrete driveway and parked under the house portico. He walked the concrete walkway to the front door. After several rings and no response, Mike walked to the white barn. He heard machinery sounds coming from inside. A small Bobcat skid loader was pushing cow manure out the back of the barn. A woman on a Ford tractor with a front loader was picking up the manure and depositing it into a spreader in the paddock. The skeletal woman saw Mike and pointed to the man operating the skid loader. The man shut off the Bobcat and approached Mike.

"Something I can do for ya, mister," said the bear of a man. He was dressed in well-worn, faded denim overalls, no shirt, brown knee-high rubber boots, and a red International Tractor baseball cap. He was fit in a tradesman's way, with a large chest, muscular arms, and ham-sized hands that looked like they could crush walnuts.

"Yes sir. I'm looking for Ted Skull's family."

"I'm his pa. How can I help you?"

"I was Ted's CO in Vietnam. I wanted to pay my respects to his family. He was a good Marine."

Mike's words were met with silence. Mr. Skull waved his wife over from the front-end loader to where Mike was standing.

"Ma, this man was Ted's Marine commander in the 'Vee-at-Namm.'"

"Well, ain't that just dandy? You here to tell us more bullshit?" said Mrs. Skull.

Mike was surprised by her tone. "No ma'am, I'm here to tell you what a good Marine he was."

"Let me tell you something, sonny," said the father. The anger in his voice dripped like acid. "He was drafted. He didn't want to go. We had only one child. He worked the farm, shouldn't hav'ta go, but they took him. Didn't matter none to them if he was entitled to one of them de-firm-mitts. They took him. They forced him into the Marines. No choice, mind you, just told him. He was goin' to be a Marine. Them city sons of bitches kilt him as sure as if they pulled the trigger."

Mrs. Skull said, "They wouldn't let me kiss him goodbye cuz he burnt up so bad. On top'a all that, damn Marines gave us that little brown bugle boy blowing taps in our cemetery. Our cemetery! He don't belong there. That cemetery for our folks. I told 'em skedaddle before I gets my shotgun. We don't want no wetback on our sacred ground. Y'all keep your stinking blood flag. I say, we just wants our boy back. Now you come ta tell us what a good boy our Ted was—we know that. We know what a good boy he is . . . always was . . ."

Tears streamed down Mrs. Skull's pale face as she spoke.

"God damn, I miss that boy," she said. Then, she abruptly turned, staggering toward her tractor with her head down, moving slowly as if she were carrying a world of lost souls.

"You best leave now," said Mr. Skull. "We don't like your kind, nohow. You bring nut-tang but misery and suffering. We about all cried out. We as sad as sad can be. You gets, now. Don't never come back neither."

Mike stepped back, rendered a sharp-salute and forcefully said "Semper Fi." Then, he turned and walked away. He did not have the heart to tell them that their son had volunteered for the Corps. Bones told his battalion commander during the initial welcome interview at headquarters that he volunteered for the Marines. He loved being a Marine. That was what he always wanted to be. He wanted to get off the farm and be his own man, not the next generation of Ohio dairy farmer.

Mike moved his bike around and drove out of Kimbolton feeling like the stuff the Skulls were going to spread on the pasture. He was surprised at their racial bigotry. All his Marines were one color—*green*. Once these men got their Eagle, Globe, and Anchor emblem, they were Marines, all of them.

The conflict between truth and perception was grinding on his soul. Mike could do nothing to mitigate their pain. He felt like an emotional sponge. All the suffering these families felt was being absorbed into his psyche. He began to question the wisdom of a war that left such a trail of bitter tears. How many families were going through like agony? *Forty, fifty, sixty thousand?* When would this futile war end? How many more needed to be maimed or killed before some could come home?

He knew he could never make these types of visits again. The burden was too great. Their pain was a gigantic cable around Mike's mind. He could almost hear the ratcheting sound as one cog after another tightened the cable. He felt the wire getting tighter and tighter. The pressure gauge on his brain was in the red. His body's klaxon blared, *Danger, danger, danger . . .* He desperately needed a place to hide. Somewhere he could feel safe.

Mike was on his bike driving by mental autopilot, not conscious of traveling south on I-77 heading toward Marietta's cantilevered bridge over the Ohio River. Without thought, Mike pulled onto Pike Street before the bridge and into the Riverfront Park. He parked the Harley and slowly walked to the river's edge. His head throbbed. His pulse raced. Sweat ran in rivulets down his back. Carefully, he sat down on the concrete-reinforced bank of the Ohio River. He put his head in his hands and tried to catch his breath. His Marine ego had given him a false sense of purpose. Did he really think he could bring any comfort to these grieving families? He wasn't prepared for the vast array of emotions. The Skulls' rejection of his mission shattered his equilibrium. He felt lost, alone, and confused, wandering without a purpose. Space and time had no meaning. Reality became an illusion. His mind drifted to another place.

Mike focused on the fast-moving dirty brown water of the Ohio River. The images he saw were of another river. The Song Thu Bon River flowed between the Arizona free fire zone and An Hoa Combat Base. One terrain feature of this Vietnamese river was an island shaped like an oval with pointed ends. The Marines called it "Football Island." This small scrap of land could be observed from the hill at Liberty Bridge. The OP, or outpost, at the bridge was part of highway security, which provided overwatch for trucks supplying An Hoa from DaNang. A battery of 105 mm howitzers were positioned within the barbwire of the OP. They protected the bridge and provided support for units patrolling the area outside the wire and road.

Mike's company rotated in from the bush for two weeks of bridge security. One of Mike's extra duties during this rotation was cantonment officer. He was responsible for the security of the bridgehead and hilltop combat base. One early morning, Mike was called to the observation tower. The tower was a tall wooden derrick topped with a covered plywood platform. The tower was built on the highest elevation of the hill. From the platform, the lookout had a two-mile, 360-degree view of the surrounding paddies. Mike climbed the long ladder to the top of the derrick. A crusty corporal on security duty handed Mike a pair of binoculars.

"Skipper, take a look at Football Island. The clearing north-northeast," said the corporal.

Football Island's predominate feature was uncultivated rice paddies covered in long grass. Some areas hinted of a once-prosperous village that had been ravished by years of war. In the middle of a relatively clear spot was a large bundle. Mike focused the binoculars and saw what looked like an animal tied to a bamboo pole. Mike adjusted the focus to get a sharper image. The object appeared human. He needed a better look. Mike asked for the handset of the security detail's PRC25 radio. He called for one of the battalion snipers to come to the tower with his sniper's rifle.

About five minutes later, the expert shooter arrived; a short, lean Marine with an attitude of superiority. Mike explained what he wanted, and the sniper got into position. The Marine sniper leveled his rifle on the sandbag and focused the sniper scope on the target.

"Jesus H. Christ! Motherfucking gooks," said the sniper in disgust.

"What do you see, Corporal?" asked Mike.

"You're not going to believe me, Captain. You best look."

Mike focused the bezel of the rifle's scope. A clear image appeared of a white man. He was nude, strung up like a trophy tiger with a bamboo carrying pole between his arms and legs. His hands and feet were tied with blue gook communication wire. He had barbwire wrapped tightly around his torso. His face was unrecognizable because of the two empty eye sockets, his mouth an ugly slash across his face. Crawling in and out of the empty orbs and toothless mouth were hundreds of large black flies. Mike pulled back from the scope and wiped his face with the back of his shaking hand. He took a deep breath and looked again. That's when he saw the Marine emblem tattooed on the man's upper arm. The blood drained from Mike's face. He was repulsed but fascinated by the sight. The cruelty and barbarism were something out of the Inquisition. Mike tried to imagine the suffering. It was beyond his comprehension to think that one man could do that to another.

For the battalion, the rest of that day was devoted to the recovery of the body on Football Island. The VC knew the Marines never left anyone behind. The body was a ruse to engage the Marines in an elaborate NVA regimental ambush. The firefight lasted into the night. Helicopter gunships, artillery, and Spookie—C47 airplanes equipped with multiple rapid-fire 7.62 mini-Gatling guns—

supported two companies of Marines in the struggle. The battle was fierce but inconclusive. No enemy bodies found; the barbwired body never recovered.

A shrill whistle blew, startling Mike. A large turn-of-the-century stern-wheel riverboat passed the park. Mike felt groggy and looked across the river into a tree. He saw blinking lights and thought they were flashes of rifle fire. He waited for the zing of passing bullets. He heard none but still ran to the nearest tree and lay flat in the manicured grass. The town hall clock chimed the hour. Mike blinked. He refocused and saw the brick wall and marquee: *Steamboat Park, Marietta Ohio*. Suddenly, he realized he made it. He was home, back in the world. Thank God!

It took a while for Mike to shake off the nightmarish flashback. Slowly, he walked to his bike. He was clumsy and confused, and had difficulty focusing. After several tries, he got the motor running. Very carefully, he pulled out of the park. He headed south. He was unsure why he was driving south, but he knew it was the right way.

Slowly, he realized the only thing he had was his mission. He had to finish his mission. His mission was south. His next casualty stop was in West Virginia. The family of Corporal Ezekiel "Bud" Yoder was in the mountain-high state. Bud was one of Captain Ruhawk's translator-interpreters in Nam.

Jerryville was an old mining town along the Gauley River in West Virginia, located on the rim of the Monongahela National Forest in the rugged Allegheny Mountains. By the early 1950s, the state considered the town abandoned. The locals labeled it a ghost town. The mines had played out. The population had dwindled to a few stubborn backwoods families. Those who remained worked for industries like timber companies or regional railroads. Noah Yoder was an engineer for the Cherry River Railroad owned by E.T. Lumber. He was the only known surviving relative of Bud. Noah was Corporal Ezekiel "Bud" Yoder's father.

Bud was just five feet five inches, but large of heart. His Marine-issue eyeglasses gave him the appearance of a bookworm. He had a quick intellect and could pick up a language as easily as picking up coins in a fountain. He spoke Vietnamese as if he were born in the country. On numerous occasions, his interaction with the locals saved the company from walking into areas that were heavily booby-trapped. Unfortunately, his cautiousness failed him the afternoon he stepped on a homemade explosive device.

Mike recalled Bud requesting a company patrol rest in a village while he interviewed some of the Vietnamese elders. The only people in the vill were old *papa sans*, haggard aged *mama sans*, and a few pregnant young women. Bud reasoned the women had to have contact with some young studs. Maybe the gooks had some worthwhile intel. During the patrol break, Bud and two security Marines trotted over a small rise down a trail to the vill. They all disappeared in a horrendous explosion. Fire, smoke, and dirt blew into the sky. A world of debris rained down.

Mike would never get over picking up a severed leg identified as Bud's because a dog tag was laced into the boot. All flesh and bones were riddled with shrapnel. As if the vision were not macabre enough, the smell stamped Mike's olfactory senses. The odor was strangely different from other battlefield smells. Maybe big game hunters would recognize the pungent smell as that of fresh kill. Maybe it was Mike's own smell of fear. Whatever, the stench was imprinted in his memory. There was something strange about Bud that day. An odor, a look, a feeling, Mike could never put his finger on the sensation. He shrugged it off as an acute field awareness, heightened anxiety, or primal survival instinct. Years later, he thought it was the feeling of the angel of death's breath on his face.

There was no easy way to Jerryville. Mike crossed the Ohio River at Marietta. He rode along I-77 to Parkersburg, then turned east. At the Clarksburg/Bridgeport intersection, he headed south. The rolling hills had changed into sizeable mountains. A twisting, two-lane road followed the Gauley River Gorge to Jerryville. The deep shadows in the valleys made Mike turn on his two bike lights as he motored onward to Webster Springs. He needed another good night's sleep before his last visit. He passed several highway signs advertising scenic views at the Webster Hotel. The idea of relaxing in a comfortable lawn chair, gazing at the mountains, was appealing.

The signs ended next to a highway historical marker indicating the famous Webster Hotel burned to the ground in 1925. Next to the plaque was a sign indicating there was a new Webster Inn several miles further down the road, advertised as the best bed-and-breakfast in the state.

The six-column, neoclassical, antebellum two-story brick mansion was impressive. The second floor had a handrailed veranda that encompassed the front and sides. A promenade-type entrance jutted out from the mansion, supported by two massive fluted columns. Hunter-green, screened, arched double doors added drama to the brick façade. Mike parked his bike and walked into the foyer. A small bell attached to the door rang. As he waited for the receptionist, he surveyed the interior. The wainscot was varnished mahogany. The floor was elaborate, dark-wood, basket-weave pattern with a light maple border. The woodworking artisanship was superb. The hallway was furnished in a heavy Victorian style, a little much for Mike's taste, but architecturally gorgeous.

"May I help you?" said a well-dressed, middle-aged woman. She wore a long gray skirt, wide black belt with large gold oval buckle, and white long-sleeve ruffle-neck blouse. Her hair was shoulder length, silver gray. In her youth, she was probably a heartbreaker.

"Yes ma'am. I would like a room with a view for the night," said Mike with a big smile.

"Oh my," said the woman when she examined Mike. She appeared startled by the road-weary biker in leathers but quickly regained her composure. "Of course, we have bedrooms and suites. All have fantastic views."

"Bedroom would be fine. Thank you."

The woman introduced herself as Mrs. Harriet Addison. She was the co-owner and proprietor of Webster Inn. Miss Harriet and her daughter, Jill, were the cooks, bottle washers, and maids. Also employed was Bugster and Scoot. Bugster was the seven-year-old granddaughter. Scoot was Bugster's border collie. Miss Harriet informed Mike that if children or dogs presented a problem, she understood and could recommend two other establishments for the night.

"No problem. I like both," said Mike.

"Very well; for your convenience, we have an informal bar in the old butler's quarters. It's self-serve until six. At that time, we serve mixed drinks and wine. The inn also has an excellent selection of beers, both domestic and foreign. Tonight, we are featuring White Tail Ale brewed locally. We hope you will join us."

"Sounds great."

"I'll make a note for the barmaid. Would you please fill out the registration card?"

"I noticed the ads along the road proclaiming the best view of the Gauley River in all West Virginia."

"We do have a wonderful vista. That information is in the tri-fold brochure with the history of the Webster Mansion." She handed him a lined card and brochure. He filled out the register form and took out his wallet to pay. Miss Harriet said, "You can settle your bill in the morning when you check out. Let me show you to your room."

"Fantastic. My bike is in the driveway. Is there an out-of-the-way place I could park?"

"Yes indeed. Please pull your vehicle around the house. There is a large gated area between the stable and inn. You will see the sign for the designated parking."

"Thank you. I'll be right back."

Mike left the inn and drove his bike around the mansion.

In the rear was a large brick courtyard surrounded by an ornate iron fence connecting the house to the stable. Both structures had a redbrick façade. The stable was divided into two separate twin-image buildings with an open, arched passageway in the center. Mike parked his Harley near the mansion's back door. When he shut off the engine, he heard a loud voice command, "Hold on tight . . . that's my girl."

Mike looked through the stable passageway and caught a glimpse of a small child riding a golden palomino. He walked through the archway to a round ring where a tall, fit woman dressed in tan boots, faded jeans, a blue sleeveless blouse, and a blue baseball cap was leading the palomino around the ring. She had her Farrah Fawcett hair pulled through the adjusting strap in the baseball cap. Her hair hung down to mid-back like the horse's tail. She controlled the stallion with a long lead line in one hand and a training whip in the other. She moved like a dancer. With a flick of the whip, the horse stopped and changed direction.

"Hold on," she commanded. "Trot," she ordered and flicked the whip near the rump of the golden horse.

The horse broke into a trot, to the delight of the saddled child. Mike watched in fascination. The woman and child were oblivious to his presence.

"Whoa," said the woman. She softly said, "Walk." The horse slowed and began to walk.

"Mommy, look, it's—" said the child as she pointed to Mike.

The woman turned. Her eyes opened wide in amazement.

The moment was awkward. "Excuse me for interrupting. I was enjoying the training session."

"You could have said something," the woman snapped. Her beautiful face slowly hardened. There was a quality of sadness and anger in her eyes.

"I apologize. I was afraid I'd startle the horse." Mike nodded and walked to the back door of the inn. He wondered what the story was with the woman horse trainer.

He entered the inn's kitchen and was immediately confronted by a small collie. The dog barked several times, and then jumped into Mike's arms. Mike dropped his gear and held the squirming animal.

"Well, this is a special kind of welcome." The dog licked Mike's face.

"Scoot, down," commanded Miss Harriet. "She's never done that before. Usually she just runs around barking."

"I must be the exception." Mike placed the little dog on the floor. Scoot ran around his feet barking. Mike knelt and petted the bundle of fur. The dog lay down, rolled over, and enjoyed the attention.

"Oh my, she really likes you."

Mike looked up and smiled. "I seem to have a way with dogs."

The back door crashed open and the small golden-haired child ran in. She came to a sudden halt in front of Mike.

"What's your name?" she demanded in a loud voice.

"Mike."

She looked at him quizzically, then turned to her grandmother and sighed deeply.

"Gram, if he said Ed, I was going to freak out. Mom is out in the paddock going bonkers."

"Oh my. Oh my. Bug, would you please sit with Mister Mike while I check on Mommy."

"Sure thing. You like my dog, Mister Mike?"

"Thank you for entertaining my granddaughter," said Miss Harriet.

"She's a joy," replied Mike.

"Bugster, please take Scoot outside."

"We're still playing," whined Bugster.

"I know, sweetheart, but Mister Mike is our guest. I have to show him his room. You know the rules."

"Will you play with us later?" asked the enchanting child.

"For sure. Once I get settled, I'll come out and we'll play."

"See you soonest. Come on, Scoot." They ran out the door, which slammed shut.

"Please pardon Bugster. She can be very precocious at times."

"No problem. You have a wonderful grandchild."

Miss Harriet showed Mike the inn that was once her family's home. The kitchen featured a large family dining table that could seat twelve, a butler's pantry with oversized cupboards, a formal dining room decorated in the blue-and-white federal style, a living room converted to an informal conversation area with fireplace and television. The mansion's library was now repurposed as the check-in area. The whole first floor was very comfortable and well decorated. The most prominent architectural feature was the curved stairway to the second floor.

From the outside, the inn looked like a two-story structure. Miss Harriet informed Mike that when the mansion was renovated, the open dance hall under the dome of the third floor was razed and two honeymoon suites were added. The second floor had eight rooms. All ten guest rooms had their own adjoining bathrooms. It took almost a year and a half to upgrade and remodel. It was difficult to keep the charm of the 1920s mansion with the back stairs, butler's quarters, and elevator, and incorporate modern 1960s conveniences.

Miss Harriet opened what Mike thought was a coat closet next to the double front doors, revealing a small, four-person elevator. They stepped inside and closed the door. Miss Harriet pressed the button for the next floor. The ride was slow.

The second floor had four rooms facing the front of the house and four rooms facing the back overlooking the stables and grounds. Miss Harriet showed Mike to room 5 in the back corner, with a panoramic view of the river.

"The third-floor honeymoon suites have a gorgeous view of the Elk River Gorge. They are well worth the extra monies."

"That's something I will keep in mind for my next visit."

"I'm assuming you're not married."

"Assumptions can get people in trouble. However, you are correct. I haven't found the right woman. Better yet, the right woman hasn't found me."

"West Virginian women can be quite compelling."

"I don't think I have enough time this trip to enjoy the sights. I hope to conclude my business tomorrow. If I can't, I would like to stay another day."

"We have a full house Friday, Saturday, and Sunday. If you need to stay another day I will help you find suitable lodging."

"That would be great. Thank you."

Miss Harriet opened Mike's room door and handed him the key.

"I hope you enjoy your stay. Remember, happy hour starts at six in the old butler's quarters off the kitchen. You are our only guest tonight. Please join us for a drink."

"My pleasure. I'll be there. Before you go, maybe you can help me. Can I make a long-distance phone call from the phone in my room?"

"The phone in your room is only for local calls. If you need to make any long-distance calls, they will have to be collect calls from the phone in the check-in area. There is a pay phone in the gas station down the block, if you prefer."

Mike put his saddlebags and sleeping bag on the large brass bed and went into the modern bathroom to turn on the shower.

The shower felt wonderful. The water was hot, the pressure high, and the travel stress in Mike's shoulders melted away. He felt refreshed. After drying off, he lay nude on the bed for a short nap. It was a little over two hours before happy hour.

He thought of his encounter with the woman horse trainer. She looked toned and athletic. Her face was Scandinavian with a thin nose and dimpled jaw. Her eyes were a cornflower blue that turned indigo with anger when she spoke to him. She was approximately six feet, with long, shapely legs and firm breasts. Thinking of her, his testosterone spiked.

After a short nap, Mike shaved and dressed in clean jeans and a blue, short-sleeve collared shirt. He walked downstairs into the butler's quarters in his go-to-meetin' clothes. The area was converted into a very comfortable smoking room with over-stuffed plaid-patterned chairs and dark-green, almost black leather couches. The room's bath was converted into a wet bar with a stainless steel bar sink and silver shelves for bar glasses. The bedroom's two outside walls were remodeled, and huge, multi-paned windows featured a panoramic view of the river gorge. Mike chose a large, two-person black leather chair with a commanding view of the cascading water. He was daydreaming of R & R in Australia when the barmaid approached.

"Good evening. Would you like to see our wine and beer list?"

"No, thank you. Miss Harriet mentioned a local brew called White Tail Ale. A bottle would be great."

Mike watched the barmaid/horse trainer walk away. She had on strapless, black high heels, a short black pleated skirt and a tailored sleeveless white blouse. Her perfect makeup highlighted her wonderful blue eyes. A large red bow held back her long sun-bleached blond hair, adding a touch of elegance. *She could grace any New York fashion runway,* thought Mike.

The barmaid got a chilled bottle from a cooler behind the bar. She placed it on a circular silver tray with a cold frosted glass and cork coaster. Carefully, she placed it on an arts-and-crafts side table next to Mike.

"Would you like me to pour your beer?"

"Yes, please."

The barmaid paused and said, "I would like to apologize for my rude behavior earlier today. You startled me. I reacted poorly."

Mike looked at her for a moment and replied, "I'll accept your apology on one condition."

She rolled her eyes, handed him the glass of beer, and said, "And what might that be?"

"I would like you to have a drink with me and dinner later."

"Drink I can do, but dinner is out of the question. I eat with my family."

From the inn's kitchen Miss Harriet shouted, "We can all have dinner together in the inn's kitchen. Mike is our only guest tonight. I've made more than enough chicken potpies. They're in the oven. Have your drinks. Dinner will be ready when you are."

The horse trainer was Miss Harriet's daughter, Mike finally discerned. For a moment, they just looked at each other, then chuckled.

Jill bent over and whispered into Mike's ear, "Nothing gets by good-old mom."

"I heard that, missy."

They laughed. Unexpectedly, Scoot ran in and jumped on Mike's lap. The beer went flying. Amber liquid covered Mike's trousers and shirt. Jill's skirt and blouse were drenched. Right behind Scoot was Bugster with a leash. She stopped in the doorway and looked at the beer-covered threesome.

"Oh my," said Bugster. Just like her grandmother.

Jill and Mike laughed harder. Scoot licked the spilled ale. Bugster giggled.

Miss Harriet came to the butler's doorway. "What in the world is going on?"

Mike returned after taking a quick shower and changing clothes. He was now dressed in faded jeans, a gray USMC gym shirt, and running shoes without socks. Jill wore khaki hiking shorts, a white cotton-knit pullover, and white strapless sandals. Mike noted she had washed her makeup off, leaving her perfect pink skin. What most impressed Mike was her braless figure. She was simply awe-inspiring, beautiful beyond words, alluring as any woman he had ever seen. Mike tried not to gawk. He was lust-struck. She handed one of two beers to Mike and placed the other on the kitchen table next to him. His eyes followed her. Mike was literally devouring her with his stare. She sat down across the table and avoided his look.

Miss Harriet said a simple grace, then announced, "Let's eat."

Dinner conversation varied. Jill and her mother told stories about some of their more infamous guests; the twins that stayed in the honeymoon suite, a couple with their female friend, and a midget with the Great Dane. The kitchen filled with memories and laughter. Miss Harriet inquired into Mike's visit. He gave them a synopsis of his mission. Simply stated he was in West Virginia to find the family of Corporal Bud Yoder. His address in his service record was 39 Holy Books Road, Jerryville.

"Mike, there is no Holy Books Road in Jerryville," said Miss Harriet.

"You're sure?"

"I grew up in Jerryville and know ever holler in Webster County."

"You said his name was Yoder?" asked Jill.

"Ezekiel Yoder. We called him Bud. His father is listed as the only living relative."

"Is his father's first name Noah?" asked Miss Harriet.

"I think it was Noah. Yes, Noah R. Yoder," said Mike.

Jill and her mother looked at each other and said, "The snake preacher."

"Snake preacher?" Mike questioned.

Miss Harriet said, "He is the preacher of a church called the Holiness Witness of Jesus on the Water. They believe the Holy Spirit protects them when they handle venomous snakes during their church services. Their ceremonies can last hours. During the witness part, they speak in tongues; sometimes dance in a trance, and always with serpents: cottonmouths, timber rattlers, and copperheads. If a parishioner is bitten, no one goes for help. They believe whatever happens is God's will. Several people from the church have died."

"Bud often told stories of handling snakes as a kid. Other Marines thought these were tall tales from the backwoods," said Mike.

"If he is the son of Noah, he probably played with snakes when he was a baby," said Jill.

"Is there any way I can meet Bud's father?"

"He works for the local railroad. I have no idea how to get ahold of him," said Miss Harriet.

"I think the best time to catch Noah would be at his Sunday church service," added Jill.

"Sounds like a plan. If you can give me directions to the church, I'll see him Sunday," said Mike.

Impulsively, Jill said, "I'll take you there."

"Perfect. With Miss Harriet's help, I'll find lodging for Friday and Saturday. We can meet here Sunday morning."

"I have a better idea," said Miss Harriet. "We live in a four-bedroom apartment over the stable. We have one—"

Jill quickly interrupted, "Mother, we really don't know Mister Mike very well. We—"

"Hush now. Bugster and Scoot like him. I like him. As I was saying, we have a fourth bedroom that's vacant. I would be happy to let you stay, if you are willing do some handyman work."

"That is very considerate. But I feel like an intruder in your family. I'm sure I can find a room somewhere else."

"Rubbish. You're staying with us and that's that," said Bugster in a very matronly voice. All three adults looked at her in amazement, then burst out laughing.

"It's settled. Majority rules; you're staying," said Miss Harriet.

"Well, hell's bells. I'll make it unanimous. Move in tonight if you like," said Jill with a smile of delight.

"Thank you," Mike said with humility.

They finished dinner talking about Bugster going to school in the fall. She was going into third grade. Mike said he thought she was going into sixth grade. Bugster called him silly.

"I'm as smart as any sixth grader, but school policy would not allow me to skip that many grades, you understand," said the Bug.

"Oh, I understand. I think you're a thirty-four-year-old midget who is trying to fool everyone," said Mike.

"Now, how could I be older than Mommy? You are very silly."

The adults looked at Bugster in astonishment.

Everyone pitched in and loaded the dinner dishes into a dumbwaiter next to the pantry. Jill explained they had a restaurant dishwasher in the basement. All the dishes, glasses, silverware, and platters used by the guests went to the basement for cleaning.

"After clearing, the dumbwaiter returns everything to the upstairs kitchen and we put it away in the cupboards. That way, the inn's kitchen is never cluttered or dirty." The basement also housed a restaurant kitchen and bakery. All meals and baked goods were prepared in the basement and delivered to the dining room. Webster Inn was renowned for its fresh-baked cinnamon rolls with gooey sugar frosting.

Another feature of the basement was two large commercial clothes-washing machines and dryers. "All the linens and towels are cleaned here." A clothes chute and second dumbwaiter made the guest-floor rooms easy to clean and make ready. Mike was impressed with the forethought, attention to detail, and organization. He hadn't realized the effort required to run a bed-and-breakfast.

After cleaning up, everyone went to the butler's quarters. Mike and Jill had fresh mugs of coffee. Miss Harriet excused herself. She was tired. It was Bugster's bedtime. The Bug protested loudly.

Mike and Jill sat on an overstuffed down couch and sipped their coffee. At first, the atmosphere was awkward. Mike broke the ice by inquiring about the palomino.

"The stallion's name is 'Last Chance.' Chance, for short. He was a gift from a girlfriend that could not control him. Sometimes he's high strung and can be temperamental, full of unbridled energy," said Jill.

"He looked downright gentle with Bugster on his back," said Mike.

"Looks are deceiving. He would never do anything to harm Bug or me. Anyone else is questionable."

"I saw a sign on the stable indicating you rent trail horses by the hour."

"Some of our guests like to ride. We accommodate. You know, another source of revenue for the inn."

"I haven't been on a horse since college. If someone would go riding with me, say tomorrow, I would be happy to pay for the ride. I think it would be fun."

"Is that kind of a backwards way of asking me out for a date?"

"Um . . . yeah . . . Would you like to go riding with me tomorrow?"

"Hum . . . Yes, I would."

"Out-f'ing-standing," said Mike.

"Out-f'ing-standing?"

"It's a Marine thing for 'that's great.' Now that we have a date, may I ask you a question?"

"Ask away."

"I see no ring on your finger. Bugster is your daughter. You're—"

"I'm a widow. My husband, Ed, was electrocuted during a severe thunderstorm almost two years ago. He was working with a line crew to restore power. Ed stepped on a downed power cable hidden by some tree limbs."

Mike lowered his head and said softly, "My condolences."

Jill continued as if she had not heard Mike. "You look just like him—a little thinner, a little taller, maybe a lost twin. When I saw you standing next to the fence, I . . . well—" Jill took a few breaths and hurriedly continued. "I lost my composure, then you walked away. For a brief time, I wasn't sure you were real. Moments later, Mom came out and said you were a guest. I was shaken and relieved."

Mike sipped his coffee and stared at the waterfall. He was trying to imagine the shock. It would be like seeing his mother again at some supermarket. She passed away five, no, six years ago. The mixed vibes he got from Jill started to make sense.

"Sudden loss can be overwhelming," said Mike. "My recent travels have been emotionally enlightening. The people I've met have endured anguish beyond my comprehension. I cannot possibly understand your grief. My only hope is you can see there is a tomorrow. The feeling of loss never goes away. I'm sure there is a hole in your heart. Hopefully, other people will help make the rest of your heart stronger with understanding and love."

"I thank the Lord every day for Bugster and Mom. They are my life, my love. They keep me going." There was a long pause of silence, the unspoken pain almost palpable. Mike finally broke the stillness with a question.

"I have another question."

"That should be easy after the last one."

"What is Bugster's Christian name?"

"Elizabeth Addison Bird Burns. She hates Liz, despises Beth, won't answer to Addison. Burns is Gram's name. If you call her Bird, you better run for cover."

"Bugster it is."

"Any more questions, or is the inquisition over?"

"One more?" Mike asked with mock trepidation

"Dear Lord. You are inquisitive." Jill smiled.

"Been called worse but the next question is easy. Would you like more coffee?"

She broke into a wide grin. "Yes, thank you."

After some small talk they said goodnight. They parted with a kiss on the cheek. Mike went to his room with visions of Jill as Lady Godiva. After getting into the big brass bed, he pulled the sheets to his chest, wishing Jill were beside him.

The smell of fresh coffee and sweet cinnamon rolls filled Mike's nose. He rushed through his morning shower, stripped the bed, throwing sheets and towels into the pillowcase. After depositing the linens in the clothes chute in the hallway, he descended the back stairs two at a time. His cowboy boots banged loudly on the wooden stairs used by servants in a forgotten time. He was ready for breakfast and anxious to see Jill. The kitchen table had plates full of mixed, fresh-cut fruit, golden grilled pancakes, fluffy scrambled eggs, crisp strips of bacon, and hot homemade wheat bread. The food smelled delicious. In the dining room were carafes of coffee and tea. Centered on the dining room table was a large plate of freshly baked, frosted cinnamon rolls. They looked gooey and sweet. The bakery smell overwhelmed his senses.

"Good morning," said Jill as she operated an automatic orange squeezer in the kitchen. "Did you sleep well?"

"I did, with cinnamon rolls dancing in my head served by a scantily clad Lady Godiva," said Mike.

"Quite a vision," said Jill with a smile.

"A true vision is this breakfast, a feast for a king."

"Good morning, Mister Mike," said Miss Harriet, walking in from the dining room.

"You all put on quite the breakfast spread. It all looks and smells amazing."

"Eat hardy. I have a list of jobs for you. All the tools and supplies are in the stable woodshop. The sooner you eat, the sooner you can get to work."

"Mom, Mike and I are going for a ride," said Jill.

"That sounds wonderful. Chores first."

"Mother!"

"Do what you can, Mike. Because I know you will do a professional job. I'll make a picnic basket for you to take on your ride this afternoon."

The back door slammed open and Bugster yelled, "Ride? What ride?"

Behind Bugster ran a gangly teenage girl with oversized glasses precariously balanced on her plain face. She wore a blue-and-gold University of West Virginia women's basketball jersey and cut-off jean shorts. Stopping in front of Mike, she boldly asked, "Are you the guy who looks just like Bug's dead dad?"

The emotional air seemed to be sucked out of the room. Jill and her mother held their breath wondering how he was going to respond.

Mike smiled. "I'm a doppelganger."

"A what?" said the teenager in a screechy high voice.

"Doppel-gang-er is a person who looks like another, a double— similar but not the same."

"Cool! That's one I'll remember."

"Mike, let me introduce you to Sassy. She comes to play with Bugster on the weekends," said an exasperated Jill.

"Pleased to meet you, Sassy," said Mike. In the background, Jill silently mouthed "babysitter." Mike nodded.

"Girls, we are going to work on your manners today," said Jill. "It is very rude to barge in and interrupt adults when they are talking."

"We're sorry, Mom. When are we going riding?"

"We are not. Mister Mike and I are going for a ride today."

"Why can't we go?" asked Bugster.

"This is for adults only."

"That's not fair."

"Bugster, we have had this discussion before. If you have a problem, we talk in private, not in front of our guests, understood?"

"Yes, ma'am. But—"

"Bugster!" Jill said forcefully.

"All right. Gee. Come on, Sassy. We know when we're not wanted." They turned and ran out the back, the screen door banging closed.

Jill yelled after them, "Don't slam the door."

"Come on and eat before everything gets cold. The kids will be in when they're hungry," said Miss Harriet.

Everyone took a plate. As Mike loaded his plate, Miss Harriet asked Jill, "Honey, where are you going for your ride?"

"I think we'll have lunch in the high pasture at Overlook Point."

"That has the best view of the Gauley Valley," said Miss Harriet. "After breakfast, please show Mike his room. I left a to-do list on his pillow. The list is prioritized. If you have any questions, please ask me. Jill can show you where the tools are."

"Sounds good to me."

"Mother, can he eat first?" said Jill.

"If he's quick about it."

They chuckled. Mike now understood why the inn ran so well.

After breakfast, Jill showed Mike his room above the stables.

Access to the stable's apartment was through the tack room. The room smelled of leather, saddle soap, and boot polish. As Mike climbed the open wooden stairs, he noted the tack room was the same size as the stalls, twelve by twelve feet. The walls looked like shiplap hickory. The floors were wide-plank rustic pine. The ceiling cross members were hand-hewn red oak beams. On the walls were halters and bridles. Western saddles were on poles horizontal to the floor and attached to the wall about waist high. Under the stairs was an oversize *S* rolltop desk with accompanying cane office chair. The desk was piled high with assorted papers and books.

At the top of the stairs was a landing with an old eight-paneled wood door that opened into a large living area. Mike walked into a family room with a barn-beamed cathedral ceiling. Two large, dark-brown leather couches were centered around a cupboard with a TV. The room was comfortable and inviting.

"Hello, ladies," said Mike to Bugster and Sassy. They were glued to the TV, watching cartoons. Neither girl responded.

"Girls," said Jill in a loud voice.

"Oh. Hi, Mom," said Bugster.

"Manners please," scolded Jill.

The girls said together, "Hi, Mister Mike."

Jill shook her head. "Your room is the second on the right. That room shares a bathroom with the room across the hall. My room is the second on the left."

"OK. We share a bathroom." Mike smiled.

"The bathroom doors have locks."

"I feel safer knowing I can keep you out," Mike quipped.

Jill rolled her eyes and smiled. "I wasn't implying—"

Mike chuckled.

"Anyway, straight ahead is a pantry with clothes washer and dryer. If you put out your clothes from the beer party outside your door, I'll be happy to wash them."

"Thank you. I have other clothes that need washing. If the machines aren't too complicated, I can do it."

"Suit yourself."

Mike felt a little sharpness in Jill's voice. Had he missed something?

"Everything you need is in your room. If you have any questions, I'll be in the inn."

Jill turned and started to walk away when Mike asked, "Is it OK if the girls help me with my list? I'm sure I could use the help."

"Can we, Mom? Can we?" squealed Bugster.

Jill's scowl turned into a smile. "That would be wonderful; anything to get you two out of the apartment before your eyes turn square."

"Come on, ladies. The list is long, and the day is short," said Mike.

Mike was going to need some basic carpentry tools. The workshop was adjacent to the tack room, table saw, drill press, planer-joiner, router table, and all the hand tools laid out for functionality and ease of use. The walls were lined with jigs and set-up devices. It appeared to Mike that several projects were interrupted by Ed's sudden death.

Mike found a handmade toolbox and asked the girls to find the tools he requested. Once he was prepared with all the tools, he yelled in a commanding voice, "Fall in." The girls looked at each other. They had no idea what he meant. He explained what needed to be done according to Marine training, then again said, "Fall in." They quickly complied with giggles. "Follow me." They marched out the stable in single file with Mike in the lead calling cadence.

By eleven o'clock, the trio had pared down the list. They replaced several floodlights, planed a screen door so it would close smoothly, and cleaned a clogged downspout. Next task was to reset several pavers in the patio. Jill found the "gang" looking at a light switch in the stable. The cover was off, and the wires exposed. Mike was explaining what had to be done prior to tackling any electrical job.

"We have to make sure the main power switch is turned off and locked out."

"Excuse me. Girls, Gram has lunch ready for you in the inn. Wash up."

"But, Mom, we're not done," said Bugster.

"Bug, this list is only half completed, and we've got all day tomorrow. Ladies, it was a pleasure. I loved working with professionals. I will mention to management that I believe you should be rewarded for your efforts." Mike came to attention and saluted the girls, saying, "Jobs well done. Detail dismissed." The girls giggled. "Off to lunch, girls. That's an order."

Spontaneously, the girls gave Mike a hug, and then ran to the inn.

"Well, you are a charmer," said Jill.

"I'm just one big, loveable Marine."

"Why don't you get cleaned up while I saddle the horses?"

"Roger that." Mike bolted up the stairs. He ran to his room, took a quick shower, and changed into another pair of jeans and T-shirt. He pulled on his cowboy boots and ran back to the paddock.

Jill led the saddled horses out of the yard. She handed a white, straw cowboy hat to Mike. It fit as if it were made for him. She smiled. She wore brown cowgirl boots, faded skintight jeans, a form-fitting, tan cowgirl vest and a light-brown felt cowgirl hat.

Mike was once again smitten by her good looks.

"I'll lead the way. It's about an hour's ride uphill. Your horse's name is Blossom. She's a sweetie and experienced trail horse. Ride light on the reins. She'll follow Chance anywhere."

"Lead on," said Mike.

They traveled a well-worn equine trail that had been a logging road years before. The path was full of switchbacks as it ascended the mountainside. Eventually, the trail began to fade. When they reached a grassy meadow, the horse trail had become a game trail. There was barely room for one horse on the overgrown path. Jill turned in her saddle.

"Just over the ridge is Overlook Point. Not much farther."

Mike's butt was sore.

When the meadow ended, a very steep wooded slope started. Mike decided to give his horse and butt a rest. He would walk Blossom over the ridge. Jill was ahead of him out of sight. The trail soon filled with wild rose bushes. The dense growth made the trail difficult to follow. Mike stopped to listen for Jill breaking trail. All he heard was voices. Someone was talking with Jill directly in front of him. It sounded like an argument. The vegetation was so thick he could see nothing but green.

Mike slowly walked Blossom toward the voices. The trail gradually opened to a scrub pine area. Ahead, Jill was off her horse. She stood next to Chance, trying to pull the reins from a heavyset man with a dark scraggly beard. He was dressed in a pair of dirty farmer's overalls held up by one button. The denim barely covered the man's massive hairy chest. A beat-up straw field hat shaded the man's eyes. All Mike could see of his face was large, brown-stained teeth set in the black beard.

Mike yelled loudly through the trees, "Hello!"

The bearded man turned in surprise. He bent over to retrieve a shotgun on the ground. The man cradled the shotgun in his arms like a duck hunter without relinquishing Chance's reins.

"Well, lookie here, if'n it ain't Mister Football, hiz own self. I'z heard you gots fried a while back. Cooked black as any goose, so be told. Goes ta show ya, I been in these here wood too damn long."

"Well, partner, it looks like you have," said Mike as he walked closer. "Now why don't you let go of Miss Jill's reins like a gentleman."

"Gentleman? Nobody called me dat before."

"Always a first time."

"And if'n I don't, what's ya gon' do?"

"Well, I'll have to take that pretty little shotgun and put it where the sun don't shine." Mike smiled.

The bearded man belly laughed. His whole body shook like a bowl of Jell-O.

"You da funniest man. Never remembered ya ta be dat way."

"I'm not," said Mike, as he steadily moved closer.

Suddenly, Mike felt a gun barrel pressed into his back. He stood still.

"Me neither. Behind you is my little brother Stanley. If'n I tells him so, he'll put a groundhog-size hole in ya backside. Isn't dat right, Stanley?"

"Sure is, bro. Let's mess him up now and do her."

"Not now. We bein' gentlemen and all. I'z wants to parlay with Mister Big Talker. Move his skinny heinie up heres."

"Ya heard Edsel, move."

Mike held his ground. Stanley poked him in the back with the shotgun barrel. Mike didn't move. Stanley pulled back and poked him harder. On the third jab Mike spun. The shotgun sailed by his back. Stanley pulled the trigger, blasting dirt and stones into the air. Mike grabbed the shotgun by the barrel and pulled it back into Stanley's stomach. The impact knocked the wind out of him. Mike jerked the shotgun forward, freeing it from Stanley's grip. Then, with a two-handed upward stroke, he hit Stanley in the forehead with the butt of the shotgun. Stanley collapsed, hitting the ground like a loose horse turd. Mike racked another round into the chamber, dropped to one knee, wheeled and aimed up the trail. He took careful aim down the barrel. To his surprise, he saw Edsel retching on the ground, holding his crotch. Jill was on her horse, moving toward Mike and looking angry.

"The shotgun blast startled Chance. The reins pulled out of Edsel's hands and he just stood there looking dumber than normal. So, I kicked him in the balls," she said.

"OK! Please let me know if I ever look dumber than normal." Mike smiled.

"Let's go home. We'll find Blossom down the trail. She bolted when the shotgun fired."

"Hold your horse." Mike rolled Stanley over and pulled his wallet out of his back pocket. He rifled through the wallet until he found a driver's license. He pocketed the ID and tossed the wallet into the bushes. Then, he went to Edsel.

Through his pain Edsel wheezed, "I'z gon' finds ya . . . I gon' skin you alive." He sucked some air and continued. "After dat, I'z gon' cook your balls an' I'z gon' feed 'em to ya wolf bitch."

"That so? Well, partner, think about this." Mike hit Edsel in the temple with the shotgun butt. Edsel went limp and sprawled spread eagle in the weeds. He lay there like a highway-flattened bullfrog. Mike retrieved Edsel's driver's license and tossed the wallet into the pine grove. The shotgun Edsel carried was an expensive over-and-under Italian model manufactured by Ivo Fabbri. Mike took Stanley's shotgun. He examined the well-crafted gun like a true professional. He laid it down, took the Winchester pump, and swung it like a baseball bat against a large, loblolly pine tree. He tossed the mangled gun on the comatose Edsel. He walked back to Jill carrying the Fabbri.

"Let's go home. I've lost my appetite," said Mike.

"Put your foot in the stirrup and swing up," replied Jill.

Mike swung up, got comfortable, and put his arm around Jill's bare midriff. Her flesh felt fantastic. He wondered if the rest of her felt as good.

"Ready?" asked Jill.

Mike started to turn his head when he felt a hammer-like blow to his skull. His hat went flying. The bark of a tree in front of them exploded as the report of a high caliber rifle echoed in the hills. Jill spurred Chance and galloped down the trail. A third rifle shot sailed high. The sound mixed with the noise of galloping hooves. By the time they came to the main equine trails, Mike told Jill he felt dizzy. She slowed Chance to a walk and turned to look at Mike.

"Oh my God," said Jill as Mike slowly slid off the horse.

CHAPTER 10

NIGHT RAIN

A WHITE DOT APPEARED, and then disappeared. When it appeared again, Mike tried to push it away but couldn't move his arms. The light danced in his one eye. The beam struck his other eye. Mike tried to kick, but he could not move his legs. Behind the beam, he could barely see a figure covered in white.

"Get the damn light out of my eyes," Mike snarled.

"Mister Ruhawk, how do you feel?" said an unfamiliar voice.

"Like I was kicked in the head by a fucking mule."

"A colorful description for a severe concussion. You're very fortunate. No fracture. Do you feel dizzy?"

"No."

"How many fingers am I holding up?"

"Three."

"Good. What day of the week is today?"

"Friday."

"Good. Do you know where you are?

"I was in Webster Springs, West Virginia."

"You still are. Now you're in the Webster County Memorial Hospital."

"What the hell happened?"

"Someone shot you. A bullet creased your skull on the right side and lacerated the top of your right ear. I had to put a few sutures in your head and ear. Everything should heal nicely. The bigger worry is the concussion."

Mike tried to feel the side of his head, but his arms would not move.

"I apologize for the restraints, but you became belligerent. We can remove them now."

"Thanks."

A male nurse loosened the web nylon straps holding down his head, arms, and legs.

"Is that better?"

"Yes."

"My name is Doctor Young. I work in the ER."

"Doctor, there was a young lady with me. Is she here?"

The doctor smiled. "Miss Jillian is in the waiting room. Would you like to see her?"

"Very much."

Jill walked into the ER room, saw Mike, and started to cry. She rushed to him.

"Everything's OK. It's going to take more than a couple hillbillies to kill this jarhead."

Jill rapidly started her narrative of the shooting. "There was blood all over your head. You fell off Chance. I thought you were dead, oh my God."

"Slow down, missy. I'm fine. They'll let me out of here in a jiff. I'll sign some papers. Then, they will release me."

■ ▮ ▮ ▮ ▮

Before Mike left the hospital ER, the Webster County sheriff, two WV state troopers, and the local ATF agent visited him. He told each the same story of the confrontation. Jill had described the men. Mike did one better; he gave the sheriff the two confiscated drivers' licenses. The sheriff smiled looking at the WV Department of Transportation laminated photos of Edsel and Stanley. He informed Mike there were three brothers: Edsel Carr, Stanley Carr, and Cooper Carr. He believed Cooper was the one who shot Mike.

The ATF agent was interested in the Fabbri shotgun Mike took from Edsel. A similar weapon was reported stolen during a home invasion in Morgantown where the housewife was brutally raped. The ATF agent said he had been after the Carrs for years but could never find their still. The brothers were known as the distillers of New River Hooch. The ATF agent speculated his team would find the still near the pine grove where Mike was shot. Mike and Jill may have unintentionally stumbled into the largest Appalachian distiller of unregulated alcohol.

When Mike was discharged, the sheriff informed him the three Carr brothers were in custody. The state police had issued an APB for the Carrs and found them after Cooper drove his brothers to the Beckley General Hospital ER. Two of the brothers had severe facial swelling. The hematoma originated from a blunt object, possibly a shotgun butt plate. The bruises were identical, elongated ovals with the imprint *Winchester* clearly visible. The sheriff chuckled, then patted Mike on the back, saying, "Nice work."

On the way back to the inn, Jill filled Mike in on what happened while he was unconscious. She was over her shock and composed.

"I turned around on the saddle to see your head was covered in blood. You said something unintelligible, then fell off Chance face-first. You were bleeding like a hillside oil spill. I took my pocketknife, cut up your T-shirt, and covered the gash. That stopped the bleeding for a short time. Then, I had a hell of a time loading your tush onto Chance. He was a good boy and stood still, but you weigh a ton. I got on and we rode back to the inn. Momma helped me get you into the car. I drove like the devil was chasing us to the hospital. While you were in the emergency, I called the sheriff.

"You've been in the ER six hours. By the time of your discharge, I was interviewed by several lawman. Six different times, three before they talked to you, then three more times after they talked to you. All the officials said they would be by tomorrow so we can sign typed statements. By now, I'm sure we are the talk of Webster County. Some reporter from the *Charleston Gazette* got wind of the shooting and phoned the hospital. He wants to interview us Monday. I told him I would get back to him."

"Thank God you were there, or I'd be buzzard meat," said a grateful Mike.

"The dressing on your head looks awful. How you feeling?"

"The painkillers the doc gave me have helped, but my head is beating like a bongo drum. It's like being KO'd in a fight but never quite shaking the rung bell feeling. The doc said I should feel better tomorrow. I have to watch for double vision and nausea. You have to watch for slurred speech and blackouts. Other than that, I can leap tall buildings, stop speeding trains, and rescue any damsel in distress."

"You're amazingly crazy," said Jill, shaking her head in disbelief.

Mike grinned. "People keep telling me that."

When they returned to the inn, Mike reassured Miss Harriett, Bugster, and Sassy that he was OK. They all fussed over him. Mike had to excuse himself, saying he was tired and needed to rest. Jill helped him up the stairs and into his room.

"If you need anything, please call. I don't know what would have happened if you had—"

Mike interrupted. "I'm happy to be here for you. Today was our lucky day."

Jill held both his hands and kissed him on the lips. The kiss was long and deep. Mike became a little dizzy.

"Wow. Now I do need to lie down."

"I'll check on you later. Your luck may get better."

When Mike was alone in his room, he sat on the bed thinking of Jill's parting comment. He could not get his mind around the implications. He needed another pain pill. In the bathroom, he downed the prescription with a glass of water. He looked into the sink's mirror.

The image was gruesome. Mike had gauze wrapped around his head. A large surgical pad stuck up from his right ear, making him look like a one-eared elf. The right side of his face was swollen and discolored. His right eye had turned black and blue.

He carefully unwrapped the gauze around his head and took off his elf ear. The side of his head was shaved clean and painted with some type of purple antiseptic. Mike had a red line that ran from the upper right side of his skull to the top of his right ear. It looked like someone had taken a grooved chisel to his head. His ear was missing some meat. The doc had stitched the jagged remains. He would look like a prizefighter when the ear healed. There was some residual matted blood on his scalp. He stripped and showered, wrapped his head in fresh gauze, crawled to bed, snuggled between the sheets, and passed out.

He dreamed he was in Nam running in dense foliage. Out of the wall of green vegetation, something reached for him. Mike struggled to get away. He felt a touch, instinctively reacted, drawing back his fist to strike. Then he smelled a familiar spicy perfume. He opened his eyes. Beside him on the bed was Jill. She had her hands up, protecting her face. He lowered his clenched fist.

"What the hell, Jill. How did you—"

"I came to check on you, and then wanted to be with you," she said in a frightened, timid voice.

Mike rolled off her and sat on the side of the bed. He was naked.

"I'm sorry," pleaded Jill.

Mike was silent.

Jill rolled off the bed and stood in front of Mike in her nightgown.

She sniffled and left the room, softly closing the door. Mike sat on the bed, bewildered. Finally, he went to the bathroom and splashed water on his face. He almost struck Jill. The only thing that saved Jill was the combination of vanilla, jasmine, and rose. The perfume called Shalimar.

Mike felt unglued. He was reacting instead of thinking. He rationalized it was the concussion. He put on a pair of pajama bottoms he found in the dresser drawer and got back in bed. His head hurt. He took another pain pill. He hoped Morpheus would visit and he would sleep.

The sound of soft rain started in the courtyard's holly trees. Soon, severe weather rolled in from the southwest. The National Weather Service in Kentucky, Tennessee, and West Virginia posted flood warnings. The heavy rains arrived about two in the morning in Webster. The thunder woke Mike with booms like a battery of 155 millimeter howitzers. The lightning strikes were so frequent, it seemed like someone was flicking the room's overhead lights on and off. The driving rain intermixed with hail pelted the stable's metal roof. The staccato of ice pellets hitting a tin roof sounded familiar, a noise better forgotten.

Mike got up and closed the rain-drenched windows. Rainwater had puddled on the wooden floor. He mopped the water with towels from the bathroom. Standing in front of the windows, he thought of the monsoons. Those days of patrolling in the never-ending rain, always wet. It even rained during a NVA mortar barrage. He shivered. Lightning struck somewhere in the pasture. The smell of electrified ozone floated in the air. It was a clean, strange smell unaltered by other odors. Then, he heard the door creak open and close and immediately detected another, the smell of Shalimar perfume again.

"I'm afraid of thunderstorms," whispered Jill in a childish voice as she entered the room. She climbed into bed and Mike followed.

"You'll be safe with me," he said, pulling her to him. He covered her shaking body with the bed sheet.

Jill molded herself into his side. She draped a leg over his midsection and her arm over his chest. Her head rested against his shoulder. Her face nestled in his neck. Mike's arm was around her shoulder, his hand tenderly caressing her back. The rainstorm swirled around them. Their emotional storms subsided as they held each other. They both felt comfortable and secure in each other's arms. Unexpectedly, lightning struck one of the stable's lightning rods. The blue-white iridescent plasma danced down the grounding wire, hopped onto Mike's bedroom windowsill and danced across the floor, bouncing off the iron, brass-clad bed frame, hitting the bathroom sink drain and disappearing. Mike and Jill felt the electric charge. The hair on their arms stood upright. Instinctively, Mike rolled on top of Jill to protect her.

"The storm will pass," he said. Reassuringly he kissed her lips. The delicate kiss magically unleashed veiled passions. Their mouths and hands began to move. They matched their rhythm to that of the storm. The tempest reached a crescendo and paused only to regain strength and begin as a new gale. The wind howled, the rain intensified, and the thunder grew louder with each clap. It was hours before a gentle rain fell. In the early morning light, a heavy mist encompassed the house and stable.

Soon, sun sparkled through the wet windowpanes, refracting a rainbow of color on Mike's bedroom ceiling. Mike opened his eyes and wondered about the tempest. He was alone in the king-size bed. Had the heavenly shape that shared his bed been real or the best erotic dream imaginable? Rolling to his side, he smelled her perfume. A coy smile spread across his face. She was real. He felt exhilarated. An emotional dam had cracked. He had been intimate on a spiritual level with Jill. He held nothing back. Was it lust or love? Since he returned from Nam, he'd fallen in bed with three woman. Lust and carnal craving were the prime factors. Two had baggage that would hinder long-term relations. However, Jill made him feel fully alive.

She added dimension to his life. He could envision a family with Jill and Bugster. He felt a connection on a level never experienced.

As he started to get up, he heard giggles. Putting on his pajama bottoms, he opened the bedroom door. Scoot burst through the opening and jumped into his arms. The girls followed quickly.

"Get up, get up, sleepyhead," they screamed.

"Good morning, ladies."

They giggled. "It's past ten, and we've got work to do," screamed Bugster.

Miss Harriett yelled from the kitchen, "Leave Mister Mike alone."

"It's OK, Miss Harriett. I'm up. Now, ladies, I have to shower and get dressed. I'll be out shortly. Then it's off to work we go. OK?"

Miss Harriett appeared at the door. "Come on, girls. Let Mister Mike get dressed."

The girls ran back to the family room to watch cartoons.

"How you feeling?" asked Miss Harriett.

"My head and ear are still a little sore but otherwise fantastic."

"Quite a storm we had last night."

"Yes ma'am."

"I had to get up and shut the windows in my room and Bugster's room. I'm glad Jill closed her windows. After you've dressed and eaten brunch, we will go over the to-do list and have a little chat."

"Yes ma'am."

After Mike showered, he redressed his head. On the chair in the bedroom was a stack of his clothes. Everything was washed and carefully folded. Mike dressed in his work attire and made a bandana out of his red neckerchief to cover his head wound. Before he left the room, he stripped the bed. Bloodstains covered various parts of the sheets.

"Thank you for cleaning my clothes, Miss Harriett."

"You'll have to tell Jill. She was the laundry nun this week."

"I took the sheet off my bed. I bled on them last night. I hope I didn't ruin them."

"Clorox should whiten them up. Just put them next to the clothes washer. Have something to eat and drink. After you finish, we'll talk."

Jill entered the kitchen from the stairs. "Talk about what, Momma?" She had an edge to her voice.

"About his to-do list; several projects need explanations."

"Oh," said Jill and looked at Mike. "Good morning. How are you feeling?"

"Like a new man. My ear hurts a little, but I feel outstanding." Mike smiled.

Jill's smile lit up the room.

Miss Harriett watched the exchange and frowned with understanding. "Quite a storm we had last night," she said provocatively.

"Quite a storm," said Jill and Mike, their eyes sparkling like conspirators.

Over coffee, they discussed the work. On top of the list was some storm cleanup and repair. Miss Harriett wanted Mike to look at a drainage problem near the stable. Jill excused herself. She had to return to the inn. They were expecting more guests.

■■ ▮▮▮▮

Outside the stable, next to the paddock, was a flower garden with a potting preparation table and bench. Miss Harriett set her coffee down on the prep table and asked Mike to take a seat next to her on the bench.

"Mike, I think you're a fine young man. Educated, honorable, and considerate, but I know very little about you. Two days ago, you stopped for a night stay. Now you seem part of the family—my family—a family I will protect with my life. My only child is an adult. She has every right to conduct her affairs as she sees fit. She does not need nor seek my approval. My concern is for her emotional well-being and that of my granddaughter. A little over a year ago, she lost her husband. He was a good man. The first year was difficult for the family. We coped. Now we have a new life. We laugh, play, and work. Jill is not a one-night stand. Do not hurt her. If your intentions are to love 'em and leave 'em, please pack your bags and go. Am I clear?"

"Yes ma'am." Mike sipped his coffee, gathering his thoughts. "I respect you and your family. It is not my intention to hurt anyone. I came to West Virginia for one reason and one reason only—to visit the family of Bud Yoder. I feel it's my duty to honor those Marines under my command who sacrificed all. I will do my duty. Your daughter and granddaughter are very special to me. They have shown me there is life after death. I've only known them for a very short time, yet I feel I've known them all my life. The one thing about life I know for sure is we can't guarantee the next second. Every breath we breathe is special. Any moment a bullet or power line or something else can extinguish our spirit. Today, I'm living in the moment. The past can't be changed. The future is unknown. Now is the only reality. Today is a gift and I'm going to live it. I understand your concern. Honor and integrity are principles I live by. I will do the right thing."

■■▮▮▮▮

Mike and the girls worked hard. Several tree limbs had fallen during the storm that needed cutting. Mike used a chain saw. Bugster and Sassy stacked the wood in a horse-drawn wagon. They raked the small branches and leaves onto a tarp, and then dumped it in the wagon. Next, they weeded the large vegetable garden behind the stable. During the afternoon, three law enforcement agencies visited. Mike and Jill signed the necessary documents. The Carr brothers were going to jail for a long time. By dinnertime, the list had shrunk to one job. They had to muck the stalls. Together, they quickly completed the smelly task.

Sassy's mother stopped to pick up her daughter at six. She was a string bean of a woman known as the town gossip. Mike introduced himself. She was delighted to meet the "dopey gangster." Mike didn't correct her. Her goal was to find out as much about Mike and the Carrs as possible in the shortest amount of time. She was visibly disappointed when Miss Harriett said dinner was getting cold and Mike had to clean up before he could join them.

Sassy's mother squeezed Mike's arm and expressed her desire to see him again. Mike politely smiled. They waved goodbye. Sassy and her mother drove off in their white Ford station wagon with fake wood paneling. Miss Harriett walked back into the stable, muttering something about a world filled with the wagging tongues of hens. Mike chuckled.

At dinner, Mike praised Bugster's work. He insisted he could not have completed his chores without the help of the girls. Bugster beamed. Miss Harriett was delighted. Jill advised the group that there was still one guest room unoccupied. Their guests, the Larimores from Michigan, had not checked in yet. She would staff the desk until they arrived.

The Michigan couple didn't arrive until after ten. It was close to eleven by the time Jill entered the apartment. There was only one light on in the family room. Mike was reading a cowboy novel, sitting on the couch. Curled up next to him was Bugster. She was in her Kanga PJs snuggled in a Pooh Bear blanket. Scoot was at her feet, curled into a ball. On the floor was a stack of children's books.

"Hi," Jill said in a whisper. "See you've had a reading marathon."

"Bugster is brilliant. Either she's memorized these books, or she reads better than half of the Marine officers I know."

"A little of both."

"You look like you've had a very long day," said Mike.

"Yeah, I didn't get much sleep last night; very bad storm," said Jill with a sensual smile.

"Very bad indeed." Mike smiled.

Jill bent over and gave Mike a deep, passionate kiss.

"What's the weather going to be like tonight?" asked Jill.

"Possibility of intermittent showers," said Mike. "Why don't you put Bugster to bed? I'll grab a couple beers. We can discuss the weather in detail."

Mike and Jill sat at the old, porcelain-topped foldout kitchen table. Miss Harriett and Bugster were asleep in their beds. The light was muted. The atmosphere romantic.

Jill looked radiant. Mike thought about what he was going to say all afternoon, but now, face-to-face, he had second thoughts. Ever the optimist, he forged forward. *Be honest and tell it like it is.*

"I have to report to my duty station in Quantico on Friday. That means I must leave Tuesday, at the latest. I plan to make the Marine Corps my career. If I were a reserve officer, my enlistment would have a specific service length. Something like three years active duty and three years inactive reserve duty. At the end of those six years, mandatory service would end. But I'm a regular who serves at the leisure of the Corps, hopefully twenty years or more.

"My duty stations are assigned. Some assignments are what's called unaccompanied duty, meaning without dependents, like wife and children. Marine life is difficult for families. The Corps philosophy is 'If we wanted you to have a wife, we would have issued you one.'"

"Why are you telling me this, Mike?"

"I guess I trying to say I'm leaving and don't know when I'm coming back."

"Did you enjoy last night?" asked Jill.

Surprised by the question Mike said, "It was spectacular."

"Would you enjoy another thunderstorm?"

"I've prayed for rain all day."

"So have I."

"I don't want to hurt you," Mike said.

"You don't want to hurt me! Well, I don't want to hurt you," said Jill.

Mike looked at his beer bottle.

"Look at me," demanded Jill. Mike looked up into the beautiful, violet-blue eyes. "I'm not some fragile flower or insecure young girl looking for love. Lonely yes. Needy no. You made me feel like a desirable woman again. I thought I had lost my passion for life when Ed died. Obviously, I have not. I like you a lot. Maybe it's love. Maybe it's something else. Nevertheless, I'm not ready to change my life for anyone right now. My life is my daughter, my mother, and the inn."

They looked at each other. The silence seemed to stretch for an eternity. Each weighed their emotions on a risk scale. What would they gain, and what would they lose if they continued? Finally, Jill said, "I'm going to take a shower and get into my most seductive night gown. Put some perfume behind my ears and other places. If you would like to see rain tonight, leave your bedside light on."

She got up from the table and put her empty beer bottle in the wastebasket under the sink, then walked to her room.

Mike slowly rose from the couch and turned off the family room light. He walked to his room and without any hesitation turned on his bedside light.

About midnight, Miss Harriett got up to take some ibuprofen for the pain in her knee. She looked down the hall and saw light coming from under Mike's door. Hopefully, her talk with Mike had been successful. She walked down the hall to check on Jill. The old wood floor squeaked loudly as she tiptoed down the hall. Jill's door was locked. She smiled. Her daughter was safe and secure.

■▬ ▮▮▮▮

The sun had just broken the horizon. The first beams of morning light danced through the trees. The scent of honeysuckle drifted on the gentle breeze. Small creatures greeted the morn with chirps and squeaks of delight. Jill and Mike woke in each other's arms. They kissed. Flesh upon flesh made each feel like the center of the universe. Later, they took a shower together, giggling like kids during their first co-ed skinny dip. They dressed and went to the inn. Mike helped in the bakery. As a reward, he enjoyed a fresh cinnamon bun. When Miss Harriett arrived in the basement kitchen, most of the breakfast cooking was complete. She thanked them, then went upstairs to lay out food for her guests.

After breakfast cleanup, the dishes placed in the dumbwaiter, guests sat in the living room drinking coffee and tea. They talked about their plans for the day. Jill, Bugster, Scoot, Miss Harriett, and Mike retired to the apartment's kitchen for coffee and hot chocolate. Jill and Miss Harriett had inn-cleaning duties to complete before any recreational activities. Mike volunteered to play with Bugster and Scoot until Jill was free. Miss Harriett estimated all the rooms would be readied by noon. After the inn was tidied up, they all could have lunch together. Then Jill and Mike could go to church. All went according to plan.

Mike and Jill drove toward the church of the Holiness Witness of Jesus on the Water. Jill was dressed in a yellow patterned sundress. Her hair was tied back, held by a long yellow ribbon. She wore flip-flops. Mike was awed by her natural good looks. He felt homely compared to her beauty.

Mike wore a pair of black slacks altered for the occasion by Jill. They were her late husband's. The short-sleeve white shirt he wore was his. He had cleaned and polished his cowboy boots. The only apparel that seemed out of place was the blue bandana around his head.

Jill drove the inn's green 1952 F10 Ford pickup. On the truck's doors, painted in gold, was *Webster Inn, Webster Springs, West Virginia*. They turned onto a narrow, two-lane, poorly maintained asphalt road. There were more potholes than asphalt. Next they turned onto the only public access to Jerryville. The lane followed the winding Gauley River. Jill asked Mike to keep his eyes open for an unimproved road on his right that was marked by an eight-foot white cross.

Crudely painted on the cross's horizontal beam was *Jesus on the Water Church*. The dirt road was more like a hiking trail. There were numerous deep ruts and washouts. The trail followed a steep grade until they reached a plateau filled with an array of wildflowers. Black-eyed Susan predominated. Nestled in the holler in the middle of the meadow stood a one-story structure covered by a rusty silver metal roof. They parked in front of the building next to twenty to thirty varied vehicles. The parishioners' economic stratification was noticeable in the type of ride they drove. A new Cadillac was parked next to a rust-bucket pickup next to a small, aged church bus. When they turned the truck's engine off, the music from the church filled the glen. A loud bass put down a strong four-four beat, and an electric guitar played out the melody of a song.

Mike looked at Jill. "Gospel?"

"It's 'I Saw the Light' by Hank Williams," said Jill.

Hand in hand, they approached the church. The outside was whitewashed, rough-hewn cedar boards with one double-hung window on each side of dented double metal doors. The aged wood showed areas of repair. Above the doors was a simple white pine wooden cross. When they opened the doors, the congregation exploded in song. *"Now I'm so happy, no sorrow in sight, Praise the lord, I saw the light,"* the chorus sang.

They stood in the back of the church. The room was tramp-steamer, belowdecks, boiler-room hot. They immediately started to perspire. The windows were open but provided little ventilation. The one-room building was packed. No one seemed to notice them. On a flimsy plywood platform in the rear of the room was a thin balding man in black slacks and a long-sleeve white dress shirt, buttoned at the neck. He was holding an electric guitar.

Jill whispered, "That's Pastor Noah with the gi'tar."

CHAPTER 11

SERPENTS

THE PASTOR SPOKE INTO a stand microphone. "My brothers and sisters, raise ya voices to Jehovah and sing loudly one more time 'One Day at a Time.' We'll start with the chorus." He strummed the guitar and cried out,

One day at a time, sweet Jesus,
One day at a time.
That's all I'm asking from you.
Just give me the strength
To do every day what I have to do.
Yesterday's gone, sweet Jesus.
And tomorrow may never be mine.
Lord help me today, show me the way
One day at a time
One day at a time.

The assembly sang loudly. When the song was finished, Pastor Yoder asked if anyone wanted to give testimony. A sickly woman in a well-worn skirt and threadbare sweater near the front spoke out.

"Pray for me."

The pastor yelled into the mike, "Pray for Sister Jane."

"The Lord helps me. Satan was lookin' at me from the bottom of some Tennessee mash last night. He tells me I'd feel better if I'z had one more shot."

Pastor Noah yelled into the mike, "Be gone, Satan, be gone."

The congregation responded. "Praise the Lord."

Sister Jane raised her hands. "I'z fell on da floor an' asked for Jesus' help."

The congregation responded. "Praise the Lord."

"Sweet Jesus said, 'Be healed. Now go be witness, give testimony,'" cried Jane.

The congregation responded. "Praise the Lord."

Pastor Noah jumped off the stage, seized Jane by the shoulders, and screamed, "*Kneel.*"

They all knelt together. He placed his hands on her head and said, "Do you accept the Lord Jesus Christ as your savior?"

Jane and the congregation screamed, "*Yes!*"

"Do you reject Satan and all his works?"

Jane and the congregation screamed, "*Yes!*"

Pastor Noah sprang to his feet and jumped around. "*Sing hallelujah!*"

The bass picked up the beat. A tambourine kept tempo. The music grew louder when the electric guitar joined in the instrumental. They sang and danced until the sweat poured off their faces and soaked their shirts.

Pastor Noah jumped on the stage. "Them that's been anointed, come forth. Gather and behold the serpents."

Several men and woman gathered around Noah. They formed a circle holding hands. Noah took a huge Bible off the podium and placed it reverently on the floor in the center of those gathered. Two men brought a wooden box the size of a file drawer decorated with colorful religious icons and held it over the Bible.

"Behold, the serpents."

The men turned over the box, and a writhing ball of snakes struck the top of the Bible. The rattlers and copperheads intertwined. Without hesitation, Pastor Noah grabbed the bundle of snakes. He lifted them over his head and started to dance. He hopped awkwardly from one foot to the other, raising his knees to his chest, following the beat of the bass fiddle. Several snakes fell off the bundle and were caught or picked up off the floor by others in the circle. Everyone in the circle danced. They passed the snakes around as casually as a hymnal. Some of the snakes were draped around the dancers' necks, others slithered down the anointers' shirts. Several snakes fell on the floor. The gathering danced on and around them in their bare feet. The congregation sang, "Take me to the King." Everyone swayed to the rhythm of the song. Jill and Mike stood transfixed by the spectacle.

Pastor Noah shouted out, "The Bible tells us in Mark 16 verse 18, 'They shall take up serpents. If they drink any deadly thing, it shall not hurt them. They shall lay hands on the sick and they shall recover.' Luke 10 verse 19 tells us, 'Behold, I give you power to tread on serpents and scorpions, and over all the power of the enemy. Nothing shall by any means hurt you.'"

Stepping to the front of the platform, he bowed his head. The congregation went silent. The music stopped. The anointed swayed. Noah held the snakes in front of him and said in a whisper, "Lord, we see ya serpent clearly. We needs your help ta see Satan's serpents."

The congregation said, "Amen."

"Jesus, we knows you waz tempted by the devil in the wilderness. We needs ya help. We be tempted by devil's serpents every day."

The congregation said, "Amen."

"Holy Ghost, show us the truth, the light, the way. Help us see the two-legged snakes that walk among us."

The congregation said, "Amen."

"Father, Son, and Holy Ghost, help us poor sinners to embrace your love and cast out the serpents. Say amen."

"Amen."

He lifted his head and shouted louder, "Say amen!"

"Amen," the congregation wailed.

The music started and the snake handlers started hopping. The pastor started to sing with passion, "Love Has Come." The crowd joined. They sang with unbridled emotion. Some stood with their hands in the air. Others fell to the floor babbling incoherently.

> *Glory, glory, hallelujah*
> *Thank You for the cross*
> *Singing glory, glory, hallelujah*
> *Christ has paid the cost*
>
> *Every knee shall bow, every tongue confess*
> *that God is love and love has come to us all.*
> *Every heart set free, everyone will see*
> *that God is love and love has come to us all.*

By the end of the song, several people had passed out, others were speaking in some unknown language, and some just kept singing.

Jill whispered to Mike, "I need some air. I feel a little dizzy."

Mike took her by the arm and led her out the front door. The music and singing followed them like a tsunami. They felt the strength and conviction in the raised voices. Mike guided Jill to a huge maple tree. As he got closer to the shade tree, he realized a small, wizened black man was sitting on a folding chair next to the tree trunk.

"It gets so hot in dat church, even da devil won't go in," said the man. He slowly rose from the chair as if it was a struggle to stand.

"Put yo missus here. Cool breeze blow off da pasture."

"Thank you," said Mike.

"I'z gots ice cold water, cola, and New River Hooch. Two bits for water and cola, gots ta get a buck for the hooch—my supply gone dry."

Mike and Jill knowingly nodded.

"Is it OK to dip my clean handkerchief into the ice water?" asked Mike.

"Sure. Dat be fine."

Mike pulled a clean, red bandana out of his back trouser pocket. He submerged it in one of the two metal wash tubs filled with ice, then placed it on Jill's forehead. He gave the man, who identified himself as Otis, a buck and got two glass milk bottles filled with iced spring water and two iced colas from the tub.

Otis unfolded two more chairs. Mike sat next to Jill. He wiped her face and wrung the cool water over her neck. Jill's hair and the front of her yellow dress became drenched and transparent.

Mike whispered into Jill's ear, "Your puppies have cold noses."

Jill looked at him, confused, then followed his gaze to her braless breasts. Her hardened nipples pressed against the fabric. She giggled and whispered, "I'm just a country girl. Don't worry, in this heat everything will dry quickly."

"You alls are first'ez, ain't ya?" said Otis.

"If you mean the first time to this church, you're right," said Mike.

"I'z always can tell. Them snakes more than normal people can take da first time."

"The pastor is extraordinary," said Jill.

"He be dat. He be dat. But yo shoulda seen hiz son. Dat boy could charm them snakes. He never gots hisself bit. No, no, he didn't! Even as a littl'bitty baby, he just laid with them evil serpents. He just laughed and laughed. Pay them no account. Now he be some'en special."

"Was his name Ezekiel?" said Mike.

"Dat be his boy. We call him 'Little EZ.' He be playin' with them snakes since he could crawl to da altar. He never gots hisself bit. No, no, he didn't! Now, Pastor Noah, he been marked, he has. I'z can't count that number."

"You been here a long time?" asked Jill.

"Pastor Noah my third pastor. Number one and number two are

in da ground next to da back door. Gots bit ta death by them serpents. Marks all over themself, true, true, they did. Watch them die, I did. God's will that."

"Must have been awful," said Jill.

"Unholy dey be. I'z part of them chosen I am. Dem snakes don't likes me none. I'd clean up after church, afraid one of them evil snakes might bite me, ya knows. Now I don' go into da church till Pastor Noah tells me them snakes gone. I'z takes care of da church and land. Gots me a cabin up da holler, I do."

"Otis, how long before church services end?" asked Mike.

Otis looked at the sun. "I'd say before the sun set."

Mike looked at his watch. That could be three hours. In the next moment, they heard the congregation sing "Onwards Christian soldiers."

"They all be out soonest, they will. Dat be the last song," said Otis.

When the song ended, the doors opened, and the parishioners streamed out. Almost all made their way to Otis for ice-cold refreshments. Jill and Mike finished their drinks. Jill had recovered. Her dress dried. They gave their empty bottles to Otis. When they saw Pastor Noah emerge from the church, they introduced themselves.

"I'z believes I knew your father," said Pastor Noah to Jill.

"I'm sure you did. He knew everyone in the county."

"I saw you all when ye came into church. I hope ye found inspiration in our tabernacle."

"An extraordinary display of devotion," said Mike.

"If ye believe, anything is possible."

"Amen," said Jill.

"I have a feeling faith is not what brought you to our church," said Pastor Noah.

"Yes sir. Your son brought me here," said Mike.

"My son?"

"Yes sir. I was his commander in Vietnam."

"Praise the Lord."

Jill said, "Amen."

"I've been on my knees talking with the Lord. He told me to be patient, all will be revealed. Now here you are. Blessed be his name."

"Pastor, I wanted you to know he was a fine Marine. He died doing his duty for his country."

"He was a special boy. He was sent to us to do God's work. When he was called to the Marines, we all prayed hard."

"He worked hard and saved many lives."

"Praise the Lord. Did he kill a horde of godless devils?" The pastor's demeanor changed from a gentle preacher to a hardened evangelist.

"He participated in several firefights," answered Mike, dismayed by the question.

"Did he kill any commies, Satan's soulless multitude, the Asian swarm that devours their babies? Tell me! I demand to know!"

"There was death and destruction on the battlefield," said Mike, taking a step back from the pastor.

"Praise the Lord," said the pastor as he raised his hands to the sky. "Ezekiel is surely in the arms of the Lord. He did the Lord's work in the unholy land of Gods enemies. He walked through the valley, his head anointed; now he surely dwells in God's house. Glory, glory, hallelujah."

The pastor reached out and seized Jill's hands. He fell to his knees and bowed his head. Jill looked bewildered and frightened.

"Lord, you showed my son the way. He gave his life for you. Help this woman find your way. Help her find peace and love in your arms. Keep her safe from all Satan's temptations. I ask this in Jesus' name. Amen." He got up, kissed Jill's hands and said without emotion, "Our next meetin' is Wednesday at seven. God would be pleased if he sees you in his tabernacle."

He let go of Jill's hands, nodded to Mike and walked to an older Chevy pickup. After carefully putting his guitar in the front seat, he got in and drove down the dirt path out of the meadows. Jill and Mike watched him leave as if in a trance.

Mike muttered, "Holy shit."

Jill said, "Amen to that."

Otis walked up to them with a huge grin. "He somethin', ain't he?"

Mike and Jill rode back to the inn in disbelief, Jill emotionally shaken. Pastor Noah had struck a powerful moral cord with Jill. Mike tried to rationalize his reaction to the pastor's hatred. He led numerous Marines who were Asian American. They were good Marines. Bud Yoder's best friend was a Kit Carson Vietnamese interpreter/scout named Jimmy Nuen. Could the reaction be how Pastor Noah coped with the loss of his son? On the other hand, was it something more fundamental?

When they pulled into the inn's driveway Jill said she wanted to clean up and change clothes. Mike suggested they have dinner together. She agreed. He asked her if she knew of a place that had a menu that included fresh fish. Jill said there was a great restaurant in Sutton, about a half hour drive. He requested that she wear something appropriate for a motorcycle ride.

They went to their separate rooms after saying hello to Bugster and Miss Harriet. They both locked their doors and met in the bathroom. Jill hugged Mike and started to cry. Mike stroked her hair.

"Never let anyone control your emotions. They're yours," he said. "Sharing is wonderful, but control by others leads to abuse. What we saw today was a freak show. It's some backwoods twist on the Bible. A charismatic preacher who charms snakes and people using Scripture to justify his outlook of the world; it's not God's way."

"What is God's way?"

"First Corinthians 13:13, 'Faith, hope, love abide, these three, but the greatest of these is love.'"

Jill looked at Mike with surprise.

"Pastor Noah isn't the only one who can quote Scripture. Now, do your thing. When you're through, rap on the door and I'll get cleaned up." He kissed her. "I love you."

Jill's eyes opened wide in disbelief. She smiled. "Get out of here."

Mike sat on the four-poster brass bed in his room thinking of what he just said. *I love you.* Why had he said those three words? Was he trying to make Jill feel better, or was it a thoughtless act? That was the problem. He was spontaneous. He had just made this relationship very complicated. He screwed up the Marines' seven Ps: Prior Proper Planning Prevents Piss Poor Performance.

Jill rapped on the bathroom door. "It's all yours. Meet you in the kitchen."

■■ ▌▌▌▌

Mike had on his biker attire. Jill wore black cowgirl jeans, calf-high, black cowgirl boots, a long-sleeve lipstick-red blouse, and a black leather cowgirl vest. Her hair was tied back with a black ribbon. She looked fantastic. Bugster was upset that she could not go. Mike explained that it would be unsafe to ride three on the bike. She retorted with "Take the truck." Jill mitigated the situation by offering a special dinner tomorrow night. She would cook Bugster's favorite honey glazed beef ribs. They would have cake and ice cream for dessert. Miss Harriett told them to enjoy the evening. She and the Bug would make it a movie night.

The Harley roared in the confines of the river gorge as they rode toward Sutton. The highway gently wound around the Appalachian hills. The fading sun cast long shadows in the valleys. The temperature dipped with the darkness. They drove around Lake Sutton at twilight.

The restaurant was situated at the end of the lake with a commanding view of the calm, dark waters. The small Italian eatery called LaPlaca's catered to the local crowd. The parking lot was full. They waited for a table. They were finally seated in the noisy bar section.

"The wait and noise are well worth the meal. It will be delicious, especially the grilled parmesan fish," reassured Jill.

Mike and Jill ordered the grilled parmesan red mullet with pasta. Jill suggested they try LaPlaca's own Primitivo Red to accompany the fish. The food was so good Mike thought about ordering a second dinner. Their conversation was limited due to the bar noise. The waiter suggested they have after-dinner cappuccinos on the patio deck. They gladly agreed.

The patio setting was intimate, with glass tables for two lit by red candles in hurricane globes. The sky was clear, and dazzling stars dotted the night, inviting romance. They touched their demitasse cups together.

Mike said, "To our many blessings."

Jill said, "To the future."

Mike put down his cup. "Jill, we should talk about our future."

"Mike, I'm not sure of 'our' future. You're the wild card. Being practical, we only met three days ago. My life was boringly ordinary until you showed up. In a little over seventy-six hours, we have been shot at, slept together, and had our faith tested. Tonight, you even said you loved me. I feel like my world is spinning out of control."

"I understand."

"No, I don't think you do. Last time my world spun like this was when I became a widow. It took over a year to feel like I had some control. I prayed a lot, I dedicated myself to God and my daughter. I started to live again. Then, this unbelievable man rode in on his big Harley. You brought passion back that I thought I'd lost. Today, I realized I'm very attracted to you . . . but I don't love you. Not yet. Sex is great, beyond great, but it's not love. Love comes with discovery, shared experiences, time, trust . . . at least for me."

Mike looked at her with a new respect. She was punch-in-the-gut honest. He sipped his coffee and looked at the calm water. Mike stalled for time to get his emotions under control. His feeling ran the gauntlet from rejection to disbelief to relief. He put his hand on the table. She placed hers on his.

Mike asked, "Can we be friends?"

Jill leaned across the table and kissed him on the forehead.

"Best friends. Always."

He squeezed her hand. "Best friends forever."

The ride back to the inn was enchanting. The headlights became beacons cutting through the night veil, displaying strange shapes of nature. Darkened trees loomed like monsters with twisted arms. Their branches seemed to intertwine, making the highway appear as a tunnel. Nocturnal animals appeared and quickly disappeared, like phantoms. Flickering lights deep in the woodsy homesteads offered hope of a safe sanctuary. Mike felt like the burden of guilt had been lifted from his shoulders. Jill leaned against his back with her arms tightly wrapped around his waist. He felt relaxed in her embrace.

They pulled into the inn's driveway. Mike parked the bike. Jill thanked him for dinner. She told him she wasn't sure if she would share his bed tonight. Jill assured him they were best friends.

Mike lay in bed reading his Western when he heard a knock on the door. He smiled. When he opened the door, he was surprised.

"Good evening, Miss Harriett," said Mike. He was glad he put on the pajama bottoms.

"I wanted to check to see if everything went okay at church."

"Yes ma'am. It was quite a show. I had the opportunity to give my condolences to Pastor Yoder."

"Good, I'm sure he appreciated the gesture."

"I think so."

"Good night, Mike." She grinned as she turned down the hallway.

"Good night, Miss Harriett."

Mike got back into bed and turned off the bedside lamp. He put his hands behind his head, wondering how long it would be before Jill joined him.

The military alarm clock went off in Mike's head. The bedroom was bathed in a gray, murky light. A heavy fog had rolled in during the early morning hours. His wristwatch indicated it was 0529. He was alone.

Mike dressed in his running shorts, running shoes, Marine PT shirt, and head bandana. After stretching and his daily-dozen warm up, he planned to run the equine trail. The apartment was peaceful as he was the first up. Silently, he went downstairs and out the door. Slowly, Mike started to jog. Within a few minutes, he found his rhythm and ran with measured effort. As he ran, Mike thought of Jill. Obviously, he was not as good as he thought. Jill was a no-show. Mike accepted he was nothing more than a chauvinistic pig. The only thing he truly cared for was the Marine Corps. Could he ever have an honest relationship without thinking of the Corps first?

Mike knew he had to get through today. He had a medical assessment this morning and had to meet the sheriff in the afternoon. That evening, he would party with the Addisons. When he got back to the inn, he would check with Miss Harriett to see if she had more chores before leaving. He needed to check in with Belmont Bay Marina in Virginia. He wanted to ensure his apartment was ready. He had phoned them earlier in the week to check on his uniforms and personal gear he sent from California. So far, all was Jake. The big question for the day was how he would interact with Jill. Was friendship enough for their relationship to last?

When he returned, the girls were busy in the inn.

Bugster saw him in the stable.

"Where have you been?" demanded Bugster. Scoot ran in circles around his legs.

"And good morning to you," said Mike.

"We thought you were a sleepyhead, still in bed."

"I was doing my daily workout and three-mile run."

"Do you do that every day?"

"I try. My job requires that I stay in good physical shape."

"And just what is your job?" said Bugster with her hands on her hips.

"My job is to 'keep this country safe from all enemies foreign and domestic,'" said Mike, reciting his Oath of Allegiance to the United States of America.

"That's a big job," said Bugster.

"Some say there is none bigger."

Mike told Bugster he would be outside once he cleaned up.

A little while later Mike and Bugster walked into the kitchen of the inn. Miss Harriett and Jill were putting away clean dishes.

"Good morning, ladies," said Mike.

"Good morning," they responded.

"He was running so he can keep us safe," proclaimed Bugster.

"Really," said Jill.

"We thought you might have slept in this morning," said Miss Harriett.

"No ma'am, just doing my Marine thing."

"We saved you some breakfast. I'll heat it for you," said Jill with a welcoming smile.

"That was thoughtful. Thank you."

The women sat with Mike while he ate. They all had coffee together. Miss Harriett said her list was completed. She and Jill had the inn to clean. He was free for the day. The back door banged open and Sassy ran in, took one look at Mike, and yelled out the door to her mother, "He's still here." Then, she turned around and said, "Hi."

The adults burst out laughing.

"What's so funny?" said Sassy.

Jill laughed so hard that coffee came out her nose. Mike looked at her and started to choke. Miss Harriett had tears rolling down her cheeks, giggling. Sassy and Bugster looked at the three adults as if they had gone bonkers.

"They're loonies. Let's go outside and play," said Sassy.

Dr. Young said Mike's stitches could come out at the end of the week. He would have some scarring that his hair should cover. Nevertheless, the doc warned Mike of the effects of repeated concussions.

The sheriff wanted Mike to look at some mug shots. Mike accurately picked out two of the Carr brothers. The Italian shotgun Mike took away from one of the brothers matched the serial numbers of the gun taken during the home invasion. The moonshiners were going to MO, the Mount Olive Correctional Complex of West Virginia, for a very long time.

On the way back to the inn, Mike check with Belmont Bay Marina. Everything would be ready for tomorrow's arrival. He would have time to settle in before reporting for duty Friday.

The inn was relatively quiet. The Addisons were in the apartment watching the evening news. The lead news stories featured the siege of Khe Sanh. The 26th Marines were crammed into a combat base, fighting toe to toe with the NVA. The match was undecided. Mike's gut twisted as he listened to the TV broadcast.

Mike asked the ladies if they would like any refreshments. Jill said she would like a beer. They walked over to the inn. Happy hour was about to start. Jill was the host. An elderly couple staying at the inn joined them for cocktails. They had family in Webster Springs and were visiting for the week. The conversation was about the importance of family. The couple was celebrating their fiftieth anniversary and first great-grandchild. Mike and Jill were inspired by the couple's devotion and love. After a second drink, the couple retired to their room. They needed a little nap before dinner. Mike watched them walk hand in hand out the room.

"What a delightful couple," said Jill.

"Still in love after all these years," said Mike.

They looked at each other, waiting for the other to say something.

Finally, Jill said, "What did the doctor say?"

"Good to go. Just have to watch for any residual effect from the concussion. Can't bang my head anymore, even with this thick skull of mine."

"That means you are leaving tomorrow?"

"I plan to get an early start."

"What are your plans for tonight?"

"Hopefully, I'll be invited to the party for Bugster. I like ice cream and cake."

"Of course you're invited. I was referring to later this evening."

"After the party would you join me for a late-night drink? I understand the inn has an after-hours bar."

"I think a night cap would be enjoyable. You have a date."

"Out-f'ing-standing!"

The dinner was Bugster's favorite—honey BBQ beef ribs, buttered corn on the cob, deep fried hushpuppies, and homemade cold slaw. Dessert was dark chocolate–frosted angel food cake and homemade vanilla ice cream. Bugster told funny stories of her adventures with Sassy. They had found a box turtle and tried to teach it to swim. They discovered the world of crawdads in the creek. Jill retold the story of the elderly couple. They were adorable. Miss Harriett said she found an emerald earring in one of the guest rooms. She spent the morning trying to contact the last occupants. Hopefully, someone would call her back tomorrow.

After dessert, they cleaned up. Bugster and Miss Harriett wanted to watch a Disney movie on the cassette player. Mike and Jill took their coffee to the inn's porch. The overcast day had cleared to a beautiful summer night. The fireflies rose from the ground, blinking their courtship dance. A whip-poor-will sang a lonesome song in the meadow. Off in the distance, two barred owls hooted. The night was alive with sounds of desire and full of promises. In the garden, the smell of honeysuckle and orchids floated in the breeze.

Mike and Jill sat on a lounge in the garden and sipped their coffees. Both were introspective.

"I missed you last night," said Mike.

"That was difficult for me to do, but—"

Mike reached out and took Jill's hand. She held his hand and leaned her head against his shoulder. Slowly, they rocked back and forth on the lounge swing. The only manufactured sound was the squeaking of the support chains. They enjoyed each other's company; neither spoke.

Their coffee went cold. The chill of the night began to seep through their clothes.

"You ready for a night cap?" asked Mike.

"I want to go to bed with you," said Jill. Her voice trembled.

"You sure?" Mike whispered.

"I've thought about it all day. This could be your last time in Webster Springs." Jill stammered a little. "I want . . . I want to feel the way you make me feel."

CHAPTER 12

THE CORPS

MIKE DROVE INTERSTATE 64 to Charlottesville, then exited toward Fredericksburg, Virginia. The ride was postcard perfect. The morning sun vaporized the dew in the meadows, ensuring the new day would be clear and beautiful. Driving over the Shenandoah Mountains in the amber light was like experiencing creation. Mike felt reborn. He was enveloped in the eastern white light traveling through the lush hardwoods of green Virginia. The warmth and splendor of the countryside reminded him of his last night with Jill.

He had never loved a woman as he loved her. He could hardly believe the depth of his passion and emotion. Jill was everything he wanted in a woman, a soulmate, maybe a wife.

Now he felt like a coward creeping off in the early morning. He left her room with a kiss on her cheek and said he loved her. She mumbled something and fell back to sleep. Mike thought it sounded like, "I love you, too."

Mike dressed and walked to the kitchen. He pulled his military notepad from his back pocket and tore off a page. He quickly scribbled a short note.

Bugster, Jill, and Miss Harriett,
Thank you for treating me like family.
I'll be back soon. Till then.
Love, Mike

Knowing he was going to be away from them for a while was a pain very different from any previous experience. Physical pain relented over time. Mike wasn't sure these emotional ties would. The only panacea for Mike was that he knew he would return. The question was how soon.

In Fredericksburg Mike headed north. He wanted to have lunch at the Globe and Laurel in Quantico. The restaurant was the honored meeting place for any Marine who stopped at the Crossroads of the Corps. Besides the atmosphere of Marine memorabilia, they served a great surf and turf. Mike looked forward to becoming part of the Corps again. He felt adrift in his quest to put ghosts in their graves. Never had he felt farther from his Marine family as his rode across country. He needed to be surrounded by people adhering to the same code of conduct and core values—his Marine family.

▬▮▮▮▮

The Quantico lunch crowd had departed the Globe and Laurel by the time Mike pulled into the parking lot. The restaurant was a two-story building with a Tudor facade. The look paid homage to the Marine history at Tun Tavern in 1776. Mike parked in an almost empty lot. He had the restaurant to himself. The inside was cool and inviting. All things Marine Corps hung from the walls: automatic weapons, swords, caps, helmets, emblems, chevrons. Mike sat at the curved oak bar that was rumored to be from the forecastle of a Revolutionary man-of-war. A lean, hard-bodied bartender who Mike guessed was a senior NCO working his B job asked what Mike would like to eat and drink. Mike ordered surf and turf and a cold draft.

A smartly dressed, medium-sized, mustached man with salt-and-pepper hair approached. He had come through the kitchen doors.

"Just returned from Nam?" he said.

"Yes sir."

"Who were you with?"

"Two-Five in An Hoa, sir."

"A very storied outfit. Quantico your new duty?"

"Yes sir. Soon to be an instructor at TBS."

"Out-f'ing-standing! Hope to see you here again. Welcome home, Marine."

"Thank you, sir."

Then the man said to the bartender, "The first drink is on the house."

"Yes sir," said the bartender.

"Thank you," said Mike. The man nodded and walked toward the entry.

Mike asked the bartender who the gentleman was.

"That's the owner, Major Spooner."

▬▮▮▮▮

After lunch, Mike drove to Belmont Bay Marina on the Occoquan River near Woodbridge. Duplexes surrounded the marina, following the contour of the tributary. They were two and three-bedrooms units. The marina's manager was the leasing agent for the eight duplexes. He was also a retired Marine gunny sergeant and long-time friend of Mike's.

Mike had first met Gunny Pete Gonzales when Pete was a staff sergeant working for 1st Marine Division G-2 in DaNang. The gunny had often debriefed Mike after recon patrols. His easy manner, quick wit, and amazing intellect impressed Mike. They became friends. When Mike learned his new post would be Quantico, he contacted the now-retired Gunny Pete. Mike hoped the gunny could recommend a place to rent. Guns said he had connections in Q-town, hooking him up with a two-bedroom unit.

The marina's office was a bait shop/boat gas station/office/housekeeping/rental desk. When the front door opened, Mike turned. Through the door came a heavyset, powerfully built fireplug of a man.

"How they hangin', skipper," said the man, thrusting a meaty hand forward.

Mike batted the hand aside and hugged the man. "Son of a bitch . . . bigger than yours."

"You only thought so. Now put me the fuck down," grunted the gunny.

"I can fraternize. You're a pukey civilian now," Mike laughed.

"Fraternize all you want. But people may get the wrong idea. Put me the fuck down." Once the gunny's stubby legs were on the floor, he did a quick parade inspection of Captain Ruhawk. "You look like shit, Hawk."

"Just being a Marine." Mike smiled.

"Yeah, head wound and all. What the fuck happened?"

"A long story. I'll tell you over a couple beers."

"Can't wait to activate the BS meter. And what's up with the Harley?"

"Another long story."

"I know, to be told over beers."

After more back slapping, Gunny Pete showed Mike his duplex. Mike was back in the Marine world and felt safe and secure behind the wire.

■■▪▪▪▪

Mike's unit was on the second floor. The front door faced the wooded slope to the rear of the marina, the land sculpted to provide an elevated parking lot. Mike opened the door and walked into an open room with a kitchen to one side and bedrooms to the other. At the end of the living room were sliding glass doors to a small balcony that faced the marina and river. The apartment interior was painted the universal light beige with matching carpet. In the center of the room sat Mike's furniture and numerous cardboard boxes.

"All your stuff's here, skipper," said Gunny Pete.

"I can't thank you enough, Guns."

"Your truck's at Starr Garage. Oil changed, battery charged, and complete mechanical PM. Give me about thirty minutes heads-up when you want to go fetch it. I can drop you off."

"Outstanding! Have to pull my uniforms out and get them to the cleaners. I report in on Friday. It's 1400 now. Pick me up at 1500. That work for you?"

"See you then."

Guns picked Mike up at 1500 precisely. They drove to the garage talking about mutual friends and where they were stationed. Mike's red 1940 Ford pickup was washed, waxed, and ready for him when he arrived at Starr's. He thanked Guns, paid his bill, and drove to the cleaners. Mike shifted through the gears like a pro.

On the outside, the pickup looked like an original off the showroom floor. The chrome grill sparkled and the split front window looked like a mirror as it reflected the afternoon sun. The real beauty was under the hood: Hurst four-speed,1962 Mustang rails, 1959 Super Marauder 430 MEL Bulldozer V8 engine with three 2300 Holley Carburetors, Edelbrock 6X2 intake manifolds, and a Hewland transmission. The truck was a screamer. Mike called his beauty "Dolly." She had never been beat on the street.

He and his dad rebuilt the truck from a barn find into a legal street rod. Mike rubbed the tan leather of the front seat thinking of the good times he had with his dad. It was the glory before the fall; their relationship deteriorated as the cancer spread through his mother's liver. His father could not understand why his son would not come home. Mike tried to explain the situation. He was deployed, in combat. His troops needed him. Their letters crisscrossed the Pacific. By the time the last letter arrived, Mike's mother had died without seeing her son, and his father would not forgive him for his absence. They had not talked since. Mike knew in the coming days he would have to address the situation with his father. For now, he needed to see a doc at the base medical clinic to get his stitches removed.

A corpsman at the clinic questioned Mike about his wound. Mike told him it was a hunting accident. The corpsman informed him a few centimeters to the left and he would have died. *Always so positive,* thought Mike. He returned to the apartment with a small bandage on his head. Back in his apartment, he began to unpack. The few items he had quickly filled the apartment. He set up his Fisher tuner and receiver. Carefully, Mike placed his two large stereo speakers in the room to get the best sound quality. Then he pulled the large vinyl thirty-three and a third record from the stiff paperboard jacket and placed it on the turntable. Tenderly, he placed the needle down on the spinning record. The sweet sound of a guitar filled the room. Mike cranked up the record and happily finished his housework, listening to Charlie Byrd.

By 2200, Mike had his bed made, clothes in the bedroom dresser, and the kitchenware stored away. He still had books to unpack and the living room to arrange. Tomorrow, he would go to the commissary for food and the PX for other household supplies. While he sat on his scuffed, saddle-brown, leather couch with his feet on a cardboard box, he made a list of items he needed. The first on the list was a garage for the bike and a case of beer for the Guns. Pete left a six-pack of beer in the refrigerator with a note on the back of an envelope, *Welcome Home Marine.*

It was time to get some sleep. As steam rose in the shower, a faint hint of Shalimar wafted in the air. He physically ached for Jill. Tomorrow, he would get his telephone installed. He would call her and let her know he arrived. To hear her voice again would be fantastic.

Mike stood in front of the bedroom's full-length mirror, his hair freshly cut to Marine standards. The base barber was careful around the long tender scar. Now, it looked like a red-striped irritation on the side of his head.

This was the third time he checked his summer service Alpha uniform. The cleaners had creased the khakis correctly. All his ribbons were pristine. His brass sparkled. The shine on his shoes was mirror-like. He was ready to report. Mike picked up his valise with his service jacket. Then he put his duty orders inside the valise. Confidently, he marched out of his apartment. It was Friday morning. Mike was going to report in early at exactly 0800. *You don't get a second chance for a first impression,* he told himself.

Mike stood at ease in front of The Basic School's S-1 administration officer. The skinny, overworked major looked over Captain Ruhawk's orders, then called for the first sergeant.

"Top, has the morning report gone out?" asked the major.

"Sir, Corporal Ditter is typing it up as we speak."

"Tell him to hold fast. We have a correction."

"Yes sir."

"Captain Ruhawk is not UA, nor has he been for the past eight days," said the major. UA meant an unauthorized absence.

"Sir?" questioned the first sergeant.

"The captain's orders clearly state his report-in date is today. He had accrued leave that was not reported to HQ by 1st MarDiv admin."

"That relieves that problem, sir."

"Here are his orders, Top. Endorse and make a copy and return them to the captain."

"Aye-aye, sir."

"Captain Ruhawk, once your orders are returned you will be escorted to the base commander's offices. You will report to Major Simmons. The MP will escort you."

"Aye-aye, sir."

"You're dismissed, Captain."

Mike came to attention but did not move. The major looked at him. "You are dismissed."

"Sir, may I ask a question, sir?"

"Captain, you have your marching orders to report to Major Simmons."

"Aye-aye, sir," said Mike. He took a step back, did an about-face, and left the office.

Mike stood in front of the first sergeant's desk waiting for the return of his orders.

"Top, I thought I was being assigned to TBS. What's going on?"

"Captain, you got me. All I can tell you is the CG has been breathing down the major's neck for about a week. Something is brewing, and if my oh-shit meter is working properly, it's about to hit the proverbial fan."

"Thanks, Top."

"Semper Fi, skipper."

Mike followed the MP staff sergeant's sedan to the base commanding general's headquarters building. Mike parked his truck in the visitor space, and the sergeant escorted him to Major Simmons's office. Mike felt like he was walking to his execution but didn't know why. The shiny linoleum hallway ended at a frosted glass door. The upper half of the door was marked in gold letters: *Adjutant.*

The adjutant's office was divided into an outer bullpen and inner walled office. The bullpen had five steel-gray governmental desks. Mike gave his paperwork to the first sergeant, saying, "Captain Ruhawk reporting as ordered."

All typing stopped and the room went graveyard silent. Mike turned and found everyone staring at him. He turned back to the first sergeant.

"What? None of you assholes ever seen a captain reporting for duty?" said the gruff first sergeant.

The bullpen of clerks quickly resumed typing at a new feverish level.

"Captain, please take a seat. The adjutant will be with you in a moment. Would you like a cup of mud?"

"That would be outstanding."

"PFC Napoleon, get the skipper a cup of coffee."

"PFC, I'm sure my escort would like a cup before he leaves," said Mike.

"No, thank you, sir. My orders are to stay with you until the adjutant dismisses me."

Mike looked at the first sergeant. The senior enlisted face was expressionless. In fact, it looked as if it were set in concrete.

Mike sat on the couch watching the office activity. Every now and then one of the junior enlisted glimpsed curiously at him as if he were some kind of exotic animal. He could see fear, curiosity, and amusement in their faces. Their body language gave Mike the impression that if he said *boo* they would all scamper out like gassed rats. The MP staff sergeant stood next to the office door watching him. The guard's gaze never wandered. For some reason, he was on high alert. Mike became agitated. *What the hell. Why am I here?* He had waited for over an hour, his patience tested.

The outer hallway door opened, and a light colonel walked in carrying a large leather briefcase. The pudgy officer walked directly to Mike, his face overwhelmed by a toothy smile.

"You must be Captain Ruhawk."

"Yes sir," said Mike as he stood.

"I'm Lieutenant Colonel Walker." The colonel clasped his hand and turned to the first sergeant. "Everything squared away with the paperwork?"

"Yes sir. The UA was a clerical error."

"Great news!" The colonel turned. "Take your seat, Captain. We will talk shortly. Top, does Major Simmons know I'm here?"

"Yes sir. He's expecting you. Go right in."

"Thanks, Top."

Mike sat again. *What the hell is going on?* He waited another fifteen minutes before he was summoned to the adjutant's office.

Mike walked in, stopping three feet from the adjutant's desk. He stood at attention looking straight ahead, about two feet over the major's bald head, focusing on the crossed flags of the USA and Corps.

"Sir, Captain Ruhawk reporting as ordered, sir," said Mike in his best military command voice.

The major looked up from his cluttered desktop. He pushed his eyeglasses off his forehead to his nose. He gave Mike a very critical look as if Mike were on inspection. After a few moments, he said, "At ease." Mike did a parade rest with both hands behind his back, his stare never wavering from the spot on the wall above the major's head. The adjutant got up from his desk and walked behind Mike.

"Colonel, he looks like a combat-hardened Marine captain should look. Neat, trim, squared away."

"Everything the Marine Corps could want in a fighting commander, Bob. He even has viable battle scars," the colonel said, referring to the scabbed red line on Mike's head. "Captain, please join us at the table."

"Yes sir," said Mike. He turned and walked to the conference table.

"Take a seat, Captain."

As Mike sat, he heard a shout in the outer office: "Attention on deck." The three officers stood as the inner office door opened. A major general, his two stars shining brightly, walked in, followed by his captain aide. All three officers stood at attention.

"At ease, gentlemen. Good morning, John, Bob. This must be the elusive Captain Ruhawk."

The general extended his hand to Mike. His grip was firm and brief.

"Pleased to meet you, Captain. I'm General Arnold, the CG of this lash up. Please sit down. Sid, could you find me a cup of coffee and not the swill Top brews. Would anyone else like a cup?"

The general was immaculate. His summer service Alpha uniform was adorned with ribbons indicating he had served in Korea and Vietnam with valor and distinction. He looked ultra-fit, like an exercise fanatic. His clean-shaved face was tan and angular. The salt-and-pepper crew cut with high and tight close-cut sides gave an overall appearance of no-bullshit, can-do attitude.

"General, we were just sitting down with the captain before you arrived," said the colonel.

"Please carry on. I'm just here as an observer."

The other officers all had the same thought: *Observer my ass.*

"Captain, when I introduced myself, I intentionally omitted my duty," said the colonel. "I'm a JAG lawyer with Headquarters Marine Corps. I have been assigned as your legal counsel." JAG stood for the Judge Advocate General's Corps.

Mike looked at him as if the man had suddenly popped a third eye with maggots crawling out both ears. Bewildered, Mike said, "Say again?"

"I'm your defensive lawyer for your upcoming court martial."

Mike toiled through the weekend on autopilot. He had difficulty focusing on simple tasks. Gunny Pete helped him drink some beer and arrange the furniture in his apartment. Guns told him the word from the NCO back channel was the deck was stacked against Mike.

"The admin men at HQ are now calling you Captain Hammer," said Pete.

"Just the nickname I wanted," said Mike.

Mike asked Gunny Pete to keep his ear to the ground and let him know of any legal scuttlebutt.

By late afternoon, Mike was alone in his new digs feeling like a doomed man. He sat on his couch, staring out the sliding glass doors, reliving the meeting in the adjutant's office. He remembered the dazed, sickening feeling as his world crumbled. Mike closed his eyes and rested his head back against the couch, replaying the nightmare as it unfolded.

A heavyset JAG lawyer had begun, "Captain, on Monday you will be summonsed to this office to be introduced to Lieutenant Colonel Brightwell. He is the prosecuting JAG officer from Headquarters Marine Corps. He will explain Articles 31 and 32 of the Uniform Code of Military Justice. Article 31 explains self-incrimination. Article 32 explains the investigation process and right to counsel. In Article 32, you have the option to military counsel and/or civilian counsel. I am here today because General Arnold wanted you to be informed of your rights and the charges as quickly as possible."

"Sir, to say I'm confused is an understatement. I have no idea what is going on," said Mike.

"This is precisely why we are having this meeting, Captain. First, let me explain why HQ is prosecuting this case. All the charges relate to actions that allegedly occurred between the times you were released from 1st MarDiv and before you reported for duty at MCB Quantico. HQ could have sent you back to 1st Division, but your alleged misconducts took place in the States."

"Sir, would you please tell me what misconducts allegedly occurred?"

"Captain, please wait until I complete these remarks before you ask any questions."

"Yes sir."

The colonel opened his briefcase, took out a folder and a yellow legal pad. He slid the pad to Mike and handed him a cheap government ballpoint pen.

"It may help you to write down any questions so we can discuss them later." The colonel opened the folder. "The first charge is Article 86; Absence Without Leave aka: Unauthorized Absence."

"You can cross that off the list," said the adjutant. "It was clerical error."

"Outstanding. Next, Article 94, overthrow of lawful civil authority; Article 95, flight, breach of arrest; Article 112 Alpha, wrongful use or possession of a controlled substance; Article 128, assault. Article 133, conduct unbecoming an officer; Article 134, adultery and trafficking in minors. Those are the articles Lieutenant Colonel Brightwell will use to file for a court martial. Do you have any questions?"

Mike laid his pen down on the lined yellow pad. He had scrawled, *#94, 95, 112a, 128, 133, 134 ????* He was at a loss for words. Mike shook his head. "No sir."

"Captain, I'm going to ask you some questions. Answer them honestly and to the best of your knowledge. Your answers are protected by the client-counselor privilege. The general, major and captain do not have that privilege. The prosecution could call them to testify if they are privy to anything you say. You can request them to leave. Do you understand?"

"Yes sir." Mike paused to think for a moment. "I believe it is in my best interest if our conversation is private."

"General, Major, Captain, if you would please excuse us."

"Colonel, when your interview is over, please send Captain Ruhawk to my office," said the general.

"Yes sir. I should be through with the primary interview in about an hour."

"Colonel, there is a conference room down the hall that will provide complete privacy," said the major. "The MP sergeant will be posted at the door. You will not be interrupted."

When the door closed on the conference room, Mike turned to Lt. Col. Walker.

"What the fuck is going on, sir?"

"That's what I'm here to find out, Captain. May I call you Mike?"

"Sure. Call me anything but guilty."

"Take a seat, Mike."

"Colonel?"

"In this setting, call me John."

"OK, John. If you don't mind, I need to pace. I'm wound tighter than a detcord, and I'm ready to explode."

"Let's run through some questions that may relieve some of your anxiety."

"Shoot."

Colonel Walker opened another folder. He took an expensive fountain pen from his briefcase, ready to jot down any notes.

"Do you know a Jessie Melrose?"

"No."

"Do you know a Bobby Hail?"

"No"

"Were you involved in an altercation while in transit at Norton Air Force Base?"

"Yes. I was assaulted by two, large black males while conducting PT."

"Did you report this to the base provost marshal?"

"No. I reported two men that needed assistance to the NCOIC at the Officer Transit Facility."

"Do you know an Edwin Diamond?"

"Yes. He's the father of one of my deceased Marines."

"Also, the past president of a known outlaw biker gang in LA. Do you know an Angela Esposito?"

"Yes."

"Did you know she was under surveillance by the FBI for subversive activities?"

"What?"

"She was being watched because of her support for SDS: Students for a Democratic Society."

"I had no idea."

"Do you know FBI Agent James LaBoon?"

"No."

"He has filed criminal assault charges resulting from an injury to his foot. Four nail puncture wounds, to be exact."

"He's a fucking pervert. A damn peeping Tom!"

"OK. Do you know Jackson Fairchild, aka King Kong, aka Kong, aka Brother Kong?"

"No."

"Did you assault an African-American man on the corner of Second Street and Main in Los Angeles?"

"I defended myself after my date was assaulted and I was threatened."

"Do you know Cosmo Popogopalas, aka Pop-Pop, aka Pope?"

"Yes. I met him on the road in Nevada."

"Did you know he was under surveillance by ATF and DEA?"

"No."

"Do you know a Bill Johansen?"

"Yes."

"Were you involved in an altercation with him at the River Roadhouse?"

"Yes."

"Did you know there is a warrant for your arrest in Burns, Oregon?"

"No."

"Do you know a Terry White Smith, aka White Dove?"

"Yes."

"Did you know she was married to a Henry William?"

"Yes and no . . . I need to explain."

"There is going to be plenty of time for discovery. Did you know Henry Williams is involved with the AIM movement?"

"Yes and no."

"Have you ever taken nonprescription drugs?"

"Not with my knowledge. However—"

"Simple answers for now. Believe me, we will get into everything in discovery. Do you know John Watts?"

"Yes."

"Do you know Phil and Frank Navarro?"

"No."

"Did you assault John Watts, Phil Navarro, and Frank Navarro?"

"If the Navarros were Watt's enforcers, then yes, we came to blows."

"Do you know there is a warrant for your arrest in Sturgis, South Dakota?"

"No."

"Do you know a Richard Miller?"

"If he's the brother of Marion Miller, I do."

"Did you transport him across state lines?"

"Yes."

"Did you know he was a minor?"

"No. He had a driver's license that—"

"Remember, discovery."

"But—"

"We'll get to all the details. Do you know any members of the Pee Street Thugs in Chicago?"

"Yes."

"Do you know Jonathon O'Malley?"

"Yes."

"Do you know anyone with ties to the Sinn Fein Organization?"

"No."

"Do you know Roger Archer?"

"Yes."

"Did you know he has sought legal counsel from the Rainbow Coalition concerning an alleged assault?"

"Is that the gay rights group?"

"Yes."

"Then, no I didn't."

"Do you know a Jerry Wisniewski?"

"If he's the brother of Peter Wisniewski, I know of him."

"Did you know Jerry Wisniewski is incarcerated for selling explosives?"

"No."

"Do you know Edsel Carr, Cooper Carr, and Stanley Carr?"

"I've met Edsel and Stanley Carr."

"Were you involved in an altercation with them?"

"Yes."

"Were you injured in that altercation?"

"Yes," said Mike as he touched the side of his head.

"That's it for the simple questions. Monday morning at 0800, I want you here. Lt. Col. Brightwell will arrive at 1000 to explain Articles 31 and 32. If his inquiry touches on any topic we have not discussed, you will invoke Article 31, self-incrimination. The prosecutor will initiate Article 32 immediately; 32 is like a fact-finding grand jury. By late Monday you will be indicted and a general court martial date set.

"Over the weekend, I want you to write down everything you can remember about your leave. Start with your arrival at Norton AFB to your reporting for duty today. Be detailed. Time, place, people, everything, and anything you can remember. Do you have any questions?"

"I'm in some deep shit, aren't I?"

"Up to your nose."

"What I can't figure out is how the charges were filed so fast. I just reported in and everything was waiting for me. I feel like I stepped into an ambush."

"The ATF and DEA have been tag-teaming you since California. They each placed a tracking device on your motorcycle. You found one but not the other. Their documents indicate they think you were involved with the Comancheros brokering drugs and weapons. You piqued the FBI interest when you shacked up with Angela Esposito and drove to Kuna to see Williams. They got pictures, statements, and warrants."

"How am I going to fight this?"

"If that's what you want to do, I'm ready and willing. That's why HQ assigned me. I'm good, very good. Some say I'm the very best defensive dog in the JAG kennel."

Mike could not remember the walk to the CG's office. He was in a daze. He remembered the general telling his aide to get three BLTs and sweet teas.

"Captain Ruhawk is having lunch with us," said the CG.

The general and Mike sat down on hardback wooden chairs around a small conference table in the general's office. They talked about small unit tactics and Quantico activities. When they finished lunch, the general asked his aide to leave so he could have a private talk with the captain.

"Captain, I've been reading your service jacket and fitness reports. You leaped quite a few very qualified officers to become a very young captain. You're one hell of a combat Marine. Two Silver Stars and a Bronze Star, three Purple Hearts, outstanding leadership report. You're in the top two percent of your peer group. HQ is reviewing a report from 5th Marines regarding your actions in Hue. A Navy Cross may be in the works. The Corps need more men like you in Nam. There could be stars in your future if this situation is handled correctly.

"Problems arise when combat Marines return home. To go from blood and guts to bell-bottoms, hard rock, and free sex is difficult. It can be mind bending. The civilian population has no idea what's happening in the rice paddies of Nam. The decisions the combat officer has to make each day would take a civilian committee a year of group discussions. Civilians watch TV and make judgments based on ten minutes of edited film. This war will be lost in the news long before a gun can win it. The media will pounce on any story that shows the failure of our fighting men and their leaders. Especially a story like a decorated Marine officer who likes to beat the snot out of civilians."

"Sir," Mike started to interject.

"Son, it doesn't matter if the charges are true or not. The first causality of war is truth. That's a quote from some hack politician during WWI. Sometime in the next couple of days, you will need to ask yourself what is best for the Corps. You will have the opportunity to set the example or be the example. Life is about decisions. I'm betting you will make the correct choice."

CHAPTER 13

THE CHOICE

MIKE'S EXTENDED MORNING RUN and strenuous workout didn't help his mood. He sat on the couch in his red Marine running shorts and red Ohio State gym shirt contemplating his dilemma. All he could think about was the lawyer's questions. As he mopped his forehead with a small green towel, he replayed the scene once more.

"Captain, on Monday you will be summonsed . . ."

A loud knock on the door stirred Mike from thought. He looked through the spy hole at the base commanding general's aide. He was dressed in dark-blue slacks, a white, collared, short-sleeve Izod shirt, and slip-on boat shoes. He looked like an Ivy League graduate from a wealthy East Coast family. Moreover, that was exactly what he was. A smile like a possum playing dead was a giveaway that his visit wasn't just happenstance.

"Hello," said Mike as he opened the door.

"May I come in, Captain?"

"Sure."

"Very nice housing."

"Thanks. It's Captain Rapp, correct?

"Please call me Sid."

"OK, Sid. What brings you here?"

"Wow, is that a '03 Springfield?" said the aide-de-camp, walking across the room to the far wall. Mike had displayed his M1895 Winchester-Lee Navy Rifle, M1903 Springfield Rifle, and M1942 M1 Grand Rifle on the wall with his Marine officer's Mameluke sword.

"A Rock Island with all the matching numbers," said Mike with pride.

"May I take a look at the rifle?"

"Sure."

Sid took the World War I 1903 Springfield rifle off the wooden rack and did a quick inspection of arms to ensure it was unloaded. He sat on the couch examining it closely.

"Do you know the provenance?" questioned Sid.

"Sorry to say no, got it from a collector at an Ohio gun show. The serial number indicates it was manufactured 1916 to '17. You into military arms collecting?"

"Not really. I just picked up this Colt 45 auto. I think it is a 1911, maybe early World War I. Would you like to take a look?"

"If you have it with you."

"I'll be right back." Sid hurried out the door. He returned with a cold six-pack of beer and the Colt 45.

Mike held the door open for him, feeling a little uncomfortable. This meeting seemed too contrived.

"Had the cold Bud in the back seat, so what the hell? Let's have a few brews and talk 45s." Sid handed the Colt to Mike and put the beer on the large, old oak map cabinet that now served as a retro coffee table. Sid popped the tab on a couple beers while Mike checked the handgun to ensure it was clear.

"Not sure if the Colt is a 1911 or 1911A1. What do you think?" asked Sid.

"What I think is you know perfectly well the difference is the 1911A1 has scallop cuts in the frame on both sides of the trigger."

Sid looked at Mike. A sheepish smile appeared on his face. "Want a beer?"

"Sure."

"The general said you were smart."

"I don't have to be smart. The aide of the CG just does not drop in on a fellow officer he has only met once to talk about gun collecting. And, oh by the way, he has a 45 and a six-pack of ice-cold beer in the car."

"That bad?"

"Virgin in a whorehouse bad."

"I guess direct is better?"

"Hi diddle diddle up the middle, Captain."

"Fair enough. Everything I say is off the record, agreed?"

"Agreed."

"The general briefed me about your situation. He respects you. That says a lot. The general wants the best outcome for the Marine Corps and you. On Monday, Lt. Col. Brightwell will inform you of Articles 31 and 32. Next, he will read the charges. Your counsel will request you be transferred to H&S Company, Base Command. Lt. Col. Brightwell will agree. You will be restricted to base and residence. A date will be set in November for a preliminary hearing. Your counsel will agree, to all."

"It sounds like a rigged game."

"Not rigged, but orchestrated. The general is being directed by '8th and I' to find an honorable solution as quickly as possible."

"The commandant?"

"The pressure is coming from on high. I'm not sure how high. The Corps PR people are shaking in their booties about the possibility of negative publicity. The media has been piranha-like since Tet. They're looking for something to tear apart. The press is telling the public the war is lost. We have to get out now before any more boys come home in body bags."

"I get that part, but how do I fit in?"

"The Marine Command Group thinks you could be a flash point. Headlines like 'War Hero Goes Nuts' or 'Crazed Marine Attacks Innocent Civilians.' You get the drift."

"I'm fucked," said Mike under his breath.

"Not necessarily so. Sometime between Monday and Friday you will be offered several options."

"Can't wait to hear this," Mike said bitterly.

"Option one, plead guilty. Dishonorably discharged, no brig time, but you will have to face the outstanding civilian warrants. Option two, resign your regular commission. You will be honorably discharged. The Corps will help you with federal charges, but you will have to face the other civilian warrants without the help of the Corps. Option three, stand trial. The process could take up to two years. During that time, you will be stationed at Quantico. The H&S commander will make life miserable for you. You'll get every shitty job that he can think of. You'll become the pariah of the officer corps, court outcome questionable, very messy for the Corps.

"Or, option four, you can request overseas duty. We can have you on a plane to DaNang in forty-eight hours. You would be assigned to 3rd MarDiv. They are in short supply of qualified rifle company commanders. All federal charges dropped. We will ensure your civilian warrants disappear before your tour is completed and any mention of your activities during this leave and following Marine UCMJ proceedings will be expunged from your military record. You'll be free and clear when your thirteen-month tour ends with a clean jacket and no civil action pending. In all probability your Navy Cross will be approved."

Mike sat and stared at Sid. An awkward silence followed Sid's proposal. The general's aide became so nervous he started to fiddle with the rifle.

After an uncomfortable five-plus minutes Mike said, "When does the general need an answer?"

"He would like your answer after Lt. Col. Brightwell leaves Monday morning. The longer you wait, the more likely the press will find out. Then, the media frenzy will start."

Sid left the apartment, leaving the beer. Mike had several more thinking about his options. He picked up the telephone and dialed a number from memory.

"Hello, Webster Inn. Hello? Hello, Webster Inn." It was Jill. Mike gently hung up the phone.

He put his head back on the couch and closed his eyes. A single tear rolled down his cheek. He mourned the loss. As he pondered his decision, his mother's face appeared before him. She was laughing with delight about something Mike's father had said. It was a quote from Wordsworth:

Who is the happy Warrior? Who is he?
That every man in arms should wish to be?
It is the generous spirit, who, when brought
Among the tasks of real life, hath wrought
Upon the plan that pleased his childish thought:
Whose high endeavors are inward light
That makes the path before him always bright:
Who, with a natural instinct to discern
What knowledge can perform, is diligent to learn.
Who, doomed to go in company with Pain,
And Fear, and Bloodshed, miserable train!
Turns his necessity to glorious gain

He could hear his mother's voice saying, *"Man plans, and God laughs."* She always had great insight.

Mike had spent the night writing a narrative of his leave for his defense lawyer. He was tired. He was angry. He was disappointed. As he looked at the twisted papers in the wastebasket, he had to make a decision. What was best for the Corps? What was best for him?

Was there a compromise? In his heart, Mike knew there was only one choice. His Marines would shout, "Semper Fi, do or die, Marine Corps! Semper Fi, Semper Fi, Semper Fi!"

261

EPILOGUE

THE FUTURE FOR JESSIE Melrose and Bobby Hail included bad conduct discharges from the US Air Force for drug possession. Both became multiple offenders of the California judicial system. They received life sentences as incorrigible criminals after their third major felony.

***

Angela Esposito became a cardiac surgeon specializing in pediatric cases. She married a family physician and moved near Santa Rosa, California. They had four daughters. She still looked at every motorcyclist hoping for a glimpse of her former lover. Her brother was released by the NVA March 24, 1973. He became a colonel in the USAF.

***

Edwin Diamond sold his Harley-Davidson dealership and retired to Ensenada, Mexico, where he continued to work on motorcycles. His wife became a favorite among the children of the barrio. She always had fresh-baked cookies for them.

FBI Agent James LaBoon was forced to retire from the FBI due to questionable conduct with a female agent. He became head of security for Billy-Mart.

Jackson Fairchild, aka King Kong, aka Kong, aka Brother Kong, became a civil rights leader in California. He earned a master's degree at UCLA in political science and was elected to Congress, representing the constituents of the 43rd District, Los Angeles.

Cosmo Popogopalas, aka Pop-Pop, aka Pope, was stabbed to death in a rival gang fight on the floor of the Golden Nail Casino, Sparks, Nevada, December 1971.

John MacDowell became sheriff of Lyon County. His only son, JR, followed in his dad's footsteps and became a deputy in the same county. Maryann MacDowell had three more children, all girls. She was diagnosed with ovarian cancer, but her treatments were successful.

Bill Johansen became a wealthy condominium developer. He lost his fortune after serving two years in jail for spousal abuse and went on to live with his sister as a recovering alcoholic.

▬▮▮▮▮

Terry White Smith became executive director for ICFPS, Indian Children Foster Placement Service, for the state of Washington. US federal officers killed her husband, Bill Williams, during the standoff at Wounded Knee, April 26, 1973.

▬▮▮▮▮

John Watts died of cardiac arrest in 1981 while serving a federal prison sentence for tax evasion. His enforcers, Phil and Frank Navarro, appeared on a TV weight-loss program, but their segment of the program was deleted because of suspected steroid use. They next opened a health food store in Rapid City that eventually filed bankruptcy protection from foreclosure. The state investigated the pair for distribution of prescription drugs without a license.

▬▮▮▮▮

Marion Miller and his brother, Richard, shared a bedroom at a private mental rehab facility in Madison, Wisconsin. Richard was bludgeoned by police in 1968 during the Chicago Democratic Convention riots. He suffered traumatic brain injuries.

▬▮▮▮▮

The Pee Street Thugs were disbanded when the Crypt Gang from LA took over their territory in the early 1970s. Several members were killed in drive-by shootings.

▬▮▮▮▮

Jonathon O'Malley retired to Dublin, Ireland, where his son ran a pub and sponsored an annual 4th of July 10K run in honor of Timothy O'Rourke, USMC.

Roger Archer remained in Columbus, Ohio, where he co-founded a successful advertising agency. The firm specialized in ad campaigns for expensive lingerie for woman and men. He and his life partner became gay rights activists.

Jerry Wisniewski was convicted of selling stolen explosives. He petitioned the state for parole for exemplary behavior while incarcerated.

Mr. and Mrs. Skull sold the dairy farm after Mr. Skull's devastating fall from a ladder. They moved into a retirement center in Kimbolton. Mr. Skull developed dementia after a stroke caused by the fall. He had trouble recognizing his wife of fifty-two years and didn't remember having a son.

Jill Addison and her mother continued to run the bed-and-breakfast. Jill married Dr. John Young five months after Mike rode out of West Virginia. Four months later the newlyweds were the proud parents of a baby boy. The couple went on to have two more children, one of whom moved to New York City and became the CEO of Manhattan General Hospital. Their only son became Lieutenant Young USMC, a decorated ground commander in Operation Desert Storm.

■■IIII

The Carr brothers were convicted of murdering a fellow convict while in lockup. They were given life sentences without parole. In prison, they were known as the Three Stooges among their white Aryan brothers.

■■IIII

The church caretaker, Otis, buried Pastor Noah R. Yoder next to the two other pastors at the church of Holiness Witness of Jesus on the Water. A coal slag slide caused the pastor's demise. He was inspecting a railroad switch near Divinity, WV. The railroad listed his death in their FAR (federal accident report) as an "Act of God."

■■IIII

Mike Ruhawk reluctantly took option four, the best option for the Corps. He served seven months of his third tour before a NVA sniper found his mark. The sniper's 700-yard shot was nudged by a wind gust and hit Mike in his left hip, shattering the bone. He rehabbed successfully but was medically unfit for duty. The 5th Marines somehow lost Mike's paperwork for the Navy Cross Award. Before he was honorably discharged as a major, the now-famous "Hammer" married his college sweetheart, Catherine Ann Burkhart. The couple settled in Pepper Pike, Ohio, with their three children. Mike became the chief operating officer of a Cleveland company that made rubber bogie wheels for tanks, steel hubs for military trucks, and compound metal treads for tracked vehicles. On January 11, 1980, the company's board of directors announced Mike's promotion to CEO. Mike then informed the board that the company would be listed on the New York Stock Exchange that spring.

The new office of the CEO had a metal plaque that sat front and center on his desk. It read *Improvise, Adapt, and Overcome.*

ACKNOWLEDGMENTS

I would like to thank my family, especially my wife, who has heard me praise the Marine Corps for years. They are my rock.

To all Marines, who are my brothers, "You have chosen the difficult path. Stay the course, honor your brethren, and remember *Semper Fidelis.*"

CPSIA information can be obtained
at www.ICGtesting.com
Printed in the USA
LVHW020100171219
640668LV00009B/301/P